FICTION   Bausch, Richard,
BAU   1945-

          Something is out
          there.

C2010

DATE		

DISCARD

ALSO BY RICHARD BAUSCH

Real Presence

Take Me Back

The Last Good Time

Spirits and Other Stories

Mr. Field's Daughter

The Fireman's Wife and Other Stories

Violence

Rebel Powers

Rare & Endangered Species: Stories

Good Evening Mr. & Mrs. America, and All the Ships at Sea

The Selected Stories of Richard Bausch (Modern Library)

In the Night Season

Someone to Watch Over Me: Stories

Hello to the Cannibals

The Stories of Richard Bausch

Wives & Lovers: Three Short Novels

Thanksgiving Night

Peace

SOMETHING IS OUT THERE

SOMETHING IS
OUT THERE

STORIES

Richard Bausch

Alfred A. Knopf   New York 2010

The following stories have been previously published, some in slightly
different form: "Trophy" in the Fiction Issue of *Golf World;* "Something Is
Out There" in *Murdaland;* and "Blood," "The Harp Department in Love,"
"Immigration," "Overcast," "Reverend Thornhill's Wife," and "Sixty-five
Million Years" in *Narrative Magazine.* "Byron the Lyron" appeared in
The Norton Anthology of Short Fiction: Seventh Edition, edited by
Richard Bausch and R. V. Cassill (New York: W. W. Norton, 2006).

Library of Congress Cataloging-in-Publication Data
Bausch, Richard, [date]
Something is out there : stories / Richard Bausch.—1st ed.
p. cm.
ISBN 978-0-307-26627-9
I. Title.
PS3552.A846S59 2010
813'.54—dc22   2009027437

Manufactured in the United States of America
First Edition

For my whole family . . .

Perhaps you know Malraux's *Anti-memoirs*? His priest tells us that people are much more unhappy than one might think . . . and that there is no such thing as a grownup.

—Robert Stone, *Damascus Gate*

Contents

SOMETHING IS OUT THERE

THE HARP DEPARTMENT IN LOVE

This morning, while Josephine Stanislowski is tearfully packing winter clothes into a big box for the attic, her friend and
neighbor Ruthie calls about the surprise party she's having for
her husband, Andrew, celebrating his graduation from college.
It's a party Josephine helped enthusiastically, several weeks
ago, to plan. "Oh, God, it's Friday, isn't it," Josephine says
before she can catch herself. "That's right."

"You didn't forget."

"I lost track of the days, Ruthie. Sorry."

"You all right? You sound like you've been crying."

"I had a pepper and egg sandwich," Josephine says, and is
dejected about the lie. "It made my nose run."

"You sound awful."

Excitable, garrulous Ruthie knows only the outlines of
Josephine's situation—Monday, after a big blowup, John
Stanislowski moved into the little efficiency downtown, his old
studio overlooking the river; he says he's through. Josephine
has told Ruthie the change is temporary, so he can work on his
new music.

"The cake isn't ready," Ruthie goes on. "And the idiot just
called to say he's getting off an hour early."

Josephine manages the automatic response. "Uh-oh."

"I won't be able to get everything laid out and the time's all messed up now and I can't get in touch with everybody," says Ruthie. "But he'll come right by you. Do you think you could delay him for me?"

It's a fifteen-minute walk from the university. They both know he'll stop and buy a quart of beer at the little Korean one-stop, as he does every day. So, twenty minutes.

"I'll—I'll pretend I need help with something," Josephine gets out. "Should we have a signal when you're ready for him?"

"Let's say the signal will be that I'll call you. And don't let him get suspicious. Make it something good."

"I will," Josephine tells her. "I have a big heavy box of clothes that has to go in the attic."

"You're packing his clothes away?"

"Winter clothes. Mine, too. I do it every year."

"I guess he's not coming to the party."

"Actually, he said he might."

"It would mean a lot to me."

After a brief pause, Josephine says, "Call when you're ready."

They talk a little about how Ruthie wants things to go, and Josephine hears herself pretending she still has any interest in it. Somewhere she finds the strength to say, "It's gonna be perfect, Ruthie."

"You always make me feel better," Ruthie tells her. Then: "Oh, I'll kill them if that cake's not ready. I've gotta go, honey. Bye."

"Bye," Josephine says. But the connection is broken.

She puts the receiver back in its cradle, and walks into the living room of her now empty-feeling house to sit with a guitar on her lap and cry. She plays a few desultory chords, trying to get control of herself. Major chords. What John Stanislowski to his students used to call happy chords, being ironical. Then, without explaining or introducing it, he would play a Bulgarian song in G minor and make them want to dance, and when it was done he would reveal the fact. Nothing inherently cheerful or sad about the major and minor keys, he would say. She can hear his voice. The guitar smells of cedar. It's a new one, bought only last month. The odor is familiar and something she has always loved, but just now it's a little suffocating, so she sets it in its stand on the other side of the room. She has spent most of the morning folding the clothes. It's a task she has performed every spring for the past four years—packing the heavy flannels, the sweaters, and the corduroy slacks. It's important to keep to routines as much as possible. She goes back to work, stuffing the big box, sniffling into the busy silence and searching her mind for excuses she might use to escape having to attend Ruthie's party. She mulls over possible lies to tell, different scenarios of feigned illness and emergency. Nothing seems right; it all sounds like evasion. And there's the business of delaying Andrew.

When the box is packed at last, its lid forced closed and fastened, she gets down on her knees for leverage and pushes it out into the hallway. Reaching up, she opens the attic stairs, but then lacks the heart to do more. A tide of anxiety washes over her. She moves from room to room, looking at the pictures on the walls and the books in the bookcases, the musical instruments—guitars, banjos, mandolins, a piano, even a harp—trying to be brave, trying to concentrate on it all as home, her home. But her stomach hurts, and it's hard to breathe right.

"Oh," she says aloud. "You are so wrong about me." It's as if Stanislowski's standing right there.

. . .

This predawn she had a dream about turtles, and remembered her childhood fascination with them, her mother talking about how they carry their homes on their backs. The dream felt occult, as if meant to impart something to her about her childhood and her mother, or take her back to a version of herself then. She didn't get another minute's sleep. The night wore on like silence during a bad argument.

Now she dusts the surfaces, and straightens things, puts last night's saucer and cup and cheese plate away. She wanders into the bathroom and blows her nose with toilet paper, washes her face, and puts on some makeup, exactly as if she's someone to whom appearances matter. Then she goes into the kitchen and makes herself a peanut butter and jelly sandwich. She can't finish it. She lies down on the sofa and thinks about staying awake for fear of bad dreams.

Waking with a start, she realizes that she has been asleep for more than an hour.

It's become afternoon, somehow. She sits up and stretches and then stands up. The house feels so goddamned unpleasantly spacious.

She lies back down on the sofa and tries to read, but the words dissolve into worry. Finally she dozes still more, and wakes up from another dream, one that leaves only a sense of itself as disturbing. She supposes it might have been about the turtles again.

On the refrigerator are photographs of her and Stanislowski being happy together, playing music, standing in a crowded piazza in Rome, on the corner of Beale and Second with friends, entertaining guests out on the back lawn of this house.

The two of them have lived here for almost four years. He's Stan to friends and family. Professor Emeritus of Music at Memphis School of the Arts. A fixture, a feature of the cultural landscape. Thirty years older than she is, he has lived in many houses; but this is her first—the first mortgage, and the first place she has occupied for more than a few months. Now she's alone with two cats and the musical instruments. No matter how many lights she turns on, the rooms seem gloomy and forlorn, nobody else here except the cats, whose names are Cat One and Cat Two. They're outside types; she lets them in at night.

Ruthie's husband works the front desk in the physical education building at the university. On sunny, warm days he walks to and from work. He comes along in the late afternoons in summer with a quart of cold beer in a paper bag, sipping it as he goes. He's been going to night school for the past five years seeking his degree in history, the first in his family to go to college. For the party, Ruthie has invited all his friends from school, along with a few neighbors, and his mother and father, who have flown in from Chicago. It's a special day and Josephine helped plan it because Ruthie has what she calls S.O.D.—special occasion disorder. The condition, Ruthie says, manifests itself as anxiety and confusion and an inability to focus on the practical matters of preparation for any social gathering; it's a kind of paralysis, really, and she's not kidding when she talks about it. The only thing for it is an organized and concerned friend like Josephine, who designed some of the banners with which Ruthie will festoon the porch and the front hall, and wrapped the presents, and even mapped out the rearrangement of chairs in the front room. She also took care of the invitations, and this week she e-mailed one to Stanislowski at his school address, to remind him. He called to ask what she could be thinking of; he never liked Andrew particularly. "Ruthie invited us both," Josephine told him. "As you know. And of course she'd like you to come."

"You tell her anything?"

"You need space and time to work on your new music."

"That's funny."

"I'm telling you what I told her. And maybe you'll write some new music."

After a pause, he said, "I don't know about this—party. I doubt I'll be there."

She kept silent, trying to control her breathing because he would hear it through the line.

"If I'm not there by the time it starts, I'm not coming."

"Okay."

"I wish it was last year," he muttered.

"Come home," she said, listening to him breathe into the phone, and then clear his throat. Was he crying?

Earlier this spring, at an outing with her painting class, she got separated from the others with someone named Bradford Smith, a classmate who had seemed only marginally interesting as a fellow student, much less a friend. They got lost in the woods. The two of them had a long afternoon, which became a surprisingly pleasurable interval of talk and telling stories and laughing about being lost. It began to feel like one of those movies where strangers are thrown together and learn mutual respect and affection, and then something causes them to take a turn toward each other in seriousness, with music. The afternoon ended in an embrace and a kiss, and resulted in a few meetings over the next month, for coffee, or a short walk— nothing more, finally, than a kind of flirtation (for Josephine, it was strangely an accession to the wish to recover the dreamy zaniness of the first day), and it never went farther than that one kiss. Smith was closer to her age and there were elements of common experience and culture that they shared. It was a form of relaxation for her, talking to him—it was even, in a way, a little lazy. But then he got strange and moody, and started talking about love, and just as she was trying gently to remove herself, things went very badly awry. Saturday morning Bradford Smith, in an absurd misguided romantic fervor, approached Stanislowski at the entrance to the music building and expressed his belief that he had won Josephine's heart. Stanislowski, having worried about her in that way from the beginning, knocked him down, and then came home and packed a bag.

"Nothing has changed," she told Stanislowski over the phone. "I love you."

"And Bradford Smith?"

"Oh, Stan—you have to please stop turning the knife in yourself."

"It's your knife, kid."

"Will you please." She sighed. "I never felt anything like love for Bradford Smith. I never felt anything at all for Bradford Smith. I keep saying it and saying it: I'm innocent of what you have imagined about me. I can't help—I couldn't help—what *he* felt."

"I might come in a cab," he said about the party. "And if I do, it means I'm planning on getting really drunk."

"That would be the mature thing to do. Soak yourself in alcohol."

"Go down blazing," he said.

"Live like a song lyric, huh? I used to know high school boys who talked like that."

"In your long-ago youth. What was it, six years ago?"

"The point is, it's immature talk, Stan."

"Well, I'm a bit past immature, wouldn't you say?"

"It's infantile, nevertheless."

"Are you preaching at me?"

"I hope you'll come to Ruthie's party. Really. And I'm not preaching. Really." She hung up, and heard the click on his end as she did.

He taught music at the university for thirty-five years before retiring last May. He has emeritus status, and still teaches a class there—a Saturday-morning community seminar in composition. Because his hands are arthritic he can't play very well anymore, but he can still write. Lately, he doesn't like much of what he has written, and she believes that this has weighed on his mind along with the other matter. His discouragement about the music is all wrong as far as she's concerned: his new music is wonderful; it is some of the best he has ever written. It has passion, a richer vein of it; the whole feel of it is less intellectual.

Most of the musical instruments in the house belong to him, though it's true that she's the one who mostly plays them now. This has been so since they first bought the house together, four years ago, deciding to live together. She was once his most gifted student. They've been married now for a year and nine months.

He's sleeping on the daybed in the little studio downtown.

Josephine told Ruthie about his doubts concerning his music, but kept the rest to herself. Ruthie's a good listener, the kind of friend whose hopes and concerns seem completely transparent in their simplicity, and whose instincts are all predicated on the assumption that the people around her are mutually interested in keeping to the principles of considerate and loving behavior. She has a way of blocking out everything else. It's what John Stanislowski calls her wall of sweetness. He wondered aloud about Andrew in the first weeks of their acquaintance, because Andrew is often wild and unruly, and he drinks too much. "They're not slightly compatible," he said.

"I think compatibility's always a mystery, though, don't you?" Josephine said.

"You're talking about us."

"Oh, God, sweetie," she said. "No."

Now she sits at the window and picks a little soft melody on the mandolin. "Hickory Wind." It makes her feel like crying again, so she stops. This is her favorite spot in the house, and she often sat here while Stan worked in the other room. Here is her neighborhood, like a tranquil scene from memory—as if he were indeed still in the next room, in that brooding but happy silence of his striving—such an agreeable, peaceful street, a shaded row of houses, each of them alike without exact duplication. There are brick fronts, clapboard sides, little porches, awnings, green shutters, tall black wooden fences and short metal ones, storm doors—those wonderful black wrought-iron doors of Memphis—and storm windows, slanted roofs and angled ones with cupolas; perfectly kept lawns with fat shrubs and long hedges trimmed flat as little walls, and charming flower beds—a lovely residential avenue in the city, not far from the university. Even now, it calms her, gazing out. It's the place she used to dream about, growing up. The only thing that announces it as part of the city is the bus that pulls by now and then, not even often enough for her to have figured out what its schedule might be.

She can't understand how she could've let Bradford Smith get so close. And perhaps it was no more complex than that there was something thrilling about being admired that way. And something alluring about the ease of it, since he was so undemanding. "I'm human," she told Stanislowski, "and I didn't do anything wrong." And the part about being human was the worst thing she could've said. Stanislowski seized on it: "Of course. There it is. You're human. You're young, he's young. You desire life, right?"

She puts the mandolin down now and picks up a guitar. She can also play the piano, the bongos, the drums, the flute, and all the woodwinds—though those instruments don't interest her as much, and since Stanislowski doesn't play them, there are none at the house. She prefers the guitar, the mandolin, the banjo, and the fiddle. She almost never plays the harp, and it sits there in the dining room looking like a small sculpture by Picasso. She expressed this once to Stanislowski, who was amused by it and took to showing the harp to people as a piece by the artist. And it made him laugh out loud when she was asked, a year ago, to teach something about the instrument to a group of visiting Japanese students, and she introduced herself as the university's Harp Department. It became a standing joke between them. "The Harp Department wishes to have dinner," she would say. And he would answer: "Is the Harp Department hungry?"

"Oh very."

"May I ask if the Harp Department has any plans on doing the cooking?"

"No, I believe the Harp Department is too tired for that and would like instead to be spoiled by her husband."

"Well," Stanislowski would say, "whatever the Harp Department wants."

Sometimes prone to theatrics—he once stood in a restaurant and demanded quiet in order to report that Josephine had written a beautiful piece of music that day, and he wanted everyone to toast her—Stanislowski is a man of prodigious learning with an ability to quote from all of it, and he's more entertaining, more involving, than anybody she has known in her life. He makes her laugh, and fills her head with ideas, musical and otherwise. She has endured his temperamental fits as people endure weather, because when things have been right she has felt so happy. Bradford Smith, she sometimes thinks now, was like the letdown that follows long concentration, like drinks and talk on a sunny patio after work on something you love, deeply. He made her feel drowsily at ease, at least until he started getting strange; Stanislowski makes her feel alive, and alert. He has said she makes him feel that, too.

His intellectual gifts are in fact matched by her own. And nobody thinks in these terms anymore—it's only something she's aware of in his company. She has felt her own powers when with him, and this is sustaining in its way, when it isn't intoxicating. It has helped her with her music, helped her see into it more confidently.

But he can be difficult when the mood is on him.

He knows where all her tender places are, and hasn't shied away from using the knowledge on certain occasions. He knows, for instance, that her first fifteen years were spent traveling from city to city in the deep South with her mother, who was an exotic dancer. She never knew her father, never even knew who he was. There were sojourns here in Memphis, and in places like Tupelo, Jackson, Corpus Christi, Galveston, Biloxi, Mobile, and New Orleans. Hotel rooms, trailers, flophouses, motels, late-night buses from one town to another, night rooms with discarded clothes on the bed and the blinking of a neon sign out the window; meals in diners, fast-food joints, cafeterias (once in a cafeteria when she was eight, she saw an old man die while trying to finish a bowl of chicken soup as if gulping it from a mug; the soup ran down either side of his mouth and his eyes did something funny and in the next instant he put the bowl down with a clatter, in a tremendous hurry, clearly trying not to let it fall and make a mess, and then sat forcefully back in his chair and was dead)—there were hired tutors, mostly people who put her to work doing something rote and left her to her own devices; and there were babysitters who taught her to smoke and to cuss, and one had showed her the guitar, and helped her learn "Tom Dooley." Two chords, C and G7. The start of everything else. She took to plaguing her mother about the instrument, and finally her mother got her a used Gibson concert guitar. She spent hour upon hour, blistering her fingers, learning to play it, and she discovered that she could hear things others couldn't. She haunted the music stores, and offered to work for lessons. She found that she possessed this ability to hear her way inside the notes of songs, and to pick up the instruments that fell into her hands, and play them. This began her journey away from her mother. By the time she was sixteen she was elsewhere, far from the dancer, living with a jazz drummer, on the road, trying all the drugs and all the other things, too, including the sexual explorations of the kind she had come to understand were her mother's own province.

In Stanislowski's mind, now, she's still journeying. The Bradford Smith business has confirmed his perception of himself as one of the stops along her way. He used to joke about this in the first months they were together.

It used to be a joke.

And apart from their respective ages, they do have very different backgrounds. He grew up with doting parents who recognized his gifts and who sheltered and supported him accordingly, sending him to private schools in Philadelphia and Boston. He was one of the youngest people who ever attended Harvard, and then he went on to Juilliard. He spent two years in France studying with a man who had been a late protégé and friend of Copland, and, earlier, of Satie. It's the kind of lofty education that makes him ill-equipped to deal with life at the level of dirty dishes piling up in the kitchen sink or trouble with the heat pump in the middle of winter. She understands this. His whole existence has been the studio or the concert hall with one orchestra or another, several of which performed music he composed; but aside from a year with the Berlin Philharmonic, he has spent the bulk of his career hidden away in this old Southern town, at this college, as a teacher. He's had three previous marriages, all to women with no musical gifts and no musical ambitions either, and all ending in divorce. The wives are prospering in other lives far away, with other husbands, and children.

Now, clouds shift over the houses and moving treetops. But wide clear blue spaces show, too. The clouds themselves are lined with that ashen color of rain squalls. Josephine rattles a little on the mandolin and tries to think of a pretense to delay Ruthie's husband, something other than the box of clothes for the attic.

The thought of the clothes brings her playing to a halt.

She puts the mandolin down. The box of clothes won't take ten minutes. She thinks of bringing up her trouble, asking Andrew's advice as a man, but Andrew is decidedly not someone you ask for advice and indeed he won't believe she's the sort who might seriously ask for it. With Andrew, you are always trying to think up something amusing to report. He likes stories and thrives on them: whenever he's present the talk becomes narrative; he tells stories and he elicits them—he makes Ruthie tell them, even through her natural reluctance to be the center of attention—and the stories are always funny; it's always about the laughs with Andrew.

And here he is, strolling a little unsteadily along the sidewalk with his paper bag–wrapped bottle of beer and his black-leather briefcase, looking completely carefree. He wears loose denims, and a gray button-down shirt with one side missing the button, so the collar sticks out a little. She steps out onto her front stoop and crosses the small space of grass to the edge of the sidewalk.

"You look like a street person with a portfolio," she says.

He sips from the bottle and smiles. "Want a taste?"

"I never drink before dark." She's managing it, showing him nothing.

"Well, it's dark up under the house." His smile widens. "I had a couple glasses of champagne at the school. My boss, because I'm a graduated guy now." He stands there. A stranger might consider him a bit of a simpleton. He has one of those faces—the little boy that he was has never quite left the features of the grown man. There are the round cheeks, and the wide grin, the eyes that turn to little dark half-moons when he's amused.

"Come on," he says, offering it. "It's so cold."

To her own surprise, she takes it, and holds it to her mouth. It is, as he said, quite wonderfully cold. It's also dry and tastes very good.

"Hey, save me some of it," he says.

She decides that they can stand here and talk for a time; it's something she can do for Ruthie. Handing back the bottle in its tight brown wrap, she watches him take another long pull of it. Across the street, a couple walks with a baby in a stroller.

They're talking quietly—a big, heavyset, balding blond man and a slender, dark-haired woman taller than he. She's pushing the stroller. They cross at the end of the block and walk on under the shade of the big sycamore there. Mottled shade from the tree moves over them.

"Imagine a street just like this in 1896," Andrew says. "This kind of light. And a couple with a baby in a stroller, walking along. It would've looked about like this. The stroller would be a pram or whatever you call it, and the clothes wouldn't be spandex, but essentially it would look the same. It *was* the same, of course. A young family out walking the baby."

"Yes," she says, a little impatiently, remembering that she always liked his odd way of seeing things.

"But, then, think of this—those people walking the baby in 1896, *and the baby* they were walking in the pretty sunlight—*all* of them are dead now."

"Yes?" she says. "What's your point?"

"I don't know—graduation's got me thinking about things." He takes another pull from the bottle and offers it to her. "Well, it's Truth. Right?"

She waves the beer away. "It's meaningless because it's not worth saying. Everybody knows about it, without the indulgence of reminding themselves."

"Indulgence." He smiles. "I guess you told me."

"Well, right?"

He shrugs. "Ruthie says I'm morbid, anyway. But I bet your husband would agree."

She wants something else to talk about. He drinks more of the beer, and they both watch a car go by—two elderly people in a long tan Lincoln, the woman wearing a white baseball cap and staring straight ahead, her lips an unimaginably dark red, and the man looking at the house numbers, craning his deeply lined neck. Josephine stares after them. The sight sinks into her, and she experiences a sensation like ice water pouring down the inside of her spine. She doesn't want to be alone; it terrifies her to think of it. She puts one hand to the side of her face, and then lets it drop to her side.

Andrew says, "You look like you saw a ghost."

She says, "Can't you think of something pleasant to say?"

"Well, I'm just fumbling through life, you know." He takes the last pull of the beer. "You all right?" he asks abruptly.

"Did Ruthie tell you about Stan going to stay in his studio?"

He folds the top of the paper bag over the lip of the bottle. "Yeah."

"It's—it's only temporary. So he can concentrate."

"I can't believe the fool'd move out." He stares at her. She wants to repeat that it's just a temporary thing. So Stan can work. The lie exhausts her; she doesn't, just now, have the breath to say it. The light and scattered shade seem to be moving, seem to be coming at her. She sees butterflies lifting from the dark green bushes in front of the house across the street, and the old woman who lives there, who never speaks to anyone, is standing on the front stoop with her black knobby cane, trying to get up the courage to take the first step down. The sight races at Josephine as if from a terrible distance.

Andrew touches her arm. "Hey."

"I'm okay. Just got a little light-headed there, probably from the beer." She notices that his eyes are a little glassy. "How much champagne did you have?"

He says, "Stan's an idiot, if you ask me."

She can't help the look that comes to her face, the silent nodding admission that things are as bad as they can be. "Listen," she says, "can you come in for a second? I've got a big box of clothes I need to get up in the attic."

"Lead the way," he tells her, handing her the bottle.

They go up to her door and in, and she puts the bottle into the recycling bin under the kitchen sink. There she takes one deep slow breath. "If you've got another one, I'd sure be grateful for it," he says from the living room. She gets a bottle of Moretti Italian—Stan's favorite—from the refrigerator and walks in there, where he's settled on the sofa with one of the guitars in his lap. He can play, too, but amateurishly. To his credit, he isn't the type of part-time musician who imposes, or has illusions about, his ability. She puts the beer down on the coffee table and sits across from him, glad of the opportunity of extending things for Ruthie's sake. She says, "Play me something."

"Naw." He holds the guitar out to her. "You."

She takes it. There isn't anything else to do. She tunes both E strings to D, plays a few soft riffs, something she has been working on, a song for Stanislowski. He drinks the beer, and then leans back, watching her. Finally she returns the instrument to its normal tuning.

"Wish I could do that," he says. "I have to use an electronic tuner. How can you do that?"

"Don't know." She smiles. "It's something you're born with. Perfect pitch."

"*I* wasn't born with it."

"I didn't know I had it until Stan."

"You don't have yet another beer around, do you?"

She puts the guitar down and goes into the kitchen to get him the beer. "You want a glass this time?"

"Sure."

She hears the guitar, a few slow bluesy notes. It stops. When she comes back into the room he's standing at the picture window, looking out at the street. The old lady across the way has gotten to the second to last step. "I tried to help her once. She wants no help. She cussed at me, no kidding. You'd've thought I was making a pass at her."

She hands him the beer and the glass, and goes over to the guitar. They sit across from each other and he drinks the beer, watching her play. She does the opening of the adagio to Rodrigo's *Concierto de Aranjuez.*

"There's something so sexy about a woman playing a guitar."

She plays on for a space, concentrating. One of her weaknesses when she plays, according to Stanislowski, is that she watches her own left hand on the fret board.

She glances up from playing and sees that Andrew's staring at her. He has drunk the beer, and he holds the empty glass with its traces of foam on the rounded sides. Some of the foam is still on his lips. He wipes it away with the back of one hand. She stops playing the adagio, and begins finger-picking the pattern to "Landslide."

"I love that song," he says. "Can I have another beer?"

"If you do," she tells him, "you won't be able to stand."

"Tell me about what happened with Stan."

"He—needs space to work." She sighs, and puts down the guitar.

Her dream last night was that she was lying at the edge of an ocean, looking out at the emerald-turning-to-brilliant-blue of the water with its bands of whiteness up close, a perfectly innocent sweet afternoon, bright sun and pale sky—and suddenly turtles came out of the surf. They were small, yet in the province of the dream she knew them to be giant sea turtles, slithering up the beach toward her. The trail of their approach was precisely toward her, inscribing a wide fan of which she was the focal point. Realizing this, she was aghast, but she couldn't move, and then she was aware that she was dreaming, and so she began trying to wake up, and she did wake up; she was in the bedroom, and Stanislowski was there, but the turtles were there, too, very small now, like the pets in the little aquariums, and yet her dream-mind continued to categorize them as the gigantic slow sea turtles that made their heavy trail across the beach sand and laid the millions of eggs. Stanislowski got up and went out of the room and didn't see the turtles and she was begging him to do something about them. He didn't hear her.

And didn't hear her.

And she woke up again, alone in the house with the cats and all the musical instruments. She remembered a story about a woman who died and her many cats devoured part of her face. She got up, trembling, and spent an hour in the other room, playing the harp for the celestial feeling of the notes in the stillness, and for the difficulty, which teased her out of thought.

But it all comes back to her now like a missed heartbeat. She tries to collect herself.

"You just got that look again," Andrew says. "I'm making you nervous."

She wants Ruthie to call now. She walks back in the kitchen and opens another Moretti, and brings it back to him. "This is the last one I've got."

He takes it. "You don't want any of it?" He pours it.

"I'm fine."

He drinks, looking at her over the lip of the glass. Then he smacks his lips. "So, what'll we do now?"

"Well, I've got this box of clothes."

He stands. "Okay." She wonders if he knows about the surprise party.

"Here," she says, going into the hall, where the box is, and when she reaches up to pull the attic door down, he stands close, so that his arm comes against her shoulder.

"Let me," he says, and pushes in front of her. She thinks of the alcohol he's had. He goes up to take a look. She sees his black shoes on the steps; he isn't wearing socks. When he backs down he has that simpleton's smile on his face. The box of clothes is against the wall, on the floor. He claps his hands together and then bends down to lift it. It's bulky and heavy, and he nearly falls back on the first step, but then steadies himself, inching upward, one-foot-up-and-standing, one-foot-up-and-standing, using the metal braces at the sides of the stairs, and the box as something to lean into, going up. He makes it with a lot of loud breathing, and when it's done, he comes back down and closes everything.

"There," he says. "Now what?"

"I don't have any beer left," she tells him. It comes to her that she has always felt that there was something missing in Andrew, something vaguely not right.

He moves toward her, and she steps back. "Andrew?"

And his arms are around her. "I feel so sad for you guys," he says, leaning in. "I wish I could make it better." She presses her hands against his upper chest, turning her head. His mouth brushes her cheek, her nose, her neck, and he keeps leaning with her. The two of them struggle briefly, he's trying to find her mouth, and then he says something, only she can't hear what he's saying because her own voice is sounding, a string of words she comes to understand are at the level of a scream, ending in "Jesus Christ!"

He steps back from her, tries to take hold of the frame of the bedroom door, and misses, falling so that his shoulder hits the frame, and he lets out a cry and straightens himself, clutching the hurt shoulder and staggering toward the living room, where he sits heavily on the sofa and bends forward over the pain, head down. "God," he murmurs. "I'm drunk. Sorry. Forget it. God almighty—"

She's standing over him. "Oh, Jesus Christ," she says. "Oh, Jesus Christ. Oh, Jesus Christ."

He sits up, still holding the hurt shoulder. He looks like he might cry. But then his expression changes, becomes that of someone who has been grievously and unjustly treated. "What the hell—I just wanted to hug a friend who's hurting."

She says nothing.

"A friend can kiss a friend."

They're both unable, for the moment, to speak. There's just the sound of their breathing. Instances flash through her consciousness, like a kind of mental static, of her and Stanislowski in the company of this man and his wife.

"You come out and have some beer with me," he says. "And then you invite me in after telling me you're separated. Jesus. You offer me drinks. You play guitar for me. Come *on*. I was just being a friend."

"Get out," she says.

"Well, it doesn't matter because I was just going to hold you like a friend."

"Okay," she says. "Fine. Fine. But I didn't want to be held."

"Stan never wanted me around," Andrew mutters. "*You* did."

It seems to her now that there have indeed been moments of a kind of pleasure in him. As with Bradford Smith. She has a fleeting sense of wonderment at the notion that there might be something she emanates that invites this sort of thing. But here is Andrew, holding his sore shoulder, looking at her with rage, his eyes accusing her, and his wife less than a city block away.

"Ruthie—your wife, remember her?—Ruthie asked me to stop you. Okay?" And then she tells him everything, all the plans. She speaks in an exhausted, sad, slow murmur.

Another moment passes. He won't look her way now, and he simply sits there with the one hand clutching his shoulder, rocking back and forth slightly. "Ruthie's—doing a party," he says, dumbly, merely repeating it. Now he stops rocking. He's very still, very quiet, seeming to contemplate everything.

Suddenly a terrible, braying laugh comes from him, an alcoholic, hacking, hellish noise that seems to come from somewhere other than his throat.

Josephine staggers from him to the dining room, sick to her stomach, and then around to the kitchen. She only wants him to leave, disappear. She never wanted anything more in her life. Out the window over the sink, she sees a cab pull up, Stanislowski. It thrills her; it makes everything else all right for a second. And then it is absolutely the worst thing she can imagine, another increment of badness. The house with its two outdoor cats and its musical instruments and its quiet and all the calm passages composing songs—all of this seems intolerably fragile, almost unthinkable anymore. She hears herself talking to Andrew: "Go home," she says. "*Now*. Get out of here."

He comes to the entrance of the room. "Nothing happened," he says. He sounds as though someone is already challenging him about it. His face is the color of paste.

They hear the door. Stanislowski comes shambling in. "I need some cash for the damn cab," he says, looking at Josephine and then at Andrew. "Hello, Andrew."

The phone rings, as if on cue. They all stand completely silent and still in the sound of it. It rings four times, and at last Josephine picks it up.

"Hi, we're ready!" Ruthie says. "Send him on his way."

"Okay," says Josephine.

"What's wrong—you really do sound awful."

"No," Josephine finds the breath to say. "Fine. It's fine."

"He's standing there and you can't talk, right?"

"Right. Yes."

"Send him on. Wait one minute and then follow."

"Stanislowski's here, too," Josephine tells her. They're both looking at her.

"That's great!"

She puts the receiver down. There's another pause. Stanislowski stares with his dark blue eyes at Josephine, one hand out, palm up. "The cab," he says.

She retrieves her purse from the dining room, brings out a twenty, and gives it to him.

"Better head on home," he says to Andrew. "Josephine and I are fixing to have a very personal conversation."

"Nothing went on here," Andrew says. "I swear to you."

Stanislowski looks at Josephine. "What the hell is he talking about?"

Josephine doesn't answer, so he turns to Andrew. "You want to tell me what in the living hell you're talking about, there, Andrew?"

"She asked me to put a box of your clothes up in the attic."

"Okay."

"I was coming home early and Ruthie asked her to delay me. There's a party for me."

"I know that," Stanislowski says.

"That was Ruthie," Josephine says to Andrew. "Go on, go."

Stanislowski stares at them. He smiles, but the smile dies on his lips and then he's just waiting there in the doorway. He looks old. For the first time in her life with him, she sees his age as a separate thing, a fact about him, like something that might be explained to her. At first she's happy about this—it's a realization of just how much his age has *not* meant. But then she sees him start out the door, and move away.

"Get out," she says to Andrew. "Christ!"

He moves slowly, through the door and out. She waits. She doesn't want to be within ten feet of him. Finally, making her way out onto the sidewalk, she looks one way and sees the empty prospect of the street with the houses on either side, and Andrew in it, walking unsteadily toward his house. Up the other way, her husband has paid the taxi and is just walking along behind it as it pulls away. She calls his name and he turns and stops. It's as if he doesn't really know where to go. She walks up and embraces him. "Stan," she says. "Let's just stay home." She puts her face into the cloth of his shirt, letting go, crying. Everything she has been through with him and everything that has brought them to this trouble is rushing through her. She steps back, and looks into his face.

"We've got to go now," he says. "And I want to get drunk."

"Oh," she says. "God. You're—oh, Christ." She turns from him and starts back to the house. There isn't anything else to do, nothing else she can think of. She hears him walking behind her.

"Josephine," he says.

Approaching them from the other direction is the young couple walking the baby in the stroller. The man is pushing it now, and Josephine sees that the woman is really quite a bit taller than he. She stops to admire the baby, wanting Stanislowski to catch up to her. He does. Not quite looking at each other, they chat amiably with the couple about the fine weather, and they make a fuss over the infant, so pretty, only three months old. It's as if Josephine and her husband are two separate people, strangers to each other, who have stopped to gaze upon the child. Josephine leans down and smiles at the small, round, faintly disgruntled face, cooing, Stanislowski waiting there behind her with his terrible doubts and his fears and his hurt. She touches the top of the baby's head and then sees that the two people are staring, and she realizes that tears are streaming down her face. She walks away, back to the house and in. The door slaps to behind her. The rooms are darker now, the sun having crossed over to the other side of the house. She sits in the living room with the guitar, and begins to tune it down again to the drop D. The window looking out on the backyard is full of the late light. He comes in and sits down, sighing wearily.

"I'm sorry. And we can't not go."

She says, "You know what? *You* can go. Or you can go back to your studio, okay? Really. Go. Take the car, take a cab, or walk it, hitchhike, steal a car for all I care about it."

He's looking at her. His face is haggard, pale, and grieving. "Look, I didn't think you and Andrew—" he says. Then: "Really." He sighs. "And have I made it so you have to worry about everything so much?"

She doesn't answer.

"We can't fail to show up. It'll mean more than it could possibly really mean."

"You're not making sense."

"It's a surprise party to which we've said we'd go. We have to go."

"So we'll go," she tells him. "But when *I'm* ready to."

After a brief silence, he says, "It always calms you down, music. Me, it agitates. That's one of the little differences between us."

She begins to perform the song she's been working on. It's a thing she can do, play this instrument, any instrument. She can make them come alive. People have spoken of their amazement. She's good. And she's innocent of any wrongdoing, too—guilty of nothing but the need to be admired. And she still loves him.

"Is that new?" he says quietly, tentatively. "That's new."

She doesn't answer. Doesn't look up. The thought comes to her that this will never change between them; he'll always doubt her feeling. She sees herself growing tired of it, weary enough to leave. The idea frightens her, and she stops playing for a moment. But she has command of her emotions now. She wipes her eyes and adjusts the tuning slightly while he watches.

"That was beautiful, what you played." His voice is small, heavy with his sad imaginings, and with regret. "I've missed you, sweetheart. I've missed you bad."

"I've been right here." She resumes playing. The music as she has composed it involves a modulation into F sharp. She executes it, and then plays the melody line through in a slower tempo.

"That's brilliant," he says. His praise has always meant so much to her. "That's just a wonderful piece of music."

"Thank you," she says.

"But you're watching your playing hand again."

She lifts her eyes and stares directly back into his, and, with a brittle smile, plays on.

BYRON THE LYRON

She was eighty-nine and had lived a long, rich life, and she told her one son, Byron, that she was ready. Byron Mailley wept, putting his head down on her shoulder. Georgia's shoulder. They were in her hospital room—the hospital wing of Brighton Creek Farm, the assisted living facility she had resided in over the last decade. She patted the back of his head. Always her most charming gesture of affection toward him— since he was nine or ten, and learning the complications of being a bookish boy on a street full of rough characters. Her name for them. She had a way of setting all his problems in terms of the books they read together in the evenings because he couldn't sleep. The books were all adventure: Hardy Boys and Nancy Drew, Robert Louis Stevenson, Theodore J. Waldeck's book *Lions on the Hunt*, written from the point of view of the young lion. Byron the lyron, she called him. It was their little joke, just between them.

Byron the lyron had night terrors, panic attacks.

Fears of cancer, fears of madness, split personality, delusions, polio, tuberculosis, the atomic bomb, the death of parents. His father gone—first with the military, flying jets, then just gone. Remarried far away. Far away was good, actually, because Father had wanted Byron to be tough, and had worked to accomplish it: drill-like discipline early; a looming displeased powerful presence early. Byron tried hard, and couldn't make the grade, as Father put it. There were fights between Georgia and the old man about the boy. The old man was gone but the panic attacks started not long after he left.

Night was a terrible prospect. He'd sit crying, nine years old, and she, pregnant with the child she would lose, her husband gone away, sat up with Byron, patiently holding him, humming to him, patting the back of his head; then, on into the next year, the terrors recurring, and it was really just the two of them for good (her words). And she'd read other things to him: Dickens, the Bible—laughing about all the *begot*s, and showing a slight impatience with the heavy seriousness. Well, it was explaining, after all, *everything*. But language is fun, too, she told him. Play.

Let's play.

He had always felt that she was more friend than mother.

Now he wept, and she patted his head and murmured, "Stop. Stop."

So he stopped. *Brave girl*, he thought. But kept still.

"Tell me what happened," she said.

She meant this about Reese. "I'm not crying about Reese," he told her. But partly he was. The look in his own eyes, he knew, admitted it. She patted the side of his face.

"Just tell me."

He kissed her hand, and held it. "Georgia," he murmured. "What will I do?"

"Tell me about Reese."

Last week, after twelve years, Reese had announced tearfully that he was leaving—this just two days past a big surprise party, Byron's fifty-fifth birthday. He'd invited everyone

Byron knew, going back to school days. Even Ms. Evelyn Wasson, his seventh-grade teacher. She read a wonderful tribute she had written about her certainty that Byron Mailley would make something of himself. Such a bright, look-right-at-you little boy, she said, with her endearing habit of using hyphenated expressions in her talk. She went on about Byron, about his work as a magazine photographer, his time in Rome in his twenties, sending her postcards and pictures he had taken of the magnificent places and the wonderful people he had come to know. Several other people spoke as well. Reese stood there proudly, smiling during it all. He'd arranged everything. He led the applause and finally offered a toast to Byron for his generosity and his goodness. Nobody more kindly than Byron, taking Reese in at such a time in his life, offering love, nurture, tolerating his neuroses, his failures of love and sensibility. A true artist, Byron. Not Reese—who was, in fact, a fairly successful painter. He said uncharacteristically self-deprecating things all evening. He had put together a show of some of Byron's photographs.

Byron's mother, ill, failing, already in the hospital wing, couldn't be there, but Reese made a tape, and took it over there the next morning and played it for her. She was listening to it when Byron came to see her that evening, not twenty minutes past the revelation, delivered in the upstairs hallway of the house, in a weepy regretful voice by Reese, that he must find his way alone for a time, and was leaving. Byron had been an emotional nursemaid all these years, surely Byron could see this, that Reese would never reach any kind of autonomy if he stayed any longer. "We can be friends," Reese said. "I so want that, Byron."

Byron knew there must be someone else for Reese, now, though it was true that Byron had done plenty of nursemaiding from the beginning. Reese had been Georgia's physical therapist; that was how they had all met—Reese, a young artist, working for Blue Ridge Orthopedic Clinic to make enough money to put food on the table, had worked with Georgia after her knee replacement surgery, and Georgia had introduced him to Byron. Reese came over to see Georgia and to work with her, and then it was just visiting. They made each other laugh. Reese was sad a lot of the time and had other troubles, mostly having to do with confidence in his work, and confidence in general. There was a neediness in him, about which he often teased. It was charming, though like most teasing it hinted at the truth. Byron and Reese began going to see Georgia together, and everything progressed quite naturally to the next stage. They had lived together quite happily, it seemed to Byron, but then Reese had begun to do well enough with his painting to quit the physiotherapy, and there were, Byron had to admit, subtle changes.

The kindest way of seeing this was that Reese was being honest in his own self-deluding way; he had depended on Byron so long, and now wanted to strike out on his own. Byron chose to look at it this way. He was by nature kindly. Not that kindness came easily to him: kindliness is work. And perhaps Reese felt the necessity of the big surprise party and the tributes in order to salve his conscience for what he knew he was already doing. But the hundred and twenty townspeople who came to the party wanted to honor Byron. They all loved him, and for good reason.

Georgia reminded him of this, looking at him now, her still-dark hair spread on the pillow so lovely. "You know you could never hide anything from me. It hurts when someone leaves you. I felt it, too, you know."

"I don't want to talk about Reese anymore," Byron said. "Let's talk about something else."

"Reese was here, today, too, son. Earlier."

Byron couldn't speak for a few seconds. "Well, he's moving out."

"He wants to come see me tomorrow."

Byron shrugged. Again, there was a pause. "I guess that's between the two of you."

"Tell me about your party," she said. "The good parts."

But she was drugged, and the drowse began to work in her. And he felt uncomfortably sullen, because she had talked so casually about Reese coming to see her. He spoke halfheartedly about Ms. Wasson and her memory of him writing to her from Rome. Try as she might—and she did try—Georgia's lids grew heavy; they closed and opened in that sluggish way, the eyes glazing over. Feeling the pressure to bring it up anyway, Byron went on to say that Reese had planned the party and seemed very happy doing that—deciding on the guest list, on the way it would all go. He drove a hundred miles west and south, to the Tennessee line, and bought five hundred dollars' worth of fireworks, using his own savings account. Byron, seeing how much he apparently needed this, let him have his way about it. It was not in Byron's makeup to seek this kind of thing. He liked a party; he was gregarious and—people talked about it—he had wonderful ability as a raconteur and storyteller, could do any accent in the world, and would do so, telling a joke, so that the experience of it was positively dramatic. But in truth, he was also rather self-effacing. He had known so many punk jerks parading themselves during his time in Rome and New York. All those years hustling photographs. His strongest sense of how life ought to be lived had always involved the old idea that one didn't let the right hand know what the left was doing. One was generous without considering who might know it. No telling how much can be accomplished if we don't care who gets the credit. Byron had performed all sorts of kindnesses, the source of which the recipients of those kindnesses never knew. No one ever knew. Not even Georgia, who knew most everything else.

She slept now. He adjusted the blanket across her slowly rising and falling chest, kissed her cheek softly, and stood there weeping silently for a moment. Then he moved to the door and out. It would be soon, the doctors all said. A week, two weeks. Her heart was so tired; it was giving out slowly. Byron went to the nurse's station and reiterated that he wished to be called if there was the slightest change. Each of the last five nights, he had left Georgia sleeping peacefully. She claimed no nightmares, no frights. It was all right. He held her hand and she went in and out of sleep, and when they talked it was nearly as it always had been—her interest in the world hadn't flagged at all.

Outside, in the chill of early March, he walked to the car and got in. The street was windy; the traffic light wavered and threw its red light on the walls of the buildings at the first intersection. Byron drove there and waited for the light to change. The street looked empty, and the emptiness of it seemed a kind of anguish coming at him, not for himself, but for Georgia, lying alone in that narrow room in the coming night. He turned around in the middle of the intersection, drove back to the parking lot, and hurried into the building, hoping she hadn't awakened, even for a moment, in his absence. At the nurse's station the woman gave him a past-visiting-hours look. He nodded at her and went on to Georgia's room, and took his chair.

When she woke again, she wanted to talk about the party, so he told how the fireworks went off among the branches of the trees and scared everyone; how there were hurrahs and shouts of excitement, and how everyone had a good time. As he talked, he remembered calling her from the bedroom telephone. She had sounded so chipper, so happy for him. He heard the weakness, and the slight breathlessness, but she had her wits about her in spite of the medicine, thinking to ask if his new next-door neighbor, Mrs. Ewing, had brought her dog with her to the party—Mrs. Ewing being one of those people who treated her dogs and cats better than she ever treated any human being, including her own daughter, Marvina, who was a good friend of Georgia's and Byron's. Mrs. Ewing had recently come to Marvina's house to restore order, as she saw it, Marvina being undisciplined and still single at forty-three.

Eight years ago, Georgia, Byron, and Marvina went to Rome on one of Georgia's whims. Georgia had lived there briefly when she went to Europe before the war, and she said she wanted to be in the city with Byron, to see where he had lived and walked and been happy. One of her dearest friends was an opera singer who lived near the Pantheon. They all sat out on the Piazza Navona, drinking Campari and soda, and the opera singer, whose name was Umberto, broke into an aria, drunk and happy, leaning toward Georgia as if to serenade her. He was a big, florid man, who kept saying, When will you come live here with me? It was all joking, because Umberto already had a companion, Pietro, who had lost a leg in the war, and now served as his personal secretary. Georgia kept saying that she wished Reese had been able to make the journey—but Reese was recovering from shoulder surgery.

Over the years, Byron often thought of returning to the

ancient city, and he would trouble Georgia about it, believing that she was settling in too well at Brighton Creek Farm. She knew this of course, and she would say, "I'm happy. Really. I can go anywhere, just closing my eyes."

He stayed in her room until well past midnight. She slept again, breathing easily, perfectly still, no slightest stress in her features. He nodded off, and shook himself awake; it happened several times. When he went home at last, he couldn't sleep. Reese had come in and taken most of his things. A row of his paintings leaned against the downstairs wall, with a note attached: he'd be by to pick this up in the morning. There were a few items of furniture, a few books, some bric-a-brac. It had always been Byron who did most of the collecting of things. Reese never kept many books; yet the empty places in the shelves showed.

The lights were on next door at the Ewings', so Byron went out and walked the sidewalk in front of the two houses. A clear, cold night, with a moon and moon-shadows everywhere. If Marvina wanted company, she would see him and come to the door. This was how they had navigated socializing since Mrs. Ewing had moved into the house. Marvina had never been one to keep regular hours and was often awake all night. She liked to sleep in, and frequently took naps in the middle of the afternoons. Alma Ewing had attempted to put a stop to all that. Like most people concerned with morality in others, Alma believed that early-to-bed, early-to-rise was the most healthy way of living. Tonight Marvina was up—he could hear music—but she didn't come to the door, and finally he went back into his own house, and got into bed. He could still hear her music—the Rolling Stones—and she was probably playing it loud to annoy her mother. Perhaps it was partly the music that kept him awake.

. . .

Early the next morning, he heard Reese downstairs, collecting the last of the paintings, and realized that there were two voices. Byron buried his face in his pillows and tried not to hear anything, his heart hurting so awfully he wondered if he were not having a coronary: how physical heartbreak was! He would never have believed it. He thought he had felt it before; but this was completely and terribly new. The rattling downstairs took a very long, bad time, but at last it ended. He took the pillow away, got up slowly, rubbing his chest, and walked downstairs. Paintings gone. The house to himself. He sat at the kitchen table with a cup of coffee and wept quietly.

Perhaps an hour later Marvina walked over to ask if there was anything she could do. He'd showered, shaved, and dressed, and he felt slightly better. It was just itself, the same pure pressure under the heart, the same band of deep aching. He had gathered some of the cards and letters that had come from Georgia's far-flung friendships—many of these people were bedridden themselves, or housebound. They ranged as far away as India, and as close as next door (Marvina).

She wanted to bring something for Georgia to read. She was also contemplating a basket of fruit—Georgia had always loved Bosc pears, and they were particularly good now. But then she also had no appetite to speak of.

"What do you think?" Marvina asked.

"Your music was on late," Byron said. "Were you up late?"

"I took a pill and went to sleep. Did it keep you up? I meant it to keep Alma up."

Byron smiled. "Did it?"

"Alma's sleeping late," Marvina said.

They smiled. He was astonished that he could smile. It rose up in him like the freshest air.

They went together to the small grocery store down the street. Marvina drove. They bought several pears, some apples, and clementines. She found a small straw basket in the little boutique next to the grocery. She bought it, and a linen cloth, which she folded over the fruit. It looked enough like a gift basket. Georgia liked things homemade, this way. Something that took time to make was much more valuable and fine as a gift. Every year in early fall she began fashioning the things she would give for Christmas: knitted mittens and scarves, calendars she had made out of old photographs, cards with cutout trees on them, decorated frames, corkboards. Every gift had something of the person it was intended for—a theme or a special flavor reflecting her feeling for that person.

"She'll like the smell of the clementines," Byron said.

"Some flowers?" Marvina frowned. "No."

They said little on the drive over. It was bright, chilly, windless; the little puffs of scattered cloud seemed utterly motionless in the wide, pure blue. At the hospital Marvina got out first. Byron carried the basket of fruit. In the room, they found Reese sitting with Georgia, who was asleep.

"She hasn't waked yet," Reese said. His eyes were rounded with shadow. He didn't look at Byron, or at Marvina. Byron moved around Georgia's bed and took her hand. It was warm. He squeezed it. There was the slightest squeezing back. Perhaps he had imagined it.

"Tell her I was here?" Reese said, looking sorrowful.

Byron nodded at him. Marvina and Reese went out, then, and he was alone with Georgia and the basket of fruit, in this room that was so institutional and clean, with its dull art and its cheerful paint and its television. He went around to the chair and sat down, but the chair was still warm from Reese. He stood quickly, reached over, and took his mother's other hand, and she opened her eyes.

"It's hard on poor Reese," she said. "I think he's confused."

"You were awake."

"For some of it. Some." She squeezed his hand. "He just sits there looking at me and trying not to cry. I didn't let him know I saw."

"I think he has someone else," Byron said.

She squeezed his hand again. "Maybe not."

Byron told her about the two voices he had heard.

"Could be a friend."

"I don't understand him," Byron said. "Does he not know I'd tell you he left me?"

She shook her head, but didn't speak. A moment passed, in which he thought she might have gone back to sleep. Then: "I'm so tired, son."

He sat down again, still holding her hand. "Marvina drove me over here. We brought you some fruit."

The little squeeze, again. He began to have to fight tears. He had wanted so to be cheerful, to get Marvina talking and gossiping about her mother. Georgia would like the idea of Alma Ewing sleeping late, having been kept up with *Hot Rocks* playing at volume.

Presently, when it was clear that Georgia was sleeping again, he let go of her hand and went to the door of the room. At the far end of the hall, two nurses stood talking. There was no sign of Marvina or Reese. He went back into the room and sat down, and took Georgia's hand once more. Just in time. She turned slightly, and looked at him.

"I smell clementines," she said, and smiled.

He reached for the basket, but when he turned back around, she had gone back to sleep. He ate a pear, and waited, and began quietly to cry again, the tears running down his cheeks. When he heard Marvina talking to one of the nurses, he slipped into Georgia's little bathroom and ran water over his face, wiped his eyes, dried himself with one of those brown paper towels. His nose was running, like a kid's, with crying.

In the room, Marvina had opened the curtains wider to let in more sun. Georgia was still asleep.

"Reese is a mess," Marvina said.

"I don't want to talk about him," Byron said. "Really, Marvina." He offered her the chair, and she declined, standing there looking over the fruit, picking up a pear and setting it back, finally settling on a clementine. When she opened it, the fragrance went all over the room. A nurse brought another chair, Marvina having apparently asked for it earlier. Byron thought of these humble practical arrangements in a kind of nightmarish light, as if their very ordinariness were a flaunting of the awful facts, the plain objective world brandishing itself at him, while his mother slipped away forever.

Georgia Susan Michael Townsend Mailley. The *Michael* was there at her father's insistence, after his younger brother, who was killed at the Marne River in 1918. A picture of this young soldier hung on the wall in her parents' house all their lives. Soft features, round eyes, small straight mouth—an open, intelligent, innocent face. Hard to imagine him being shot in the neck, bleeding to death on a barbed-wire fence in the rain and sludge of a terrible May morning all those years ago. Georgia had kept the picture on the foyer wall of her own house for most of Byron's growing up. It had lain in a box of her things for the years she lived at Brighton Creek Farm. Byron, according to his grandfather, favored the long-dead uncle. Georgia had resisted the name for him, incurring her father's wrath. As she had often done. She had, he would say, confounded him at every turn—in fact, he had taken it upon himself to warn others about the difficulties of raising a daughter. He would call friends when their wives had children, to congratulate them if they had sons and to commiserate with them if they had daughters.

Georgia married young, and then left that marriage after a period of only weeks; the fellow reminded her too much, she said, of her father—it was her father, though, who had it annulled. His frustrations with her over the years were tinged with admiration, no matter how dismayed he seemed. Georgia had done more in the world than all the sons of his friends and associates. After the marriage episode, which took place her last year of high school, she went on to Radcliffe, graduated early, then traveled to live in Europe. She didn't return until just before the outbreak of hostilities in 1939. One of her favorite stories was how, in June 1934, working for a foreign press service as a secretary and occasional feature writer, she had climbed partway up a lamppost to set eyes upon Adolf Hitler himself, a ridiculous-looking little Chaplinesque man standing in the back of a big black automobile with one hand up in that farcical salute. Later that day she was ejected from a café for imitating the führer's stance. She would laugh, telling the story. "I was young, you know. Only twenty or so."

Byron got his storytelling ability from her. He'd also gotten the adventuresome, generous spirit—though he would never attribute this kind of thing to himself. Others, who knew them both, did. Georgia was her own country, some said, meaning it as the highest praise. An empire, was Georgia, with her several careers, her loves and tumultuous friendships and loyalties. No one ever left her willingly except one—the second husband. The military man. He had flown for the air corps over Germany, and after the war he flew for the airlines, three years of that before reenlisting. He was a retired colonel somewhere out west, the last Byron heard, with a fourth wife and a pair of young twins. Probably ramrod straight, those twins, Georgia would say.

She had outlived so many of her friends and companions, most of whom were older than she had been. There was something about her that drew people to her, from her earliest life. Who could imagine a girl twenty-something years old traveling alone, employed by a wire service, to write about conditions in the new Germany? But she had done that. She had also been in plays off Broadway, and written a memoir that was published, about life in England just after the war—the rebuilding of London. And when she had Byron, with the air corps chap, as she called him, she settled in this little Virginia town to raise her son, her family. She thought she would have more children—hoped for half a dozen, anyway. But things changed rapidly: hostilities in Korea—and at home—caused her husband to go away, and she lost the second child unexpectedly, at almost eight months. Byron had memories of the long night when that happened, pacing in the too brightly lit waiting room with his grandfather and several friends from the library where she had gone to work. He would never forget the look of fright on his grandfather's face. "I'm afraid we're going to lose her," the old man said.

How strange to think of that now. He held her hand, and wept a little more, trying to keep it from Marvina, who ate another pear and then called her mother to wake her. That was the announced purpose of the call, and she said it to please Georgia, who had opened her eyes long enough to nod and smile.

"No answer," Marvina said.

"Poor woman," said Georgia.

A little later, she asked Byron for a piece of paper. It hurt to talk. She signaled that her throat was sore and dry. Marvina got her some water, and she sipped it carefully, seemed to hold it a long time in her mouth. Byron was afraid she might pass out with it still there, and choke. But she swallowed it, and then wrote on the paper: *Byron, I'm dying.* He looked at it, and then at her face, with that strange peaceful smile. She wrote again: *For a clementine.*

Marvina, reading over his shoulder, sobbed and said, "Oh, God. Georgia—if that isn't typical of you." She was laughing and crying at the same time.

"I'm sorry," Georgia said, rasping. "That was mean."

Byron shook his head, and helped calm Marvina down. Georgia wrote another note, asking for some music—she had brought with her a complete set of the Sinatra-Dorsey recordings, and Byron put it on for her. She had two songs she especially liked from those years: "April Played the Fiddle" and "Everything Happens to Me."

They put the music on, and sat listening to it. A nurse came in and worked on the IV lines, then asked Byron and Marvina to leave, so she could help Georgia go to the bathroom, and take a spritz bath. They went together down to the cafeteria and had a cup of coffee. There were several other people there, all looking tired and worried, clearly wishing they could be anywhere else. At one table a pair of young girls sat with an older brother, and they had balloons announcing the birth of a sister. The balloons were tied to the chair in which one of the girls sat. They were eating pastries and ignoring one another.

"Guess I'll call Alma again," Marvina said. "Poor woman."

"Tell me about Reese," said Byron.

She shrugged. "He's confused. Sick at heart. You know how he feels about Georgia. And you."

"He's seeing someone else, Marvina."

"I think he was feeling smothered by everyone's love for you, Byron. No kidding. That's what it sounded like this morning, talking to him. He kept saying he didn't want to compete. He felt awful that we got there while he was visiting Georgia."

"How could he think we wouldn't come to see her?"

"He was leaving—you know."

"No, I don't want to talk about him."

She reached into her purse, brought out her cell phone, and dialed Alma, who answered this time. Alma claimed she'd been up and around, had gone out to the store to buy groceries. She asked how Georgia was.

Marvina told her about the clementine incident, winking at Byron. The clementine incident would profoundly disturb Alma. Marvina said this, after disconnecting with Alma, and then seemed to catch herself. "God almighty, what the hell am I saying?" And she began to cry.

They returned upstairs, to find that Georgia was still being attended to. The door was closed. They waited at the nurse's station in the garish light, while people moved around them and past them. An old, old man walked by, slowly, pulling his own IV apparatus with him. His slippers made a whispery noise. When the nurse opened the door and smiled at them, Georgia was falling asleep again. Movement of any kind, the nurse said, was exhausting for her. She had been a little sick.

"What a lady," the nurse whispered. "She apologized to me

for it. Imagine that." Byron wanted to embrace her. For a moment they all just stood there, appreciating the small slender woman in the bed, lying so still, breathing softly, sleeping, it seemed, without dreams.

That afternoon, Marvina had to go home for a while, and Byron told her to go on. He'd stay the night. "Oh, I'll come back," Marvina said. "I would've been here last night only—" She shrugged. Her mother, of course. Alma, for all her talk about salvaging things for her impractical daughter, needed attention. And poor Marvina had to give it without actually seeming to.

Byron accompanied her to the elevators and hugged her. She kissed his cheek, and she was sniffling as the doors closed on her. He went back to Georgia's room, and found her awake.

"I had a dream," she said. Her eyes were blazing. "It wasn't a good dream."

He moved to the chair and took her hand again. "Tell me."

"It's silly. I was doing a calendar for someone. But then something went wrong with it. All the pictures kept dissolving, and I couldn't pick them up. It swept over me, somehow. It was just awful. It was just a calendar I had ruined, but it was terrifying."

He reached for her other hand, and they sat there. He thought she might be going back to sleep, and he felt himself hoping for it.

"I'm scared," she said suddenly. "Oh, hell. I thought I'd dealt with this."

"I'm right here," Byron said.

She held tight, weathering it, enduring it; it swept through her in a trembling, her hand so tight in his that he marveled at how strong she still was. She'd shut her eyes, but was not sleep-ing. No, she was trying to put something away from her, inside, trying to master herself. When she opened her eyes again, they were still rounded and too bright. "Oh," she said. "Damn it all."

He stood and leaned over, trying to embrace her—she wouldn't let go of his hand. "I love you," he said.

"Read something to me," she said. But she wouldn't let go of him. So they remained that way until, at last, she seemed to let down, sighing, drifting a little, then jerking awake. Each time this happened, she squeezed tight again, and looked at him out of those brilliantly lighted eyes. There was something nearly supernatural in the way they shone.

After a long interval, she let go, and he sat back down. She was still awake. She stared at him as if not quite able to discern who he was. Then she patted the bed and said, "I'm sorry. Read to me?"

So he read some of the cards and letters, all expressing the hope—the faith, really—that she would come through this and be her old self. One of them was from a priest she had known in Europe before the war.

"I miss the consolations of religion," she said, interrupt-ing him.

"Do you—would you like me to see if—"

"If someone would take me?" She smiled, then. "Funny."

He was at a loss. He went on reading the letter, but then saw that she was staring beyond him, at the door. He turned, expecting Marvina. It was Reese. Evidently he had waited until Byron saw him. He came forward into the room, with his own little gift of soaps and lotions in a basket. "For your hands," he said to Georgia.

She raised one arm so he could come be hugged and kissed.

It was always the way they had greeted each other. Byron took his clumsy embrace in turn, then opened a bottle of lotion for his mother. He and Reese watched Georgia put the lotion on her hands, being careful of the place where the IV went into the back of the right one. She looked from one to the other of them. There was still that unsettling brightness in her eyes, as if the fear were still climbing inside her, and she was choosing to pretend it wasn't there. But then the nurse came in, time for changing things again, and she shooed them out into the hall. They stood there in the fading early evening light from the window at that end. Across from them several people were ranged around the bed of another woman, also old, and probably also dying; this was, after all, where they brought people from the assisted living part of Brighton Creek Farm.

Out the window was the building where she had come to stay ten years ago. They were both staring out at it. Byron feeling the pain in his lower chest, wanting not to show it, wanting to be far away from Reese. Perhaps he would go down to the cafeteria for something he wouldn't eat, having no appetite now. But Reese might go with him. Or stay and be alone with Georgia.

"Remember when we brought her here to talk to them," Reese said now. "That first time?"

Byron nodded, without quite looking at him.

"Who was that guy? I can't remember his name."

"Scottish sounding," said Byron, who remembered perfectly well the name, McCutcheon. He said, "Mac-something."

"I can't recall it," Reese said.

They were quiet. Georgia had sat patiently listening to McCutcheon talk about all the advantages of assisted living, and she had abruptly interrupted him to say, "Excuse me, are you quite serious?"

The man stared.

Georgia turned to Reese—yes, it had been Reese—and said, "This guy's an ass, isn't he?"

Byron remembered that now, and he knew Reese was remembering it, too. He almost said something. But the nurse opened the door again, and came out, and they could go back in to Georgia, who lay with eyes closed, in fresh sheets and fresh nightgown. Soon they would bring dinner. But she would probably not eat it. She had eaten a little of the clementine. Food was the one thing that had ceased to interest her particularly; it was such an effort to chew.

She opened her eyes. "Boys," she said.

"Sister," Reese said. That was what he had always called her.

"Tell me about it," she said, looking at neither of them.

Reese began to cry. Byron went back out into the hall. He heard Georgia say his name, and hesitated. But when he looked back into the room he saw that Reese was bent over the bed, holding her hand, and she was saying something to him.

Byron felt a rage rising in him, and he went down to the cafeteria and ordered coffee. He sensed, with a small stab of regret, his own abruptness toward the slow lady behind the counter, who handed him the coffee with a lackluster shrug and went about cleaning the grill. He moved to a table alone and sat, hands shaking, sipping the coffee, which was too hot. He couldn't believe his own anger. And he felt it at Georgia, too, for accepting Reese's affection, knowing what she knew. It hurt him, at a level for which he was unprepared. How could she, knowing what she knew?

But then he remembered, with a sinking at his heart, what she also knew.

He couldn't decide what to do with his own emotions. He

drank the coffee, which burned his tongue, and he sat there feeling childish. He actually had the child's thought, *I'll go away and then they'll be sorry.* "Stupid," he said, aloud. Then put his hands to his face and wept.

When he went back up to the room, he found the door open, Reese gone, Georgia lying there staring out the window. He went to the chair and sat down. They had brought her a meal, which she hadn't touched—a roll, mashed potatoes, three slices of turkey, all of it looking like a frozen dinner. She'd had a little of the apple juice, which she had apparently asked for.

"You didn't eat," he said.

"Don't be mad at me, son. I'm unable to select anymore. Don't want to."

"I don't understand," he told her, because he didn't.

"I don't know what happened with you and Reese," she said. Then she took a deep breath, so weighted with exhaustion that he was alarmed, and thought she might pass out. "I don't want to send anybody away from here," she said. "Not now. Do you understand?"

"Yes," he said.

"I'm not convinced."

"No," he said. "I do."

"Byron the lyron," she murmured. "You know I always meant it, that you were brave."

"I'm not brave," Byron said.

"Yes." She raised one hand, almost as if to wave at him. "I'll be the judge of that." It was automatic now, and she was falling asleep again. He moved the tray of food away, and then sat watching her sleep. Marvina came back in at last, with her mother. Alma wanted to say hello. Marvina had brought cards, and when Georgia woke, the two of them played a couple of slow rounds of gin rummy, on Georgia's dinner tray. Later, Reese came back, and stood off to one side, watching the card game. Everyone was gentle, and in the pauses when Georgia slipped off to her fitful sleep, they were quiet, and quite still, almost as if frozen that way in a photograph.

They all left at the end of the evening visiting hour. Georgia was sound asleep. Very still, breathing very easily. Reese kissed her cheek. Marvina and Alma did, too. Byron held her hand again for a while, and then kissed her himself. Outside the room, he took Reese by the arm just above the elbow. For a second, it was almost impossible to draw in air. Marvina and her mother had gone a ways down the hall. "I'll be right along," Byron said to them. They went on. Reese was looking at him with a kind of resigned alarm.

"I want you to be here for her," Byron said, low. Scarcely able to get it out. "She wants it, and I want it. No standing to the side. No hanging back. Please."

Reese nodded, his eyes widening slightly.

"I don't want any confusion about it. Nothing is changed between you and me if you're here for her. Only don't let her see you hanging back. This is about *her* bravery. Not yours, or mine."

"Thank you," Reese said, with a deep sigh. "You have always been—" He didn't finish. He just looked down and repeated the phrase: "Thank you."

Byron let go, and they walked side by side down to where the other two waited. He rode with Marvina and her mother back to the house. Reese had gone off to wherever he was staying now in the city.

When they got to the house, they saw that the Ewings' dogs and cats where setting up a ruckus. Marvina hurried her mother in, and then came back to where Byron was standing on his porch. He'd had the sense she wanted to speak with him.

"Reese *is* seeing someone else," she said. "I hope I'm doing the right thing telling you."

He bent slightly at the waist, from the pain. He turned from her, and looked out at the lights of his town.

"I'm sorry, Byron. And I think he's miserable." Byron couldn't get enough air again. He faced her, breathless, all dark inside, a desolation—a man losing everything. Marvina walked over and put her arms around him. "I'm so sorry," she said. "Want me to stay tonight?"

He shook his head. "I told him to keep coming to see Georgia. She wants it."

Marvina shrugged; her expression seemed to say that it was hard to explain.

No, Byron thought. It wasn't really so hard to explain at all. Georgia had said to him, quite honestly and gently, what she required. It wasn't too much to ask. He could find a way to do what she wanted. He was Byron the lyron.

Georgia Susan Michael Townsend Mailley passed away in the middle of the night, almost exactly one week later. There was no warning; it happened quite suddenly and peacefully. Her son was downstairs in the cafeteria, with Marvina, drinking coffee. Reese had left, with a promise of returning in the morning, first thing. Everyone had settled into a pattern of visiting with the failing woman, who seemed at the end to be growing stronger, and holding on. She was alert when awake, and herself, right to the end.

After her passing, the people who had stood with her at the edge of her darkness drifted to other lives, as people do—Marvina took her mother's advice and sold her house. The two women live in a duplex in the old town section of Charlottesville, Virginia. Reese went out to California with his new companion for a year or so, and then came back to Virginia. He took a job teaching art in the local high school, and continued to make money with his painting. Byron moved to New York again, and worked for a magazine there for a few months, then settled in a little walk-up flat on a narrow street in Rome. He still lives there, and not always alone. Now and then he walks out near sunset and takes pictures of the old part of the city, those ancient buildings, with their long history, their beauty and complication, their tragedy and triumph, their songs and their sorrow.

REVEREND THORNHILL'S WIFE

Keeping strictly to the early-morning ritual, Diana prepared coffee, boiled one egg, and lightly buttered two slices of toast for him, then put cereal on for the girls, and went and dressed for the day, while they ate. When they were finished, she rinsed the dishes and put them in the dishwasher. In the usual rush, she saw the twins off to school, brushing Lauren's hair for her, and nagging Kelly about brushing her teeth thoroughly to get the food particles that had lodged in her braces. All as usual. So much the exact pattern of her mornings. The ordinariness of it made her happy, and it surprised her. It also increased her sense of unreality.

From the doorway, she watched them climb on the bus, hauling their book bags. They waved to her from the windows, as they always did, and she waved back, and the motion of her own small hand crossing the plane of her vision seemed to swipe the ordinary feeling away. She felt the truth, a shock, though it was thrilling, too. Clutching her blouse tight at her throat against the slight chill, she watched the bus move off. Then she went into the living room and sat with her hands clasped tightly over her knees, waiting for him to finish shaving and dressing.

When she heard the bathroom door open, she hurried into

the kitchen and pretended to be just finishing there when he came down the hall. He kissed her on the cheek. "Have fun," he said, as he had said every morning for going on twelve years.

"You, too," she told him.

She watched him cross the shady lawn to the car. He waved, going away, and she held up one hand. She was in this now, and she did not feel guilty. After the car turned at the end of the road, she closed the door and went through the rooms, making sure the place looked right. She took some personal items of his—hairbrush, cologne, a Bible concordance—and put them in the hall closet, along with a wedding picture and several family photographs. At last, taking a deep breath to ease her trembling, she made the call.

"I'm alone."

"I'll be right over."

"Where are you?"

"Midtown. I looked up the directions online. Can't wait to see you."

She breathed into the line. "Hurry."

"Oh, yes," he said, and hung up.

She headed for the bathroom, slipping out of her clothes as she went. It was all delicious action, bright with purpose and anticipation. In the bathroom, she folded the clothes and set them on top of the hamper. On the wall opposite the shower stall was a print of four Indian maidens washing clothes in a stream, the pristine rush of blue-white water over stones. Behind them was an orderly procession of trees, mountains, and sky. She looked at the picture as if it belonged to someone else. Everything was under way; it was going to happen. She turned to the mirror and put a dash of light-pink lipstick on, standing naked at the sink, and, with a few soft strokes of her fingers, arranged her hair.

In the bedroom, she opened the closet, brought out a robe, and draped it over herself. She stopped in the hallway, held on to the wall, inhaling and letting it out slowly, repeating this five times, counting.

Movement was best. She went into the living room and lifted a blade of the closed window blinds only a fraction of an inch to look out at the street. Phyllis Copperfield, crazy Phyllis, a woman who lived by the clock, had come out of her house with the baby in a running stroller. She wore spandex slacks, and had a bandanna around her head, her hair tied in a ponytail that swung from side to side when she walked. At the top of the street, she began to run, and she was gone.

Phyllis had been one of her chief worries. They had been friendly, and Phyllis knew things, had gleaned something of Diana's dissatisfactions. Phyllis herself was by her own account going slowly crazy. Her husband was often out of town— sometimes for weeks at a time—and she was alone with a baby whom she hadn't wanted and whose demands made her miserable and sleepless. She would say terrible things about her husband, her mother, the baby, neighbors, herself, and they would have been off-putting if they weren't also funny. About the husband, whom Diana had seldom seen, she was particularly brutal: he was a man whose sex appeal improved the farther away he was; on the telephone, calling from another time zone, he was astounding. Up close, you wanted to think up a trip for him to make. A thousand miles away, he was rockets and flares. Home, he was slippers and boxer shorts with a pattern of clover on them, and beers, burps, and the rest, too. Away, he was all the primary colors. Up close, he was beige.

It was disturbing how often Phyllis's jokes about her life struck through Diana as containing truths about her own.

. . .

Now she poured coffee for herself, and sat on the sofa in the living room, one leg crossed carefully, languidly, over the other, slowly sipping the coffee. He would be no more than twenty minutes. And abruptly she decided that she wouldn't greet him like this, drinking coffee, so she hurried to finish it, put the cup and saucer in the dishwasher, and returned to the bathroom, where she ran her fingers through her hair again, and brushed her teeth.

She was waiting at the door when he pulled up. He parked down the street a little and walked back, carrying a small brief-case, keeping to the sidewalk. There was a stockiness about him that hadn't shown in the photographs online. He wore a gray sport coat, light-colored jeans, a black T-shirt. She opened the door and stood back for him, and when he came through, she experienced a coursing of blood to her head. She closed the door and engaged the deadbolt, watching her own trembling fingertips. She had never felt such excitement. He put the briefcase down and faced her where she leaned against the door. For a moment, neither of them spoke. His eyes trailed down her body and then back up. "You're taller than I thought you'd be."

She breathed, "I told you how tall I am."

He smiled. "You look taller."

They moved together into the living room and he looked at everything, removing the sport coat. "Nice house."

"I don't believe it," she said. "My God, we're actually together." She couldn't catch her breath.

He sat down on the sofa and rested one arm on the back of it, and she saw that he was nervous, too. "Took me just less than three hours. I was eighty-five miles an hour all the way."

"I'm sorry about not wanting to meet you in a motel."

"Forget it."

"It's just that I'd have felt cheap."

"This is more fun—there's an element of walking along a high cliff. We could both get busted—crash and burn."

"Not likely. The kids are at school and he's never home before five."

"What about the neighbors?"

"The whole street empties out before nine o'clock. Everybody works except Phyllis Copperfield across the street, and she's a friend. She knows about you. She doesn't know about *this*. But she's off on a run and then she'll come back and nap with her baby."

They looked at each other. There was an inevitable, though unspoken, element of evaluation about it. They had told each other so much on the telephone. She knew of his childless marriage to Marta, a good woman who was ten years older than he, and of his searching for someone, seeking to feel passion again. And she had told him of Warren's essential prudishness, a religious man for whom lovemaking was a very specific kind of performance, with such elaborate trappings of romance that she felt stifled by it all—poor Warren never got beyond his sense of the kiss and the fade-out. She had told him all of this over the telephone, several weeks ago. They had established that both of them loved their spouses, and that this meeting would be nothing more than what the Internet site on which they had met claimed to provide: people mutually looking for extramarital excitement without commitment.

"What does this Phyllis person know about me?"

"Just that I have a friend online."

"Jesus—you told her? Did you say what the site was?"

"No, no, no, no, no. I would never tell anyone a thing like

that. You're the only one who knows about that. I just told her I'd met someone I liked talking to."

"You didn't name me."

"No. *God*, no."

"Well, really."

"You haven't talked to *any* friend about me?"

"Not one, no."

"Well, Phyllis doesn't know anything."

"Look," he said. "Is it safe here for us?"

"Yes."

"And he suspects nothing."

"Nothing," she said. "Believe me. I pay the bills. I take care of everything."

"I still worry about the e-mails. I don't want anyone to get hurt."

"They're in a file on my own computer, buried in code. Trust me. It takes three different passwords to get to it."

"And you've never done this before."

"We've been through all that."

"I'd like to hear you say it, anyway."

"You're the first and only," she said.

His gaze went around the room. "I drove like a crazy man, getting here."

"You're nervous," she said. "Me, too."

"I was your first hit on the site."

"Nathan," she said.

"I don't guess it makes much difference."

"What about you?"

"Oh, I make it a regular practice. I've seen five hundred different women this way."

"Stop it."

"I'm scared," he said. "I didn't think I'd be so scared."

This was one of the things she liked about him. That he could talk this way so simply and honestly about his feelings.

"Nathan," she said.

His smile changed everything about his face. She liked that, too. "Here we are," he murmured.

Again, they were simply staring at each other. She felt the breathlessness she had experienced earlier. She held still.

He sat forward and rested his elbows on his knees. "I've dreamed about this. You're even prettier than your picture."

"You sound even sexier in person," she got out.

"Those wonderful phone calls—I never would've believed people could do those things over the telephone."

"Me, either."

He said nothing for what seemed a long time. He sat there, staring, another evaluative pause, as if the two of them were waiting to recognize each other. His eyes were slate dark, and big. They looked past her own, into her.

She began to speak, asking if he wanted a cup of coffee, but he was rising, coming toward her, and she opened her arms.

"Where's the bedroom," he said. "Where do we go?"

She led him into the spare bedroom, and while she pulled the blanket back he got out of his clothes. The speed of this surprised her. She found it awkward, as close as they had been on the telephone. It had been wild on the telephone. She had lain awake nights, replaying it all in the dark, full of yearning. He flopped onto the bed, rolled to his back with his arms at his sides, gazing at her, waiting for her to remove her robe. She let it drop to one hand, and tossed it against the baseboard. She wanted to talk more, to go slowly. "Beautiful," he murmured, smiling. It was such a good, wide smile. She crawled in next to him and when he put his mouth on her breast she patted the back of his head. "Easy, baby, we've got all morning."

He looked up. "I'm hungry for you."

"Can we talk a little first?"

He lay over on his back. "Okay. Of course—I'm sorry."

"It's just that it's so new. I want to enjoy it *all*."

"Okay." He smiled and nodded. "Me, too. I want to *savor* it."

She leaned up on one elbow and looked at him. "How are you?"

"I'm on fire."

"I'm still so nervous," she said.

He pulled her down, and began kissing her. His hands were rough—the skin was rough, callused—and she felt the power in the fingers, moving on her back and shoulders. He rolled with her, and was on top, kissing her neck, muttering words. She couldn't hear the words, and she tried to push his shoulders, wanted him to support himself a little so she could catch her breath. He did so, came to a kneeling position, straddling her. "I want to look at you."

"Yes," she said. She could feel it now, the excitement, all that she'd ached for and not had, the letting go, utterly.

"Do me?" he murmured, almost shy, offering himself.

"Oh," she said, sitting up, coming to him. "Oh, yes. I will. I will."

Afterward, they lay quietly, he with one leg over her abdomen, one hand on the side of her face. "I got married to Warren so young," she said. "I didn't know anything."

"None of us did, at one time, I guess."

"We were babies."

"Everybody says just to leave."

"Well, I won't—I can't. I love him."

He stared. "I'm exactly the same about it."

"It's just that you and I need sparks. Right?"

"That's us," he said, and kissed her ear.

They were quiet, listening to a dog barking in the neighborhood.

"There's not much else to say," he murmured. "But we keep having to say it."

"Warren told me before that this—that anything other than, well, the normal thing, you know—that it makes him feel sinful."

"You had no trouble talking about all this on the telephone. Missionary position, right?"

She put her head on his shoulder and sighed.

"Religion," Nathan said. "It's killed more people than Hitler and Stalin combined, and it's ruined the pleasure of the rest of us."

"Let's not talk about it, now," she told him.

"I think it's a sin for him to deny himself the pleasure you can provide."

"That's sexy."

He started kissing her again. She worried about her stomach a little, with the coffee she'd drunk. But she had dreamed of this, of not having to worry or hold back from being curious, the strongest element of herself, wanting to know, to feel it all, and wanting it to go on. As it did go on, and she lost herself in it, reveling in it for the difference from how things had always been. She had known this kind of experience only from books, and from some of the sites she had wandered among on the Internet. He was there for her at every turn; his imagination was boundless. The morning went fast.

Finally, he pulled the blanket with him, removing himself gently and getting out of the bed, and he stood there, looking around the room. "I expected more religious kinds of stuff on the walls."

She saw the gleam of sweat on his chest and abdomen, and the little lines of where her nails had scratched his upper arms. "No," she said. "It's just the Bible for him, you know."

"A waste."

"I thought it was sweet when he and I were first together. I did. I thought it meant he'd be true. And he is. He's sweet. He calls me angel. And I actually like it when he does that. We have a nice family life. A good life—like you and Marta."

"Marta's a fool," he said. "But then so am I."

"You're feeling guilty."

"No." He turned slightly, still taking in the room. "A little, maybe. I must not be a very nice man."

This upset her. She lifted herself slightly and looked at him. "You shouldn't talk like that. You're a wonderful person."

"Yeah. Well. I think sometimes maybe it's me, you know. Maybe I just don't stir her drink."

"Does she get any pleasure—I'm sorry. We've been through this."

He looked at her. "I gave you pleasure. I saw it and felt it."

"Oh, yes."

A moment later, he said, "This isn't where you sleep."

"No."

"Let's do it in there."

"Okay."

"One minute," he said, and he went into the bathroom and closed the door. She got up, put her robe back on, then stepped to the window and looked out through the little slit in the blinds. No one on the street. The dog was still sending its two-note complaint into the sunny air.

In the kitchen she put the water on for coffee, and then she went back down the hall to the bathroom door. "I'm making coffee."

"I don't ever drink it. Remember?"

"Do you mind if I have some?"

He opened the door. He still had the blanket wrapped around him. "Let's go back to bed."

"Let's have something to eat and then go back," she said.

"We don't have that much time, baby."

She turned the burner off and let him lead her into the master bedroom. But then she hesitated, pulled back, so that he stopped and his hand tightened on her wrist.

"I don't know," she said. "This doesn't feel right."

"You're kidding me."

"I sleep here every night."

He looked at the room, still holding her wrist. "That makes it especially good."

"Please," she said. "I know it's silly. But I just can't."

He let go, and walked by her, across to the other room. She closed the door and paused there for a few seconds. She would never have believed that her life could become as strange as this. Her heart was thudding against her breastbone. She had never felt more alive. Except that there was also a kind of macabre sense that she had opened a little crevice in a fortification on the other side of which something awful awaited—there did seem to be an element of morbidness about all this. She could not decide if it was something she remembered from her upbringing or if it was real. She was not a bad person. She was gentle and loving to her husband, the children, her parents, his, the whole family, everyone she knew. Yet the whole of her previous existence seemed unreal, now, distant, a faint rumor.

She put her hand on the wall and steadied herself.

He was waiting for her. There was a curve to his eyebrows that she had liked from the first glance at his picture online. He patted the bed by his side. And she went to him.

She said his name, and kissed along his collarbone. "Don't worry," she murmured. "It's just a silly superstition, and I'm more comfortable here. You want me to be comfortable, don't you?" He didn't say anything, didn't make a sound, moving against her.

"Nathan?"

"Don't worry," he said. And he put his face down in the pillow at her ear. "Sweet, oh, so sweet. I don't care, I don't *care*."

She nuzzled his neck and moved herself, taking him deeper, and feeling the thrill. "Oh, let's just keep *on*, baby. Let's just keep *on*." She moaned into the hollow of his shoulder.

Later, showering alone, she thought the rest of their time together might be long. It troubled her, and she hummed aloud, listening to the echo of her voice and knowing he could hear it, too. He was making coffee for her. (Getting her cup and setting out the French press and showing him how it worked provided a pleasant diversion about which they could tease—he had never heard of French press coffee. "French press," he said. "Sounds like a sex act." She smiled at him and stood quite still while he kissed the side of her neck.)

Now, drying off, she saw mental images of the children, and of Warren—unwanted reminders. She brushed them away, felt it as a mental exercise akin to this motion of drying herself with the towel. She put her robe on and walked out and made her way to the kitchen. There he sat, naked, turning the pages of the newspaper. She went and perched on his knee, kissing him. "Let's go back to bed."

"Oh," he said. "Let's."

The phone rang this time, just as she straddled him, and they paused. He moved once inside her and then held her by the arms.

"Don't answer it."

"No."

They waited. It rang and rang. Finally she disengaged herself and went to answer it. He said nothing. It was Warren, calling from work.

"Oh, hi," she said.

"You okay?" he asked. "You sound breathless. It rang and rang. I was about to hang up."

"I was in the other room. I ran to answer the phone."

"Should've let the machine get it."

"I don't have it on."

He breathed into the line.

"Warren, what is it?" she said.

"I'm going to take off early—so I'll pick up the kids from school."

"Are you sure?"

"Yeah—you relax a little."

"That's sweet," she said.

"See you in a little while."

"Okay."

She put the receiver down and turned to find Nathan getting into his clothes. "Oh," she said. "We've got an hour, still."

"You're sure."

"Yes."

But the lovemaking this time felt rushed and faintly mechanical; they finished and got dressed, and then went into the kitchen, to the breakfast nook, where she drank cold coffee, and he had a glass of orange juice. The sunlight through the leaves at the window gave a soft green cast to the room, and she had the thought that this was something she would not notice normally.

She told him about it.

"I think women get all the credit for noticing things. I think it makes them feel like they've got to."

"No," she said. "I honestly don't notice that sort of thing. Small things, I mean."

"I find that hard to believe."

She looked out at all the shades of green on the back lawn, and felt the day closing too fast, the time slipping.

A moment later, he said, "I never believed I'd do a thing like this."

"I know. God! I know."

"I've got to go soon."

She touched his hand. "I miss you already."

"Are we terrible people?" he said, and he looked like he might cry.

She smiled, through what she realized now was her own weeping. He was waiting for her answer.

Then: "Are we?"

"Yes," she told him.

When he left, he walked with his briefcase held up under his left arm, striding quickly away, without looking back. She watched him for part of it, but then worried about crazy Phyllis across the street, and closed the door. She went to the bedroom window and watched him from there. He hurried along, looking a little funny, a man with an appointment for which he was late, his coat lifting in the breeze.

She moved through the house putting things back to normal. She could feel the ghost-pressure of him between her legs, and she took another shower, washing carefully, taking extra care of her neck, her breasts, her inner thighs. She cleaned her teeth again, and looked at her mouth.

Finally she got into her jeans, blouse, flats, pinned her hair back, and went into the bedroom to stare out the window. She saw Phyllis come out and look over. Phyllis walked across the street and knocked on her door.

Diana took her time going to answer it. When she did, Phyllis went by her into the living room. "I'm sleepy. I just had a nap, and I'm exhausted and the baby's asleep. I can't stay. Tell me who he is."

"He's—he wanted to sell me a direct TV network plan."

Phyllis stared. "Come on—it's not your Internet friend?"

"No," Diana said through a tightening at her chest. "Nothing so exciting."

"I wish it was—I'd tell you to send him over to me. I'm going batshit over there."

"Can't help you. Next time I have a Jehovah's Witness, you're first on the list."

"Don't be so high and mighty."

"I'm just kidding." She held the door for her friend, realizing that she wished to extricate herself, not just for the moment, but for good. Phyllis could find some other woman to be her neighborhood sounding board. In the next instant, as Phyllis stepped by her out onto the little stoop, the realization arrived that this feeling was an aspect of something else: everything was changing. She had wanted so badly only to taste fully the passion that she believed was in her nature.

"I'm going to reserve a bed on the psychiatric ward," Phyllis said. "If *you're* not going to provide any excitement. I thought there might be something to do this afternoon other than watching the fucking idiot box and cable."

At last, alone, she lay on the sofa and tried to drift off. It would be all right to be asleep when Warren and the children arrived. But sleep eluded her.

The children came in first, a welter of noise and argument. Warren was still out at the car, collecting their book bags, and a raincoat that Lauren had left at school, last week. He came up to the door with it draped over his arm, carrying their bags.

"You should make them carry their own," she told him.

"I don't mind." He put the bags down on the bench in the hall, and embraced her. His arms were thick, and she let her hands roam over the broad shoulders of her husband, breathing the familiar bay rum and talcum odor of him. The girls were already in their room, going on about something. Even when they were agreeable these days, it sounded anyway like an argument—the voices rising, competing for attention.

"You have a good day?" he said.

"Ordinary," she said. "Nothing new."

He walked into the living room, removing his sport coat. She went into the kitchen and started dinner—baked chicken and a salad, and creamed corn. She worked quietly, hearing the sounds of her house. The girls knew they were to do their homework as soon as they got home; in the evenings he was always there to help them if they'd run into any problems; he would check on them, taking small breaks from reading his paper. He read the paper front to back every day, and indeed one of the pleasures they had always enjoyed as a couple was reading the Sunday paper together, and sipping coffee, talking over the articles they read.

He came into the kitchen to pour himself a glass of water.

She wanted to make love to him. She looked at the fine creases of the muscles in his forearm and thought of taking hold of it, pulling him toward her. But she could never be that forward with him. She had always to make him believe it was his idea. She crossed behind him and patted his upper back, then leaned in and kissed his cheek. "Long day?"

"Not too bad," he said, heading into the living room with his water.

Dinner was quiet, unusually so. The girls whispered to each other, the terms of some game they were engaged in. They had more homework after dinner—work that required them to be on the Internet. They excused themselves and went into their room, to their computer. Later, with the TV on, Diana heard them giggling. Warren, who had gone to check on them, said they were doing something with some other friends on MySpace. It was harmless. He liked to watch the comedy channel and ESPN. He flicked back and forth between them while she read, and then for a little while she was in her own room, a covey off the dining room, what must have been a sewing room for the previous owners of the house. She went online, expecting a message from Nathan, but there was nothing, and probably he had been as busy as she had been, after the long drive home.

She started to write him, and couldn't think of anything to say. Finally she wrote, *Things normal here.* And as she pushed SEND, something toppled over inside her. The room seemed to spread out away from her, and then it was as if she were shrinking in it, falling away from herself, and she put her hands to her face, holding on, using what felt like her last strength to close the computer down with its secret passwords and its dummy sites leading to other sites, leading to the one site.

She made her way into the living room, this room of her home, that was no longer home, and she found him asleep in his chair, and on television there was a comedian talking about President Bush. The first President Bush, because the jokes were about the Gulf War and General Powell. Warren could look at the same bit over and over, and laugh at it every time as if it were new. She remembered that she used to admire that about him. Turning the TV off, she took his hand and pulled gently. "Honey," she said, realizing with terror that it was rote, that it didn't come from anything anymore. He opened his eyes and looked at her, a blank expression of half-sleep. "I didn't know I was gone," he said. "I was dreaming I was eating something and not being able to swallow it."

"Can you go back to sleep?" Her own voice surprised her.

He stood, and took her arm, and they went into the bedroom together. In the little open space at the end of the hallway, they crossed the opening to the guest room, the dark rectangle of the open door, the faint shapes of the furniture in there, the dressing table and the cedar chest and the bed.

In their room, she got quickly into her nightgown, brushed her teeth, and crawled into bed, while he hung his clothes neatly in the closet, and then cleaned his own teeth. She lay listening to the electric toothbrush, which he used exactly according to directions, thirty seconds for each quadrant of the mouth, upper teeth and lowers, adding up to the two minutes. Then the flossing, and the rinsing. She still wanted him, not out of any appetite now, but hoping to recover something, to make up for it all, in some way, for herself. He came into the room and seemed surprised to find her awake.

"Hey," he said.

She smiled. "Hey."

He got into the bed, and came close, and kissed her, and then moved against her, reaching to pull her panties down.

"Darling," she said to him, trying to mean it, and feeling Time open out, the long prospect of hours, days, weeks, months, years—all of it suddenly far past her, undoable, gone.

Beyond any hope or solace. "Oh, God," she said, from the weight of it on her heart. He held her close. He was going to come over on top of her now. She took his face in her hands and said his name, and felt her own mind like a broken wall.

He was ranged above her. "My sweet angel," he said.

SON AND HEIR

They left at seven, plenty of time to go four miles, even with all the traffic lights in the city blank and dead. Everything was down, the whole region blacked out, because of the heat wave. And this was only the last week of June. Nobody could get any sleep. There were people up at all hours, walking around in the streets, trying to cool off. For Lyndhurst and his roomie, even when there had been power, the little air conditioner in the apartment window coughed and sputtered and sighed, a waste of electricity. It had been a hot spring, without rain. Miserable. But these past few days things had gotten scary. It was like the world was being cooked by the sun, the universe changing badly. All the frightening predictions of the scientists were easier to believe, having to go through the hours of each day under the enormous airless bell that had settled over everything: a photochemical inversion, the news people called it; an unhealthy mist made of diesel exhaust, carbon monoxide, and smoke.

Lyndhurst had been having bad premonitions.

He'd come along anyway, for the ride, crossing the bridge into Virginia. On Memorial Bridge, there was the slim relief of the air moving over him in the front seat of Grant's red 1965 Mustang convertible. That lightened his mood a little, until they got embroiled in the traffic in Rosslyn. The world was burning.

They had a thousand dollars, and they were going to score a supply of coke, to relieve the boredom, Grant said. Lyndhurst just wanted motion.

He hadn't been that interested in the drug. He'd begun doing it as an exploration. He told people it wasn't much different from Flonase; it cleared his sinuses. Once, when he was wine drunk, it sobered him up. But he never felt the rush people talked about, or the sense of power—the invincibility, Grant called it. But now, in this scorching heat wave that had become a season of its own, he thought of it as a way out of the unnerving minutes of the smoldering week.

He was twenty-seven years old, and as of that birthday, almost nine months ago, his father had stopped all support of him. According to his father, he had curled up in his life like a bug in a cocoon. Lyndhurst wouldn't deny it. He hadn't spoken to either of his parents since the day the money stopped, though they lived only a couple of miles down M Street. The old man was president of District College.

When Lyndhurst was nine, at a gathering in the house for the college's faculty, he saw his father kiss one of the faculty wives out in the backyard. The shadows of the house and trees on the lawn hid them from the people on the patio and in the windows of the crowded house, but Lyndhurst saw them, saw how long the kiss lasted, and later he saw the looks they gave each other as the party was breaking up—avid, hungry, gluttonous looks. Nothing was ever said about it, and the boy told no one, not even friends, what he had seen. But it made him sick in the nights, and for a long time he had trouble going to sleep. It was as if the first part of something momentous had been accomplished, and the rest of it was waiting to happen. Something awful was coming. But things went on as they always had. There were other parties, other gatherings where the woman was present, and neither she nor Lyndhurst senior gave any sign of what had taken place between them. And the boy's parents went on in their studied portrayal of a perfectly happy couple, with their exceptional son. At night, there were whisper fights that grew louder, silences that lasted days, or weeks. They began using the boy as a go-between. "Tell your mother we're expected at the alumni dinner on Friday."

"Tell your father I'm planning a headache for Friday."

"Tell her she's going. The house we live in and the pleasant life we lead at the expense of the college demands that we be present. She's going. Or else. Tell her that for me."

"I can't remember all that, Daddy."

"I'll write it down for you." He wrote it on a small spiral notepad, and tore the page out for the boy to take to his mother. She read it, then crumpled it and handed it back.

"Take this to him," she said.

And he did so. And his father wrote another note. "Take that to her," he said.

The boy did as he was told. His mother wept reading the note, and did not give it back to him. That fight lasted almost three months.

They passed each other in the halls of the house without speaking. They sat across from each other at dinner without uttering a word.

They would go to things like the alumni dinner, and force the boy to accompany them, and at these events their public affection for each other was impressive; people said it was heartening. They actually remarked about it. The shining couple.

It was as if they were acting scenes in an improvisational play about a successful college president and his charming wife and son. The boy resented the dishonesty of it, even before he had words to express it. He thought of his life in the mansion as a struggle against pretense. There was a kind of desperation in the will to break the pretty facade down. And he had done that, all right. It used to be pleasant imagining his father explaining his son's bad history to a prospective donor.

The college president's only son had been expelled from three different universities and also had washed out of basic training for the army. The years since were a blur of different jobs—delivering phone books, lifeguarding, manning the counter in a liquor store, working construction, waiting tables.

He had drifted through several relationships, too, young women with troubles of their own. Life was puzzling and mostly too big to consider beyond the present. And in some inexplicable and unexpressed way it was all intuitively in defiance of expectations—his parents' ambitions for him—and of the falsity he had grown up with.

He never thought of the future, or worried about it much, either. He had taken to considering himself an observer of phenomena, and if now and then he felt the lack of some solidness to depend on, he was interested in what he did see and feel. He was not depressed, as his father said, nor bipolar, like his mother, who wore the term like a badge. He was waiting, really—hoping for some way out of the swirl of requirements, the alarm-clock-driven, phony, professionally societal life of his parents. He believed that something eventually would occur to him, some hint of a great thing in store. Whatever it was, it would seize him, and settle forever the question of where he should be in the scheme of things. Sometimes he entertained fantasies of going to Hollywood and making it big. He had looks. Everyone said that.

Last fall, in what turned out to be the last conversation he had with his father, the old man said, "I want you to know, I'm not taking the blame for you."

"I'm not blaming you for anything. What are you talking about blame for?"

"You're going to want to blame somebody or some*thing*. It's human nature. When life comes down on you, you'll want to point at something."

"Maybe I won't want to point at anything."

"I want you to understand me," his father said. "I'm cutting you off because you're a grown man now and should be on your own. This has nothing to do with your childhood, which has been way too long in ending."

"I understand," Lyndhurst said to him.

"I hope you do. You're welcome here anytime as a man. But never again as a child."

"Okay. Whatever."

"That's an entirely typical response."

Lyndhurst took his glasses off and wiped them against the tail of his shirt.

"Here's five hundred dollars to get a start somewhere," his father said. "But that's it. I'm doing that much at your mother's insistence."

"Yes, sir."

"We both wanted you to have something to start with," said the college president's wife.

"Just so we understand each other," the president added.

Lyndhurst nodded, already planning to disappear from their lives forever, not out of anger but simple avoidance; they repelled him.

. . .

It was Grant, his apartment mate, who got him into waiting tables at Cassimino Grill, where you could pull down three hundred dollars in a night. Grant was five years older, and the perfect apartment mate. He, too, resisted the idea of planning for some future life. He wanted only to get to the next good time. He had a thing for classic cars, and this Mustang was his latest. Its engine sounded like a big train.

The arrangements for the night were his. He'd used the connection before. "I can't believe the fucking traffic," he said. "If we're two minutes late, man, won't be nobody there."

"Rush hour, in an electric disaster, man. Chaos."

"The infrastructure's fucked," Grant said. "It's like we just fell into the third world."

Lyndhurst put his head on the seat back. "I can't breathe." Lately it had been hard to speak about anything but the weather, the situation.

It was almost eight o'clock. The air that flowed over the car when it moved was like somebody's bad breath. In the SUV in front of them, several kids were pressing against the windows, cool in the air-conditioning. People were driving around in their cars to cool off. Of course, there was no air-conditioning in the Mustang.

Earlier that day, looking for some kind of relief, Lyndhurst had walked down to the edge of the river and put his legs in, though there were signs warning people off. He experienced the familiar sense that the signs were not meant for him. He was aware of this without wanting to change it. He understood it as though it were a condition or an ailment he had acquired. It was as if he could turn in himself and measure how far he had gone from the world in which everyone else lived. Moving his feet in the muddy cool water, he examined the idea. He was reminded unpleasantly of the boy he had been only five years ago, who would not recognize the man sitting by the river with his pants legs rolled up and his feet in the water. This heat wave, this photochemical inversion with its attendant blackout, had undermined him in some way he couldn't understand. It was a major catastrophe, the power failure, but people were dealing with it; *he*, himself, was dealing with it. Still, there was something at the pit of his stomach that kept gripping him. The fact of it, the going on of it, a whole region sweltering, powerless for four days now, and you couldn't even look at the television news to find out what was keeping everything down.

Looking at the whiteness of his own toes in the water, he felt a sudden wave of disgust.

It caused him to stand, and move off, back toward the glare of the street. People went by him bent on their own attempts to find a cool place to stop, or rest; there were some young men tossing a baseball on the ellipse. It was too hot even for that, though they persisted, and a man with a cart was offering them cold drinks, standing under the shade of a sycamore tree with a white bandanna covering his head, and a T-shirt that stuck to him from the sweat of his upper body. Emblazoned in fire-colors across the front of the T-shirt, in letters shaped like licking flames, were the words TURN IT UP.

"Jesus," he said now to Grant. "I'm fried."

He had called the power company a dozen times at least. "*If you have an emergency outage to report, please leave your telephone number. We are working around the clock to correct the problem.*" The voice sounded bright and bouncy, as if the speaker had already found the answer to everything.

"I went swimming today at the park," Grant said. "Too crowded. Packed. Pool was like bathwater."

"I sat in the freaking river for an hour."

"God. You sat in the river. You're toxic."

"I'm suffocating."

"Quit whining."

"I'm describing the territory."

A moment later, Grant said, "I used to think the most terrifying realization is that we live in history." This was just the kind of offhand comment he liked to make.

Lyndhurst usually ignored him. But the word *history* got under his skin. "You sound like my father," he said.

"Well, I like history."

"Since when? You?"

"The real most terrifying realization, though, is that we live in *nature*."

Lyndhurst said nothing.

They came past a lot of children playing in the brown gush from a fire hydrant. The children were running around after a beach ball that kept getting knocked back by the force of the water. "Talk about toxic," Grant said.

In some of the yards in front of the houses, other children were running through sprinklers. One heavy black man sat in a little folding chair in a wide fan of spray. He wore sunglasses, and had his arms folded across his chest, the posture of someone quite happy with the way things had turned out. Several women stood on the street corner, watching the kids frolic in the dirty-looking water. One of the women looked right at Lyndhurst. He smiled. Her expression didn't change. She seemed to glide out of his view, Grant speeding up now, entering a side street, a neighborhood, the houses set back among shrubs and trees, more substantial than those on the main drag. Lyndhurst thought of dinners on Sunday afternoons at his mother's family home in Raleigh. A house like these. At times, lately, he had to admit to himself that he missed something about those afternoons. Or he wondered at his own sense of surprised longing for it. The experience was like discovering a cut in the skin, that in the rush of the day you hadn't known you'd received. He looked over at Grant, who appeared completely relaxed. But then Grant never seemed to get rattled by anything. The blackout had actually made him cheerful; it was a change, he said. It killed the routine. That was his phrase, and he used it a lot: he was always seeking ways to kill the routine, and nothing ever seemed to get through the cool exterior.

"I just thought of a way we could make some money," he said now. "We could start a lottery about when the lights will come back on."

"We'd spend a fortune getting it started and before we could collect a penny the lights would come on."

"A risk, I admit. Should've thought of it yesterday."

The street wound toward sunlight, then dipped and widened, and here there were brick bungalows with little flower beds lining the sidewalks, and stone sculptures flanking the entrances.

Grant turned into a cul-de-sac. More low-slung houses and tree-shaded lawns, backing onto thick woods. "Here we go," he said, pulling to a stop in front of the center house, a cedar-roofed, flagstone building with a big picture window under a dark green awning. A path to the left of it led up into the woods. "Ten minutes to spare."

A thin, white-haired boy was framed in the big window, staring out. "We're being watched," Lyndhurst said.

"Probably thinks we're company," Grant muttered. "I'm gonna move us." He pulled the car around to the top of the circle and stopped again.

"They just gonna pull in here, too? Is it a house?"

"It's up that path. A little clearing in there. I lived in this cul-de-sac when I was a kid. I know these woods. I've been scoring dope there forever. There's a playground about a half mile farther on. They'll park there, see, and I'll meet them in the clearing. Get it? Fast and clean. I'm in there and out in a minute. I trust I've explained this clearly to you."

"No," said Lyndhurst. "Start over."

"How long we been living together?"

It was too hot to say much more. He took another deep breath, leaned his head against the seat rest again, then brought one hand to his forehead.

"Me-grain?" Grant said. "Well, we'll fix you right up, there, Johnny boy."

Lyndhurst had been living with Grant for more than a year, and still didn't know much more than that he liked classic cars and did various forms of recreational drugs. Although there was a woman he saw fairly regularly—and there had been times when he had asked Lyndhurst to remain away from the apartment for a night or two—he was not forthcoming about his feelings for her, or for anyone. This girl—Ramona was her name—had once sought reassurance from Lyndhurst about his roommate. She had arrived for a date, and Grant was on the phone, and he sent her outside, with Lyndhurst. There she lighted a cigarette, blew the smoke, and said, "Tell me something. Tell me anything."

"You look nice," he told her, because she did.

"He never says anything like that to me."

Lyndhurst shrugged.

She seemed a little impatient, drawing on the cigarette again and talking the smoke out. "He's a complete mystery to me."

"Just a guy out for a good time, I guess," Lyndhurst said. He felt the emptiness of the observation, and then experienced a surge of resentment of her for involving him in this way.

"What about you," she asked. "Don't you have anyone?"

The question surprised him—or his reaction to it did: he felt caught out. "Sure," he said, not returning her gaze.

"Are you like that with her? You never tell her anything about yourself?"

"I'm not seeing any one person right now," he got out.

"I can't stand this, like, feeling I have all the time like I'm not getting the real person. I mean I don't know anything, really. He digs old cars. Classic rock. He won't eat, like, onions or mushrooms or green peppers. He likes shellfish."

"Maybe that's about all anybody knows about anybody," Lyndhurst said.

She didn't appear to have heard him. "I don't know the guy."

"Well, but that's how he is. Maybe there isn't anything more."

She was small and pretty, with thin, slender fingers and almond-shaped brown eyes. There was a quickness about her, a fluid, supple easiness of motion, as though her bones were softer than those of other people. He had found himself thinking about her now and then, except that she was Grant's, had been with Grant, and there was something about that fact that left him cold. He couldn't ever quite look straight back into her eyes. Ramona didn't want simply to be charmed or entertained; she wanted it all, wanted to be there for the big things, and the longings for which there wasn't any name. She was frightening, and Lyndhurst felt that he knew exactly why Grant kept her at a distance.

"You lived in the president's house at the college, didn't you?"

He nodded.

"What was that like?"

"It sucked."

"Come on."

"It did," Lyndhurst told her. "It sucked big-time. When I was a kid I'd spend nights hiding under the fucking bed because I hated it all so much. The whole goddamn thing. That scene—one big pretension. My parents—so sweet and proud of the kid, you know, the happy family, smart and so cool and all that, but you should've heard them when there wasn't anybody around. They picked at each other, when they talked at all. They wore each other down to little shivering lumps. And they wore me down, too. You couldn't ever do anything right with them. Both of them. A couple of critics."

"You see?" she said. "I don't ever get from him anything like what you just told me. Nothing close to it."

"Hell," Lyndhurst told her. "I'm just talking about hiding from the grown-ups. That's anybody's life story."

"But it's you, like, as a boy. I feel I know *you* better now, see? I, like, know you better than I know him. That's a *lot*—what you just told me."

He thought she might actually make some move toward him. But then Grant came out of the apartment and her eyes lighted up and she was like a little girl.

"If the power comes on," Grant said now, "move the car out of the light before you start celebrating."

"Just go get the shit and let's get out of here."

The sun was slanting through the trees, lowering, sinking into red clouds.

"Darkness," Grant said. "Here it comes again, man."

"I can't freaking breathe." The shadows that lengthened on the lawns offered no relief. Lyndhurst gazed at the blank streetlamps without really seeing them.

"The power's gonna come on and we'll have a party and celebrate, because we'll have something to celebrate *with*."

They had indeed been expecting the power to kick on, every minute since the first day. The emergency services were calling it a grid failure as catastrophic as if there had been a nuclear explosion. Pure overwhelming demand had done it. The electric company had tried rolling blackouts. And then something went wrong somewhere, and they were still looking for the solution. Emblazoned across the front pages of the local broadsides was that there was no evidence of terrorism. Lyndhurst wondered where they found the power to print these circulated flyers.

Grant got out of the car, then leaned on the closed driver's side door, taking a deep breath, as if having stood up into a stream of cooler air. "Don't go anywhere."

"Where am I gonna go? You've got three hundred dollars of mine." This seemed to dawn on Lyndhurst as he spoke. "I'll be right here."

Grant strolled toward the entrance of the cul-de-sac and then made his way along the other side, and down, to the center house and the path. Lyndhurst saw him go on up into the trees and disappear. He watched the place for a few minutes, feeling doubtful about things. Sirens sounded in the distance. The sun was sinking fast, and there would be another night of pitch blackness to get through. The boy still waited in the big picture window of the center house.

Several times during the long nights of trying to sleep, Lyndhurst had looked at the fact that he was now afraid of the dark. The failure of light everywhere, the dead streetlamps and traffic lights, the dim structures of the street, which used to be illuminated—gas station signs, storefronts, fast-food joints, banks—seemed elements of something far worse than a power outage brought on by a heat wave in an energy-stressed summer. It made him want to get in the car and drive to wherever there was light. Sometimes he dreamed that he had done just that.

But he did not dream this now: he dreamed that he was doing exactly what he was doing—waiting in Grant's classic Mustang for Grant to come back. And Grant came back and got in and stared at him, and he couldn't move, and then he was nothing, and no one was anywhere.

When he felt his head nod heavily to one side, he sat abruptly forward, rubbing his eyes, and, turning to look at the entrance to the woods where Grant had gone, saw the boy from the center house, standing close enough to touch, gaping at him, mouth open, hands shoved down into the pockets of baggy white shorts. Lyndhurst heard himself cry out.

The boy just stood there, staring. He had hair whiter than silk. The darkness of his skin made the hair seem unnatural, like a wig.

"What're you doing there?"

No answer.

Lyndhurst looked at the skinny brown legs coming down out of the shorts. "Well?"

Nothing. Perhaps thirty seconds went by.

"You deaf or something?"

The kid looked eleven or twelve. He had a thin face, narrow lips, a short piglike nose. His eyes were ice blue and dry, and there didn't seem to be anything in them. Glass eyes, Lyndhurst thought. Marble eyes. Maybe he's blind.

He waved one hand across the boy's line of vision. The eyes followed. "Can't you talk? Christ—what're you doing? Say something."

The boy only stared at him, lips moving slightly, as if some nerve tic were playing over them.

"Get out of here," Lyndhurst said. "Get."

The boy didn't move. Lyndhurst looked at his watch. Almost nine o'clock. Had he been asleep that long? He glared at the boy. "You better get, if you know what's good for you."

The boy took his hands from his pockets. He was clutching a rock in each one.

Lyndhurst flinched at this, though there was no other motion. The boy held the rocks.

"Don't even think about it," Lyndhurst said, as levelly as he could.

"You with a gang?" the boy asked. His voice was very high, a girl's voice.

"No, I'm a ghost. I come from the night."

He stood there.

"I'm not with a gang, kid," Lyndhurst heard himself say. "My father's president of District College."

This information seemed to have the effect of confusing the other. "What's that?"

Lyndhurst felt some of the same confusion. He said, "Nothing, forget it. I'm not from a gang and not a criminal. And if I was, do you think I'd tell you I was?"

"Just stay away from the house."

"Did I come near your house?"

"We have a big dog."

"Okay. And you have rocks. You're protecting the castle. Where's your folks?"

"They're in the house, with guns."

"You're a tough bunch."

In that instant, the lamps along the street came on, a dazzling shocking suddenness all around, and a buzzing. Lyndhurst gave forth another cry. There were lights in the houses now, too, the sound of televisions and radios rattling in open windows. It was as if the boy had done it, as if his walking out here and standing in the dimness had brought it about.

Lyndhurst got out of the car, keeping his eyes on the rocks in the boy's small fists. "Go home, kid. Your lights are on, now. The world's back to normal. You can watch television and wait for Mommy and Daddy to come home." He felt weirdly like chattering now, wanted to tell the boy about the last strange four days. He held it back.

The boy slowly turned and walked a few paces away, then spun around and hurled one of the rocks. Lyndhurst ducked, but the boy was throwing it at the nearest streetlamp. It hit the metal dish above it with a clang and then flew on into the dark beyond it.

Lyndhurst said, "Nice shot. You trying to black us all out again?"

"I meant to hit that. That's how good I am."

"Well, fine. I'll write home about it."

"Are you a gangster?" said the boy.

"I'm waiting for a friend, okay?"

"Where'd he go?"

"He went to see somebody. He had an appointment. What the hell's the matter with you, anyway?"

"Just keep away," said the boy, turning warily, and going on toward the house.

Lyndhurst watched him go, but then followed him for a few paces. "Hey, you got a lot of crime around here or something?"

The boy went on.

"You got criminals coming around here?"

He glanced over his skinny shoulder, but said nothing, going on into the house. Lyndhurst turned, looked back at the Mustang with its passenger door still open. It seemed that every house had music and voices coming from it. Someone made a lot of noise closing the windows of one house, and a second later he heard the air conditioner kick on. That startled him, too. He walked to the car and got in. It was ridiculous to be so jumpy. The power was back on. Things could get back to normal. He had a sense of the life he had led being restored to him.

Except that it was now past nine o'clock. Grant had said it would be only a few minutes. But what constituted a few minutes?

There was the boy's shape in the window, staring. The white hair showed even in silhouette.

He looked at the place where the path went on into the dark line of trees. The whole wide sky seemed flooded now with light and noise. Finally he got out, closed the door, and crept to the entrance of the woods, keeping track of the big picture window. He turned and faced the open half circle of houses, saw the lights in them and the lights beyond, thinking of going back to sit in the car. Grant could come from some other direction. It was possible. He waited another minute, then entered the woods, walked along in the closed-feeling dimness of the path, expecting to see Grant coming the other way. The path wound up an incline and then dipped steeply leftward. The shadows were deepening, the foliage bordering either side closing, narrowing. No air stirred. The only sound was the leaves rustling as he moved through them. "Grant? It's me. The power's back on."

He stopped and waited.

"Hey?"

A whisper of leaves, and then stillness.

"Come on, man," he said, mostly to himself.

Perhaps fifty yards farther on, down another declension that flattened out and widened, he came into the clearing. He saw Grant immediately. Grant was quite quiet at the far edge, sitting against the base of a tree. Lyndhurst stumbled blindly toward him, beginning, with a sick sinking at his heart, to understand, though he worked to deny it, had to get close enough to see, to make sure, telling himself it was a prank. "Don't do this," he said. "Come on."

Grant stared unseeingly straight at the faint glow of the far sky. There was a bullet hole in the middle of his forehead.

Lyndhurst staggered back, and then began to flounder away low, gagging, coughing, back into the woods, running. Something caught at him and he fell hard, then scrabbled wildly to his feet, thrashing, and then stopping his own breath with his hands over his mouth, turning to look behind him, trying to make no noise at all, to slip away. He stumbled again, faltered through, blasting into crossing branches, losing the path and then finding it again.

When he came bursting out onto the center lawn, the boy was there, just in front of the open door of the house. The boy watched him as he stumbled to the car and got into it. He started it, heard the roar of the engine, and knew that he couldn't take it with him, couldn't be here behind the wheel. Crazily, wildly, as if it were on fire, he stood out of it, then reached back in and turned the key off. He couldn't think, looking around himself, retching, gasping. The boy watched him warily from the house. Lyndhurst removed his shirt and wiped the steering wheel, the backs of the keys, the tops of the doors, the dash, hurrying, hearing his own breathing. He put the shirt back on, some little hopeful part of his mind presenting him with the absurd thought that this would make everything come right.

"Mister." The boy had approached to within a few feet of him.

Lyndhurst started to run the other way. He took a few uncertain strides, then stopped, and turned. "Go away, kid. Please? Will you leave me alone? I'm not a gangster." He couldn't stop shaking. "God," he said. "God."

"What happened?" the boy said. He had another stone in his hand, and was poised to throw it. "Where's the other guy?"

"Just get," Lyndhurst said.

The boy didn't move, and abruptly Lyndhurst understood that he was afraid, that he had been afraid all along. He was alone, and trying to protect the house he lived in, the place where people cared for him.

"Nobody's gonna hurt you," Lyndhurst told him. "I'm as scared as you are. Can't you see that?"

"I'm not scared," the boy said.

Lyndhurst looked beyond him. "Good for you," he said. "Good." He was breathing the words. "Go back in the house. Lock the door. Because there *are* gangsters around here. You get me? And if anybody asks you, I was asleep. I never left this car." He understood the absurdity of the words as he spoke them, and he swallowed, shaking his head, then turned and strode quickly away, trying to seem calm, keeping his pace steady, not looking back. He saw his own shadow under the streetlight; the shadow lengthened and then faded, and another took its place—the next streetlight. The whole vast, now-glowing night was harrowing, fantastical, and horrible, lights flashing, sirens wailing far off, dogs barking, car horns sounding, music coming from the open, empty houses. He kept walking, and then he was running again.

He went toward the bigger glow of the city, across the bridge with the shimmering dirty river running below him. Everything looked as it always had. It was awfully itself. The city, with its high crime rate and its dangerous, run-down neighborhoods. There were people out walking, and a jogger came by in the opposite direction. Lyndhurst kept going, half-running, looking behind him, and then trying merely to walk quickly, to seem casual, fighting for breath. The image of Grant sitting against the tree kept coming to him. He was near the apartment building, where all the lights seemed to be on, and everyone was out. There were people on the balconies, drinking beer and celebrating.

The boy had seen him. The boy would tell the police about it.

In the apartment were Grant's things—a baseball cap, a pair of sandals, a beer glass in the sink. Lyndhurst got rid of his works, put it all in a plastic bag and threw it into the dumpster outside. He leaned on the iron door, in the sound of the celebrations, and fought to keep from being sick again.

When she pulled up, he tried to move to the other side of the dumpster, but she had seen him. She got out of the car and walked over, head tilted slightly, as if she wasn't sure it was Lyndhurst.

"Hey?" she said.

"He's—he's not home."

"Where is he? He said to meet him here."

"He's not here," Lyndhurst nearly choked on the words. "Go home, Ramona. Please."

"What's wrong? Something's wrong."

"Go home."

"Are you sick?"

"Yeah—sick."

"Poor Lyndhurst." She waited. "Hey, the power's back on." She seemed to want to celebrate.

"I don't know where he is, okay?" He had nearly shouted at her.

She stood there with her head tilted in that way, regarding him, and then she seemed to sink into herself. "Oh," she said, turning. "No." She walked a few steps away, and turned to look at him again. "He was going to do something with you—you were both going somewhere. He told me that. Something's happened. He got arrested. Tell me."

"I've been here the whole night," he said. "Goddamn. What do you want from me? I've been here the whole night. I didn't go anywhere."

"I was here earlier." Her eyes had narrowed, and she took a step toward him again. "I rode back out to get some beer. No one was here. You're shaking."

"I went for a walk. I went for a walk." He held his hands out as if to show his helplessness to explain anything. "I went for a walk, goddamn it."

"You don't have to shout." She stepped closer, and touched his shoulder. "Tell me."

He said, "I'm sorry. I got sick. I'm sick. Go home. Don't come here anymore."

For what seemed a long time, she stood and looked at him. His breathing was coming with a rasp. He couldn't get enough of the hot night air to make a single exhalation. He thought he might keel over.

"We could go inside and, like, wait for him?" There was something pleading in her voice.

"Don't you get what I'm telling you?" Lyndhurst said. "Get!" He straightened, and felt himself begin to gag. "Go home. Go back to your life."

"Oh, no," she said again. "No." Then she turned and walked slowly up the lighted walk to the building, and around the corner of it, out of sight. Her motions were those of a person expecting any moment to be set upon by something bad. He waited a moment, bending, with his hands on his knees, trying to gather himself. Finally he started down the street, hurrying, glancing over his shoulder to be certain that she wasn't following him. He thought of what was ahead of her this night, and was afraid she would remember him as he was now. He felt sorry for her, and yet he wanted never to see her, or hear her name, or know of her, ever again.

Not quite an hour later, he was on the street in front of his parents' house, the president's house, standing with hands on his knees again, choking for air, the muscles of his legs and arms jumping. He stood under the streetlamp, and then realized that he was in light, and moved to the shadow of the spruce tree at the edge of the lawn. The house was dark, save for one light upstairs—the one his parents had on a timer whenever they were going to be gone for longer than one night. Of course they had gone to the Eastern Shore when the power failure continued. He heard voices from the neighboring house—people who had moved in since he left home. He crossed to the side door, the one into the sunroom, where he knew a key was hidden under the mat. It was there. He went in, closed and locked the door. The quiet and the dark made him feel slightly calmer, but the air was stifling, and the memory of Grant's still shape in the clearing, with the little perfect black circle in his forehead, kept returning to him. He began to cry softly, moving through the house, up the stairs, no one home, everything turned off, all the lamps unplugged. He reached for a wall switch, flicked it, was bathed in dreadful bright light, cried out, and turned it off again immediately.

It had all begun as a lark, going for a ride in the sporty convertible, something to do. Killing the routine.

Here was the doorway to his room. It seemed that the sirens never let up; they were still sounding across the night. But it was the silence of the clearing that remained with him, the vastness of that quiet, the hugeness of it—the not-breath, not-seeing of the shape there, sitting against the base of the tree. On the table by his bed, the digital clock had not been unplugged. The little red light showing the wrong time to the minute changed, and then changed again, and still again while he watched. The night would pass slowly. One little increment at a time. His father would want to come home before morning. He never really liked being away from the house. They were probably already on their way. He had a picture of them, sitting in the car, not speaking, the silence between them heavy with all the old discontents and resentments, the radio on, the night gliding by the windows, and the lights of the city restored. They would want to be home.

He got down on his knees and crawled under the bed.

TROPHY

Today I got a letter from an old friend inviting me to come back to Virginia to help him celebrate a new opening in his chain of hot-dog stands. I might actually go. This is the ninth such invitation he's extended in the last eleven years. I always liked Jimmy, and in fact did go when he opened the first one, back in '94. I met his new wife, saw his new house, and we had a happy couple of days. We even played golf once, like we used to back when I sold cars for a living and he owned the dealership. We haven't been in very consistent touch since then, so it really would be something if I did show up again now.

Hell, I probably won't. Life's so busy anymore. But getting the invitation made me think about him, and about something that happened, on a golf course, all those years ago.

You don't know anybody I knew then, so the names won't matter, but I'll make them up anyway. And I won't tell you exactly where it happened, either. There are several public courses up and down the Shenandoah Valley in Virginia. Say it was one of those—far, far away.

One foggy Sunday morning, five of us were going to play eighteen holes. Although we knew one another and had played together in different combinations before, this was one of the few times we were all together at the same time. The others were Daryl, Harry, Anthony, and, of course, Jimmy.

We'd gone to work for him at X Motors back in the earliest part of the Clinton boom, before the bottom fell out and Jimmy's tax troubles came to light and he had to sell the lot. None of us was thinking much then about whether we would stick to this line of work. That aspect of things hadn't become quite real to us, was only a shadow on the distant horizon. We'd cooked up this day of golf essentially just to lighten Jimmy's heart, although none of us spoke about that directly.

We decided to split up this way: Daryl and I would go ahead and tee off, while Harry and Jimmy would wait for Anthony, because together Anthony and Harry could always make Jimmy laugh, and they were better golfers, too.

I didn't know this yet, but that week the corporate people, putting on the finishing touch, had told Jimmy they'd been forced by the IRS to pull his floor plan, so the IRS could collect on inventory. What this meant, if you ran a car dealership, was that you couldn't sell that company's cars anymore. The government would sell them against your tax debt.

Like I say, that was only the finishing touch. For Jimmy, things had been going from bad to worse for the last couple of years.

We had all benefited from his generosity, and we talked about him like a father or an older brother, admiring his ability to be lighthearted and to make fun of himself in his sea of troubles: business failing, payments mounting up, wife living elsewhere—a recent development—and his daughter from the first marriage not speaking to him anymore, having sided with her mother.

The major reason for the new wife trouble, really, was that the dealership consumed so much of his time—in the boom years because business was good, and in the bust years because it was bad. In fact, there wasn't much time at home for any of us then, but especially not for Jimmy. And so the wife, let's call her Elaine, twenty years younger than he was anyway, started feeling neglected and lonely. The rest of *that* story hardly needs telling: she'd moved out three weeks before.

My own wife was having trouble understanding the hours, but she managed all right; she's still with me. We're in pretty solid shape, too. But this isn't about me.

Jimmy was our friend, and in a way our mentor, too—we were in our thirties and he was fifty. He'd taken each of us in at various points as salesmen (me, Daryl) or mechanics (Harry, Anthony), and we'd spent some really magnificent, deep-laughing hours over whiskey or wine or beer, almost always at the nineteenth hole at one course or another, mostly on Sundays. Elaine also played now and then; at least that gave them a little time together. They both knew Chris, the owner of the course we were playing the day I'm remembering. Chris, apparently believing that Jimmy knew everything, told him how sad he was about the situation with Elaine, who'd played eighteen holes on Friday and confessed she was going out with somebody from her Asian cooking night class. To me, it seemed pretty harsh for her to do that, knowing Chris would talk and it would get back to us. When Chris saw that Jimmy didn't know, he tried to take it back. "I don't know, though, could be just talk."

"Probably not," Jimmy said.

"Have you talked to her?"

"Everything she says to me is straight out of Fuck You Central."

"I never heard that one," Daryl said, and laughed a little.

Jimmy said, "Well, there's nothing much I can do about it," and thanked Chris for his concern. But it hurt him; I could see it in his eyes. He smiled and took a club from his bag and made a little loosening-up swing. "Thanks," he said again, in case Chris had missed the first expression of gratitude. Then he looked down at the club head and waggled it a little, concentrating.

Jimmy was six-five and heavy boned, with great green eyes under thick brows that seemed always knitted, even when he smiled. He'd concentrate on what you were saying and remember little details about what was going on in your life, and you felt like you were important to him. He had large intelligence, and he could be very funny. And even so, all his troubles were in that face—that long, gaunt, grief-stricken, disconsolate face. Not just the recent trouble, but a pretty steady stream of bad luck: his brother killed in Vietnam; a younger sister gone off to some cult and never heard from since, probably as a direct result of losing the brother; both parents dead, evidently of heartbreak. He had a long-established habit of expecting the worst, and this assumption informed everything he said, though he'd express this as calmly as someone making observations about the news. Really, you never had the sense that he was complaining and yet no misfortune was the slightest surprise to him. He'd already imagined all of it. His life was just going that way—hard passages, failed ventures, people leaving, sorrow after sorrow.

And through it all he was interested in how *you* were doing.

None of us was very good on the links. Handicaps, we used to joke, weren't really comforting, since they'd all be so unreasonably high. Anthony was the best player in the group, though often enough he'd get up into the low nineties. Harry hadn't broken a hundred more than a half dozen times in his whole life. Jimmy could sometimes beat Anthony but was usually closer to the century mark himself. Still, when he flushed one—his swing looked so good and he was so tall and powerful that you'd swear he was a hustler. You'd hear that purely amazing smack of the club head meeting the ball, and think, God almighty, it might go into orbit. Well, you know what I'm talking about if you've spent warm Sundays treading the green paradise of possibility, as Jimmy liked to put it.

Daryl and I—well, the less said about our game the better. On a bad day, it could look like field hockey. Lots of unexpected divots, some of them traveling farther than the ball itself. And occasionally with my first swing, the ball didn't move at all.

But we always had fun. There was the talk and the comradeship of difficulty, again to use Jimmy's words. He was naturally expressive, and he liked me because I read books and he could talk to me about them, getting the gist, since for periods of time he could rarely read more than the newspapers. He used to call me truth-seeker, a term he said he liked better than *philosopher*, and I liked it better, too. More than once he suggested I might someday be able to find a meaning in all the bad luck he'd had. That's how he talked then. I swear, what he was going through, I don't think anybody else would've been able to stand it. More often than not he'd have this mild little grin, telling you about something that, if it was happening to you, would finish you off within the week.

On this day our tee time was seven o'clock. Anthony was late, so we went to the practice green and did some putting and chipping, without saying much at first. It was, as I said, foggy. Damp and humid. It looked like the weather might lift, but you never can tell for sure in that part of Virginia; up in those mountains, they've got little reflectors in the center line of the road that can glow all day long. You could look at the thick folds of fog and believe a sunny day was somewhere out there on the other side; you might even expect it to break through.

We talked some, skirting the real subject—this news about Jimmy's wife and her new friend. One of *his* favorite topics on the links was the peculiar psychology of the sport itself, and its players. He knew the jokes, of course, like everybody else, but he also made *observations* about it, and these actually had as much to do with human nature, stuff that you and I would never think of. And he thought of *me* as a philosopher. Today was no different. You remember when that plane crash-landed on the airport runway in Iowa, and they caught it on film? A lot of people died but plenty lived, too, thanks to the pilots who brought that crippled bird in. Well, NPR reported that the pro at some club next to the airport said, quote: "About half of our golfers went home, after that." Jimmy said, "Imagine how it was for the *other* half, the ones who stayed." And he did a little dramatic bit, lining up an imaginary putt and then stopping, peering off in the distance. "What the hell is that? Oh, *my God*!" He feigned witnessing the horror of a plane bursting into flame on the runway, and his lips drew tight, his teeth showed. "My God! What a terrible thing." Then he straightened up, adjusted his belt, looked at me and said, deadpan as hell, "Who's away?"

A joke from a face as forlorn as Jimmy's, believe me, it's funnier than if a clown tells it.

In any case, it got a big laugh from us, even knowing the sadness behind it.

"Golf," I said. "It's just the nature of it. So damn punishing, so steadily humiliating that you never want to give up while there's still a chance."

"That's what we keep you around for," Jimmy said, smiling at me and loosening up with his driver. "Our own Plato, leading us into the heart of things."

Harry said he'd probably have stayed to finish the round. "Couldn't do anything to help, right?"

"Well," Jimmy said, "at least you're honest."

We shook our heads at all the bad luck in life.

A few minutes later, Anthony hurried over from the clubhouse, apologizing for holding us up, and Jimmy turned to Daryl. "What're you waiting for?" he said.

For a second, Daryl looked like he'd just taken a blow to his head. I thought he must be thinking about the airplane crash. "What?" he said.

"Hit away, man."

Now he looked relieved.

"Hey, Daryl," Harry said. "You nervous? Gotta fly somewhere?"

"He had too much coffee this morning," Jimmy said.

We all laughed, since Daryl drank about twenty cups a day. He set his ball on the tee and after his usual intricate preparations and waggles, made the first shot of the day. We watched it go straight up into the fog and disappear, then drop in the middle of the fairway like something falling out of blank heaven, not more than a hundred yards away.

"A pop-up," Jimmy said. "Better than a grounder."

I walked over and got set to hit. They were all waiting, watching, and I lucked out, hit it straight and low, farther than my usual dying slice. Daryl and I rode in the cart down to his ball, and that's when he told me they were going to pull Jimmy's floor plan.

I looked back to the tee, where Jimmy stood with the

others, waiting for us to hit. He was talking, and I felt very odd to hear about this new trouble in his life. "Did he tell you that?"

Daryl shook his head. "I know, okay? It's a fact. It's happened."

"My God," I said.

Daryl wasn't even listening to me. He hit his second, using a three wood, and skipped it about eighty yards along.

"I have to face it," he said. "I can't hit fairway woods worth a damn."

We both laughed. He wasn't much good at hitting anything else, either. I took a two iron out of my bag and started over to my ball, and when I got there what he'd said finally registered. I glanced over at him. He was standing by the cart, waiting for me to hit. "How'd you know about the floor plan," I asked, "if Jimmy didn't tell you?"

He shrugged. "That kind of news travels fast."

I addressed my ball, took a swing, and made contact; to my surprise it went straight and low again, under the fog. I was doing something right, and of course I had it in the back of my mind that as soon as I tried to *repeat* the motion, it would fall apart. So I thought about what I always enjoy about playing— the being out there, the fresh air, the smell of the grass, the breezes. But the fact that Daryl knew what he knew was nagging at me.

I didn't play bad, for me. We weren't talking much, and Daryl got even quieter than usual. He was having a rough time of it. On the fifth hole, a long par five, he lost his ball in the middle of the fairway. A hundred yards wide, this landing area, and he'd hit it so good, too. "That was maybe the best drive of my life" was his verdict as we watched it sail away into the fog. We rode out there and I topped two shots in a row, and we spent the next ten minutes looking for his drive. Nothing. The dew on the grass was making a false shine, even in the grayness. We just couldn't find it. I gave him a ball, mostly to get him to stop looking, and he hooked it bad into the woods on the left side. Behind us, back on the tee, they were hooting for us to get moving.

We played on in fog that was only a little less thick, a shelf hanging over us. Sometimes, going uphill, we just went on faith, heading toward where it must've ended up by following the line on which it vanished. We didn't say much. We were all business, tee to green, as you often are when conditions threaten to close you down. He was playing a lot worse than I was.

When he mentioned stopping in the clubhouse for a drink at the turn, I said I didn't want to. We were sitting shoulder to shoulder in the cart, both of our balls on the green. "Really, Daryl," I said. "How'd you know about the floor plan?"

"I told you."

"No, you handed me a cliché."

He shrugged. "I'm not like you. I'm not all that expressive. I can't think that fast."

It came to me that I'd always felt there was something disagreeable about him, so I tried to just let this go. We went straight from the ninth green to the tenth tee, where we had to wait for some guys who were starting their round. Despite the weather, the course had gotten crowded. We hung back and watched them hit, and they were very good. I was glad we weren't playing with them. Above us the fog kept turning on itself and looking like it might burn off.

The others came up behind us. Jimmy had actually parred the ninth with a sweet little downhill ten-footer. He'd scored a 45 on the front and was happy about it, but I swear his smile and those sad-angled eyebrows made it look like he was crying. Anthony had a 36, without a mulligan. We agreed that the first nine was the real test and Anthony might actually keep it in the seventies. Jimmy said a 90 would make his day, and Harry added that it would make his *life*. I stopped listening, watching Jimmy and thinking about the business folding up. Daryl went off and bought a Coke, then stood under a big oak to drink it, as if to shelter himself from a relentless, searing sun. I remembered that he believed you'd burn worse on an overcast day. He was always worrying about his health. It was another thing I realized I didn't much like about him.

Finally we teed off. The foursome in front of us was so good that they were long gone by the time we got to the green, and we never saw them again.

I watched Daryl go from one side of the fairways to the other, hacking away. He was making me feel like a pro.

On the fifteenth hole, an easy par four except for the little pond fronting the green, he hit his second shot into the water. He walked over to where it had gone in, then turned and waved for me to bring the cart over. I'd already hit my shot— my third—over the green, but I was at least getting my shots up a little. And by now, witnessing his round, I felt positively artistic. I drove the cart over and waited, making no eye contact as he rummaged around in his bag and finally brought out a new ball. He held it out at shoulder height and took his drop, then lined up his shot, swung, and topped it into the water; this one skipped a couple times before sinking. He took another out: drop, hit, skip, plunk. And another: drop, hit, plunk—this one went straight down, as if that's what he was trying to do.

Then he removed his bag from the cart, turned, and swung it in a wide motion, like a waltz step, into the pond. He actually seemed composed, almost serene. Stone-cold calm. The bag didn't go far, just floated away from the edge slowly and started to sink. Daryl walked down the little bank and with no hesitation at all strode into the water up to his knees, and reached forward to haul the bag back out. When he emptied the water that had got into it, some clubs fell out, but he calmly replaced them, and waved for the others to play through. "I'm going back to the clubhouse," he said.

"Just put it back on the cart," I said, none too patient with him. "You can use my towel to dry off the shafts."

"It's me she's seeing," he said.

I didn't know what he meant for a second.

"I feel awful about it. But I can't help myself either."

And then I did know. "God almighty," I said. "What the hell."

He got in the cart. "I'll drop up by the green, and take a three-stroke penalty."

"Four strokes," I said to him. "You'll take four, since you're sitting at least nine over there, by the pond."

"Okay."

I didn't want him in the cart with me, but his meltdown had taken plenty of time and they weren't too happy behind us.

Up on the green, after stubbing two wedges, I missed two putts and picked up. I didn't even feel like playing anymore.

"What the hell did you do that for?" he said. "I said okay about the four strokes."

"I'm playing the course, not you," I said to him. "And they're waiting back there."

He looked at me, then sized up his putt from where he'd taken his drop, about fifty-five feet from the hole. The ball rolled down the green, through shadows and swells, snaking left and then right at the hole, like a guided robot, nearly died at the lip, and then plopped in. My spine shook, and God only knows what his did. But neither one of us said a word. He walked to the hole and retrieved the ball, then we got in the cart and rode silently to the sixteenth tee.

"How could you do it, Daryl?" I said to him. "This is Jimmy, for God's sake. What the hell are you thinking?"

"She came to me, man." He stood at the ball washer and worked it a little, dried off the ball, and teed it up. "I think all the trouble scared her. I don't think she's built for it. And she didn't like being a trophy wife, either. You should hear her on that particular subject."

"Jesus Christ," I said, so low that I didn't even know if he heard me.

This was a par three, modeled after that famous blind par three in Scotland. A little white post gave you the line into it. While he addressed his ball and started all his waggling, I stepped to the other side, teed mine up, and hit it. I didn't care who had honors, him with his fifty-five-foot putt and four balls in the water, or me picking up after taking seven strokes. I managed to get it up in the air. It was short, though, and dropped down halfway to the post.

"Okay," he said again, then shanked his far right, out of bounds. "Mulligan?" he said.

I didn't answer. I was staring back at the green we'd just vacated. Somebody, probably Anthony, had hit into the middle of it. Another ball was in the sand. I could see the trail where it had rolled down from the lip. And here came Jimmy, walking with a slight limp, carrying his sand wedge and putter. He always seemed so laggard and worn, but God, just then he looked older, too. Maybe it was the light—or just what I now knew. He waved at me, and I waved back. I felt awful.

Daryl hit again, a surprisingly straight shot that dropped down just beyond the marker. He stood back with a stupid little smug smile on his face.

"You're sitting three," I said.

He looked at me for what felt like a long time. "Okay," he said.

I kept my five iron and walked down to my ball and skulled it into the tangled wild grasses on the right. I never wanted a mulligan more in my whole life.

"You're hitting three, buddy," he said, rolling away in the cart.

I found my ball in the tall grass and tried again, and it went somewhere toward the marker. When I got there I saw it had sailed over the green, and that Daryl's was fifteen feet from the hole. He stood there waiting for me to chip, and I fluffed it, chunking it all of four feet. I started to pick it up, but that would've been more of a statement than I wanted to make. So I swiped at it again, knocking it to the fringe on the other side. I was seething, and still away.

"Should I holler for them to go ahead and hit?"

"Yeah," I said. I could barely look at him.

Over the crest of the hill, I saw Jimmy take a club from his bag, then he moved out of sight to the tee. I heard him hit, and his ball came sailing in high, right at the pin. Daryl was watching it, too. "Looking good," he yelled.

It hit, bounced once, and began to roll, missing the pin by an inch, but it was going to roll all the way over, and since I was already standing there, I just stopped it with my shoe—you know, lifted my foot at the toe, let it come in, and then clamped down on it. Stopped it dead. Hardly even thinking about it, I used my putter to edge the ball along to the hole. Daryl just gaped at me, which played into things because it was like he was watching Jimmy's shot. I pushed the ball to the lip of the cup and in, then yelled, jumped, and ran over to where Daryl was just staring at me as if he couldn't believe I'd go through with this. "Wave and yell," I muttered, "you son of a bitch."

He turned and held his hands up and walked to where they could see him clearly from the tee, acting like a man who couldn't believe what he'd just seen—which must have been pretty easy for him, since that was indeed the situation. I kept waving and yelling, glancing over to make sure he wasn't going to blow it. Now his face seemed frozen: *These are your cards, so play them.* In those few seconds I really hated him.

There was a lot of celebrating back on the tee, and finally the other two hit—Anthony's ball only twenty or so feet from the hole, Harry's a good deal farther away, on the left fringe. Waiting for them to come up, I picked up again and Daryl marked his ball.

"Take a four and pick it up," I told him. "Or so help me I'll tell him."

"You'll tell him what?" he said.

And there we were, both in a Mexican standoff of guilty knowledge.

"Pick it up," I said.

"You know what you can do with it," he said.

We saw Jimmy come over the rise, those sad eyes wide with wonder. He was like a little boy. He hurried over to the hole and looked in.

"Man," he said. "Oh, man. I don't believe it. I don't *believe* it."

Daryl was staring at me, and I gave it right back.

He bent down, picked up his ball, then looked at me again. Everybody else was yelling and clapping Jimmy on the back.

"God almighty," Jimmy said, shaking his head.

"You should've seen it," Daryl said. And given his expression, you would've sworn he believed it, too.

I hadn't even known I would do it. There was nothing at all premeditated about it. And I felt suddenly very strange—guilt way down, but mixed with happiness, or something more like exhilaration. Daryl kept congratulating Jimmy and he was really getting into it, talking to him about the flight of the ball, how it hit and rolled toward the cup, like the most delicate putt.

"I just couldn't believe it," he said. "I've never seen anything like it."

"How far did it roll?" Anthony wanted to know.

"Thirty feet?" Daryl said, looking at me.

"At least," I got out.

From the look on Jimmy's face, you could almost believe it had happened exactly like he was imagining it.

"Jimmy," I said.

"Yeah?"

"You deserve this," I told him. "Congratulations, man."

Later that afternoon, Daryl and I went out to buy some good wine, since we meant to celebrate the ace in style. We got to the liquor store without speaking a single word. I bought five bottles of Brunello, at forty-nine bucks a pop, and wouldn't let Daryl put in a dime. As we drove back, he said, "She's just a young kid who wasn't ready for the kind of trouble Jimmy's been in."

"You can tell yourself that," I said. "Don't tell it to me."

I carried the wine into the clubhouse, where other players had gathered round, and Chris was taking down the details for the plaque they'd make. The wine was wonderful and we all sat around feeling glad. In the middle of this I caught Jimmy staring off. It was only for a couple of seconds, but he was deep in thought, and knowing everything I knew, I felt that strange stirring of guilt again. Maybe no one should have even that small portion of the power of fate. I glanced in Daryl's direction, but he was drunk already and telling somebody I didn't

recognize about how he'd thrown his clubs in the pond on fifteen. By this time, I guess I was a little drunk myself.

As we were all leaving, Jimmy took my arm above the elbow
and said, "You know about Elaine leaving and all that, but now
they're pulling the floor plan on me. I'm gonna have to sell the
dealership. It's something I've been dreading for months. But I
feel good anyway. It's almost like defiance. This thing today's
going to change my luck around somehow. I can feel it."

He hadn't had more than a couple glasses of wine.

I said, "Me, too," but it wouldn't come out, quite. I choked
on the words.

That was twelve years ago. I left Virginia before the summer was
out; my wife got a really good job offer in New Orleans, and we
took it. After all, the dealership was gone, and a guy can sell cars
anywhere, right? Except that now we live in Oxford, Mississippi, and I'm selling mortgages. Before that I taught school for
a couple years—English, or Anguish, as I liked to call it.

I never saw or heard anything about Daryl again, but I hope
he's being cuckolded somewhere. Harry and Anthony, as far as
I know, are still fixing cars. Jimmy's in his sixties now and has
two houses, the one I saw in Virginia, and another in Florida,
plus a hunting cabin in Montana where he and his third wife
spend some time. Every year or so I hear from him. And it's
true that he dates his life's turnaround from that hole in
one. The plaque Chris made for him sits on his mantel, right
next to the ball itself, which Jimmy had gold-plated, for his
own trophy.

Maybe something like that can change everything, I don't
know. But I do believe Jimmy's the type who can survive and
come out all right no matter what he has to go through.

Still, it *is* so if you *think* it is so, right? And he does.

Trophy

Last Christmas, I got a card with a picture of the two of them, Jimmy and the wife. She's not as young as Elaine was, but nice-looking, with soft, kindly eyes. I liked her right away, and still do, though I saw her only that one time. Jimmy? Well, the truth is, no amount of success can change those particular features, that particular face. Happy and smiling from the heart of well-being, he still looks like he's carrying the weight of the world.

SOMETHING IS OUT THERE

By the time they got back to the house, the snow had started, coming fast in the swirling wind over the mountains to the west. Paula drove, with her elder son, Luke, in the front seat, and the younger one, Virgil, with Aunt Dora in the back. Aunt Dora spoke about the roads, how fast they became impassible in this part of Virginia, worrying aloud about her stepson Christopher's journey down the valley from Winchester, where he had been in college. No one answered her. After what they had been through today, she would of course be worrying about Christopher. But Christopher might even beat the full force of the storm, and even if he didn't, he was driving a Jeep, and he had driven in snow before. He would pull in, safe, and Aunt Dora would fall apart, telling him about the harrowing hours of the afternoon.

At the house, Luke got out, hooked up the hose, and washed away the blood on the ground at the far end of the porch. The snow was already covering it. When that was done, he and Virgil got a shovel and broom from the shed and commenced clearing a path on the sidewalk. The snow was sticking. The boys worked well together, but a little frantically. They were such good boys, and Paula knew it would be some time before they could be truly careless again.

Aunt Dora sat in the front seat of the car and watched them, refusing, for the moment, to come inside. "I'm sorry," she said. "I'm still terrified."

Paula nearly lost patience with her. After all, it was Paula's husband who had been shot, and who lay in the hospital with a bullet wound in his leg and a badly bruised lower back from the fall off the roof of the house. An hour of surgery, but Kent was all right; Kent would be fine. The doctors said so. Kent would be good as new in a few days. The bullet could easily have severed an artery, but it hadn't, and Brice Collins was in custody, after an afternoon of evading the state troopers. But they had him now, and it was over.

"Please, Dora."

"I know."

Paula turned and made her way along the path her sons had cleared, and stepped up onto the porch. There were pine boughs arranged on the railing, and Christmas lights drooping from the eves of the roof. Brice had driven up, stopped, got out, aimed the pistol, and fired, and then driven off. Kent had fallen from the far end of the porch, onto the stones of the little garden. He lay there with open eyes, and Paula knew that as long as she lived, she would remember the look in them as she approached—the desperate, almost childlike searching for some clue in her face as to how bad it all was.

He had found that he couldn't move. The leg wound bled profusely.

At the hospital, Kent got sick and thought he might die. It had been a long and terrible afternoon. He kept telling them how Brice Collins had done it. Pulled up, got out, walked over, leveled the pistol at him, and fired. He cried like a little boy, telling it. Kent and Brice had been friends since high school, and had been in business together, but there had been bad blood about the split of payments for an addition they had built onto a house in the upper valley. Kent had decided almost a year ago that he wanted to find a way out of any kind of association with Brice, because Brice had begun selling dope. Finally, the only way was to fire him, though it was a partnership. Kent had kept back enough money from the payment on the last job to cover the extra expenses of time lost while Brice drove up to Washington and made shady new friends and associations, and peddled his goods out of the trunk of the car. Brice took the firing badly but nobody dreamed he would go this far.

"Christopher, too," Kent said, and seemed to want to say more. But when she pressed him he just kept crying, coughing and trying to catch his breath, looking at her with those eyes that sought her assurance; and finally the eyes rolled back in his head and he passed out.

The doctor told her this was normal, to be expected. He had been given something to help him rest. All his signs were good; he was a very lucky man, and never mind the bullet wound in the leg, a twenty-two slug passing through. He was very fortunate to have survived such a fall.

In the house, Dora went straight to her room and lay down. Paula cleared the table and washed the dinner dishes. The two boys stood on the porch watching the snow cover the place they had washed. The snow was coming down hard. You couldn't see out to the road for the close swirling of the flakes. Night had fallen in this white roiling, a tremendous quiet. There had been very little wind at first, but now it was picking up.

Paula watched them start working on the sidewalk again. They were two years apart, at a stage where they were more like friends than brothers. At thirteen, Virgil could make the older boy laugh. It was a communication the two of them had.

With others, both were quiet and polite, calling men "sir" and women "ma'am," as their father had taught them. She and Kent were very proud of them both. Now the boys worked quietly, clearing the snow. It was just to have something to do with their hands, she knew, and her heart went out to them. She opened the door and spoke to Luke in as normal a voice as she could muster. "Sweetie, come right in and tell us when Christopher gets here, will you?"

"Yes, ma'am."

She closed the door and went down the hall to the entrance of Dora's room. Dora lay on her back, with one hand over her eyes.

"What," she said.

"He's fine," said Paula. "And Christopher will be here any minute. It's all okay now."

"It was so awful, to see him lying there on those rocks. I knew what had happened immediately. I heard the shot and I knew."

"Well, it's all right, now. It's over now."

"I can't help it, honey."

"Well—would you like a glass of brandy or something?"

"No, thank you."

In fact, Paula felt the same chill, the trembling along the length of her spine. She wanted the little details of the evening, of any evening. Dinner and television and talk and sleep. Kent was all right. "Are you going to sleep?" she asked Dora.

"No."

"Dora, please stop lying there looking at it all. It turned out okay. Kent can come home in three days, if we're not snowed in."

"How bad is the snow?"

"It's a storm. But we've had storms."

Dora said nothing.

"Chris will be here in a bit, and we'll all have some Christmas cheer. It could've been so much worse, Dora. Think about it. A man like Brice. They've got him. It's over."

"I'm trying not to think about it," Dora said. "So you stop talking about it."

"Come help me wrap presents."

"I don't know, honey."

"Come on out and talk to me," Paula said. "I'll make hot chocolate or something."

"I'm really so tired."

"We haven't done anything all day."

Dora took her hand away and raised her head. "You're kidding, right?"

"Well, we haven't. We decorated the tree. We went to the hospital."

She lay back down. "I'm exhausted."

"You're just going to stay here the rest of the night? It's not even seven o'clock."

"I'll be out in a little while. Let me get a hold of myself. Christ."

Dora was Kent's aunt, and she had come to visit because Paula asked her to—the two of them had formed a close friendship over the years. They could talk to each other; they could tell each other anything. Paula hadn't told Dora this, but she was thinking of leaving Kent—tension over money, absences, drinking, unexplained aspects of failing business, sadness generally in the bedroom. What she did tell Dora was that Kent was unhappy, had seemed so for a period of months. And in all of this there were similarities: Dora had been in the process of leaving Christopher's father when Christopher's father died.

Christopher didn't know any of this. Dora had kept it from him—and from everyone, really, except Paula. Dora felt that there was something hypocritical in accepting the boy's sorrowful affection, his worry over how she was taking the loss of a husband for whom as another human being she was sorry, but whose private treatment of her, over ten years of marriage, had earned something other than love.

Paula had been describing her own unrest to Dora, the two of them sitting in the kitchen breaking up stale bread for dressing, when they heard the shot.

The snow was sweeping across the light from the porch now. Paula opened the door again and stepped out into the cold. The boys had gone out beyond the border of the light.

"Luke?" she called. "Virgil?"

Just the wind, carrying its weight of snow. She stepped down onto the sidewalk, which was quickly being covered once more. "Boys?"

Nothing.

She went back up onto the porch and along it, to the end. And here they were, standing over the spot where their father had fallen. They were talking low. She couldn't hear what they were saying for the wind. But Luke had one hand on Virgil's shoulder, and now Virgil reached up and wiped his nose with the sleeve of his coat. He was crying. "Boys?" she said.

They seemed startled. They walked around into the yard and along the front of the porch, to the stairs, where she went to meet them. "We're all right," she said.

Luke had picked up the broom and begun sweeping the steps. "Yeah," he said. Virgil held a shovel, but just leaned on it. He had pulled his scarf over his lower face.

"Come inside now. You'll both catch cold."

She saw again the way her husband's gaze had sought her, from where he lay on his back, unable to move or breathe, and later in the hospital as he wept—the helplessness in his eyes, the stare. She shivered.

Luke had stopped sweeping. "I wish it was tomorrow," he sobbed.

She said, "Daddy's all right."

He turned back to sweeping the sidewalk. Virgil stood there, staring at her, holding the shovel. His face was white— he looked scared to the bone. She stepped down and put her arms around him.

Their life had been good; they were so fortunate. This was still true.

Yet she couldn't stop seeing Kent lying open-eyed on his back in the snow, and the blood soaking it in a widening circle at his legs. "It's a happy Christmas," she told them. "A very lucky Christmas after all. Right? It could've been so much worse."

Luke stared out at the road. "I'll feel better when Christopher gets here."

In less than fifteen minutes, the work they had done on the sidewalk was visible only as a small declension in the drift of snow. And it kept coming, the wind whistling. Looking at it all, you saw the flakes plunging horizontally, with a force. Paula walked out in it, and struggled to the end of the driveway, hoping to see the lights of Christopher's Jeep. The flakes stung her face. There was no sky, but only this massive wall of blowing snow, as though the wind had taken on nearly solid form, and here was its shape, blasting down from the mountains. The pathology of this day seemed to be expanding—the world had broken from its strand of gravitation, was flying off into the blackness.

There was no sign of life down the road.

Inside, Dora had fallen asleep. The boys were staring at television—some newspeople, treating the whole thing like a delightful happenstance. A white Christmas. The first in years. They even played a little of the song. She looked at them and thought of them as beings from another sphere of existence, another species. They were where they were, in the lighted studio, smiling, sure of life; and she was here, in this house where her vaguely estranged husband, only hours ago, had been shot.

"I'm getting worried," Luke said abruptly. "Why doesn't Chris call? There's no way he can get through a storm this bad. I bet the road's closed."

"They haven't reported that," his younger brother said.

Aunt Dora appeared in the entrance of the room and coughed. When she spoke, her voice was tremulous, filled with dread. "He's not here yet? He hasn't called?"

They all looked at her.

"Oh, God," she said. "Something else's happened."

"I'm going to make coffee," Paula said.

In the kitchen, Dora sobbed, sitting at the table with her face in her hands. "I'm a wreck," she said. Paula poured more coffee for herself, and a cup for Dora, who looked at it as though she didn't recognize what it was. The television newspeople were now talking about a big accident out on Route 66 West. Christopher would be coming south on highway 17, and would only cross under 66 West.

Kent had taken such a fall after the shot. The bullet had not hit bone, nor cut through any vein or artery; it had hit him in the lower thigh and exited a little higher out the back of the leg. They were making sure there would be no infection; the wounds were treated and closed. It was the fall that might've done something more, might've hurt him where they weren't looking. When she was very young, a boy she knew had crashed on his bicycle and injured his side—a slightly cracked rib, the doctor said. But the boy had ruptured his spleen, and died as a result of it.

Now she watched Dora lift her coffee cup and sip. There wasn't going to be any coming back from what this day had been. Her boys were talking over the newscasters on the television, and she wanted to tell them to be quiet so she could hear.

In the next instant, the boys stirred from their places— there was a scurrying toward the front door. They had seen headlights coming down the road. When she and Dora got to them, they were standing in the open doorway, in the still-blowing snow, waiting for the lights to get to the turnoff into the driveway in front of the house. The headlights came. They all watched.

"I'm going to give him hell for not calling us," Dora said. But there was no conviction in her voice.

The car came pushing by, lighting up the hillocks of drifting snow. It plowed through and went on, and they all watched the red taillights until the heavy curtain of snow blotted out the twin embers. For a moment, no one said anything.

"Hell," Luke said, under his breath. "Where the hell are they going? There's nothing down that way but Wayside Pond and the gas station."

"He'll be here," said Paula.

Dora wandered back into the kitchen and then on, to her room. The boys talked about shoveling the walk again. Paula said to go ahead; it was something for them to do. She couldn't quite voice the thought—it was too ordinary, really, almost childlike—but it seemed impossible that the trauma of the afternoon's trouble and anxiety could be added to by anything serious where Christopher was concerned. The world she knew did not act that way. She wanted to say something to the boys—to tell them that the day's misfortune was sufficient, plenty enough for anyone, and surely the world would not add to all that. But then she understood the irrational nature of this line of thinking; there was not going to be anything sensible or logical about this day. She felt a little freezing current of air under her heart, and tried to concentrate on watching the boys shovel the walk again. They barely made any headway.

When she went back into the kitchen, she found Dora standing at the kitchen sink, taking a pill. Xanax, Dora said, to calm her nerves. There was a glass of whiskey on the table, next to the open bottle: Old Forester. Dora had changed into her nightgown. "You trying to calm down or knock yourself unconscious?" Paula said.

"Sometimes this is my nighttime ritual."

Paula watched her move to the table, lift the glass, and throw it back. She set the glass down and poured another. "He's stopped for the night, and just forgot to call me," she said.

"Hey," Luke called from the other room.

They all moved to the front door again. What looked like the same car had come back down the road—and now it turned in. A man, not Christopher, got out. He was tall, big around, heavy, and he wore a long beige car coat over jeans and boots. The car coat had a hood, which was up, though not zipped tight. The man stood gazing at the upper windows of the house. Paula said, "Get back from the window," and they all moved.

"Who is it?" Dora said.

"I can't make out the face," said Paula, peering out the small opening in the curtains of the window next to the door. The man crossed the snow-covered walk toward the porch. He came up onto the stoop, looked to either side, and back out to the road.

Then he stepped forward and knocked.

The sound brought a little yelp of startlement up from the bottom of Paula's throat. Dora looked at her. "Well?"

Paula moved to the door. "Yes?" she said, loud enough to be heard through it.

"Hello," said the man. "I didn't think I'd make it here. It's bad out on the highway. Is Kent Goodson at home, please."

"He went out for a few minutes," Paula said. "Do I know you?"

"No, ma'am, we never met. I did some work for him, though. I was supposed to meet him here this afternoon but the storm slowed me down. I gotta get some papers filed with the county, you know. For permits on a renovation?"

Paula looked at Dora, and at the boys. They all stared back.

"I can come back later," he said. "Sorry to bother you. Can I just leave these papers in the mailbox?"

Paula opened the door. "You can give them to me."

"Oh," the man said. "Thank you." He reached into the coat. "I swear I never saw snow gather that quick in my life." He handed her a sheaf of forms. "They just need his signature as the contractor of record. And—well, I don't really know how I'm gonna get 'em back though." He turned a little and looked up the road through the rushing wall of snow.

Paula had the thought that the day's trouble had made her suspicious, and she looked at the man, who seemed merely perplexed at the problem. "How important are these papers?" she asked him.

"Well, you know, the guy wanted us to pull permits. And the county requires the papers. Can't really close the deal or begin the work—you know. This is a bathroom these people are adding."

She remembered Kent talking about it. She said, "Kent is in the hospital."

He came in, bigger even than he had looked standing out there, looming in the doorway, and then inside the doorway, further strangeness in this very strange and terrifying day. Paula stepped back from reflex, and she thought about how paranoid the day had made her. Dora and the boys had gone into the kitchen—Dora herded them in there as soon as Paula spoke about where Kent was.

"I'm so sorry to hear that. Truly, ma'am."

She had an abrupt sense of all of it being connected, something unfolding that she was ignorant of, and for which she was unready. He put the hood down on the coat, and snow dropped from it onto the little area rug. "Just so sorry. I guess—"

"He's going to be home in a couple of days," Paula said. "Well, three days."

"Nothing serious, I hope."

"He took a fall. He'll be fine."

The wind was pushing through the door behind him, and now he seemed aware of it. He stepped back to the frame of it, and then out onto the porch again. "I'm sorry about messing up your rug, there. I'll leave the papers with you. If he can sign them I can come back and pick them up. They just really wanted to get going while the weather's bad, you know, because this is inside work."

"I'll tell him," Paula said. What she wanted now was for him to be gone.

"Thanks," he said, and she saw him shiver. It touched her in an odd way—a poor man trying to do an honest thing in the face of suspicion that had nothing to do with him.

"Would you like some coffee?" she heard herself say.

"Oh, you're so very kind. But I better get going." He turned and started off the porch. "Oh," he said, turning. "Is Christopher around?"

"Christopher?"

"I went to school with him, and he e-mailed me he was coming down."

"He's on his way. He should be here soon."

"Well—tell him I said 'Hey.' Maybe we can get together while he's here."

"What's your name?"

"Jack," he said. "Tell him Jack Stallings."

"I will."

"Thanks for the offer of hospitality," he said. "I do appreciate it." He pulled the hood up, walking away.

She watched him go to the car, swipe the snow from the window, get in, and start it. He seemed now to be in something of a hurry. Dora and the boys had come into the room behind her. Both boys held knives. Dora had one of Kent's golf clubs. The car backed out of the drive, with some spinning of the wheels, went on back down the road, and was gone.

Paula closed the door, locked it, then looked out the window again. Her hands shook. The others moved to the front windows, and for what seemed a long while no one said anything.

"What the hell is going on?" Dora said. "For God's sake— you actually let him in."

"He knows Christopher."

"I heard that. I never heard Christopher mention him."

"Well, he's *gone*, Dora. And—look." She held up the sheaf of forms. "He had to drop these off. That's all. He was a nice man doing his job."

Dora only briefly glanced at her, then stepped to the window and looked out. "Well, I never heard of him."

Paula looked at the forms. They were all permits for electrical and plumbing work on the job Kent had talked about doing.

"Oh, hell," Dora said. "Where are you, Chris?"

There didn't seem to be any way to rest, now. They couldn't even sit down, but kept vigil at all the road-facing windows, upstairs and down. Paula and Aunt Dora waited downstairs, looking out at the monotonous swirl of snow in the porch light.

"Why doesn't he call?" Dora muttered, several times. She kept calling his cell, and getting only the recording.

"I want to know what Brice had in his mind," said Paula. "Last week I came in and Kent was yelling at him on the phone. He hung up when he saw me and wouldn't talk about it. He said it was Brice. And it surprised me because he had already fired Brice."

Dora had another glass of her whiskey and was sipping it slowly, staring out at the snowing half circle of light. "God," she said. "I think it's the dope and I think Christopher's mixed up in it some way, too. Christopher and Brice and Kent and— and this guy, whoever he was."

"Kent fired Brice. Kent's not mixed up in anything."

"I never heard this guy's name and I never saw him with Christopher. I worked at Christopher's school, Paula. I never saw the guy."

"Stop drinking," said Paula. "I might need your help with some things around here."

"I'm fine, real—" Dora began, and they were suddenly in blackness. There was not the sense of light failing, but of dark closing down on them like a judgment. And there was only silence now, except for the wind in the eaves.

"I knew it," Paula said. "I fucking well knew it. God*damn* Virginia Power."

"Mom?" Virgil said from the stairs.

"In here, sweetie."

He and his older brother made their way to the kitchen, feeling along the walls. Dora was already looking for candles, a flashlight, something. But it was pitch-black. Complete darkness. Even the streetlight by the road had gone out.

Dora hit something and glass shattered. "Christ!" she said.

"Where's the phone?" said Luke.

"Stay in here. All of us," Paula said.

They managed to get seated around the table. The dark was total. The only way they could tell one another's proximity was by voice and touching. A light on them would have shown a tableau of grace before a meal—everyone holding hands. They waited. Paula had the thought that it was just the storm, just the aftermath of the bad afternoon, the shock of having been through it. They would wait out the night, and in the morning things would look normal again. A snow covering. Bright sun on hillocks of it, and bright sky, clouds trailing in the aftermath, across cleansed blue distances. But Dora was crying now, and muttering to herself, and Virgil, too, had begun. The wind whipped at the house like something searching the dark for them, in the angles of roof and wall. There was no light anywhere, no glimmer. This was darkness pure and unalloyed as any element.

"It'll be all right," Paula said. "It's a snowstorm. What happened today is over. It's over. Brice went off the deep end, and they've got him and he'll spend the next fifteen years in prison. And a man stopped by to leave some papers for Daddy."

None of them answered her. The wind shook the windows, even louder than before. The only sound inside now was Dora's muttering and crying. Paula let go of her hand, and the others let go—you could feel the shifting in the chairs.

"Dora, stop it," Paula said. "Please."

"That wasn't anybody Christopher went to school with," Dora said.

For a moment, they were all quiet again.

"What're you saying?" Paula demanded. "Christ. You can't know *everyone* he went to school with."

"Something's happening. I know it. Where's Christopher?"

"Christopher's stopped somewhere in a motel. Probably asleep. Now stop it—stop it. Drink some more whiskey."

Dora's answer was lost in the ramming of the wind.

"You'd think my eyes would get adjusted to the dark," Virgil said. "I'm blind."

"That's how dark it is," said Luke. He had left the table.

"Watch the broken glass," Paula said.

He rattled glasses, and a drawer opened; they heard the sound of knives and silverware being moved.

"It's not in there," Paula said to him about the flashlight.

"I saw it in here, I swear."

"Don't cut yourself."

"I'm okay," the boy said. But there was such fright in his voice.

It was Dora, finally, who found a lighter, and, with that, searched out some candles on a cabinet shelf. They lit the candles. As they were lighting the last ones, the telephone rang. Paula reached for it, knocked a candle over, and cursed, but picked up the receiver and said, "Hello?"

The voice on the other end said, "Is Kent around?"

"No."

Dora and Luke both, in a frantic kind of unison, said, "Find out who it is."

"Who's calling, please?" Paula said.

She waited. They were all three watching her, intense, fixed, focused, their eyes glittering in the flickering dimness.

"Who's calling, please?" she said again.

But the connection had been broken.

"Boys," Dora said. "Take a candle and see if you can find the flashlights. There must be a couple of them somewhere."

"The utility closet, out back," Luke said. "But the wind'll blow the candles out."

"You are not going outside," said Paula. "Stay here." She picked up a candle and started toward the living room, and the doorway down to the basement. "I mean it—stay where you are."

Dora followed her. They went together in the chaotic shifting of shadow and light on the stairs. At the bottom, the candle went out—but Dora had her lighter, and they got it going again. They were standing very close in the dark, with the candle flame flickering between them.

"They were all in on it," Dora said. "They were all going to make so much money."

"What are you *talking* about?" Paula said. "Do you know something I don't know?"

"I know they were meeting about it. Brice, too."

"He *fired* Brice."

Dora said, "That was about the money. I'm sure of it." Then she began to cry. "I don't know how, but I think Christopher's in on it, too. I think that guy was looking for Christopher. I'm afraid he'll hurt him. Christopher dropped out of college, Paula. He was going to bypass it all. He told me that over the phone. He said he was going to make so much more money doing what he was doing and when I asked him what it was he wouldn't tell me. And something's gone wrong and Brice felt cut out of it and others got cut out of it—I heard Kent say that. Those very words. 'What about the others that get cut out of this?' I heard him say it. And I never saw that Stallings guy before. I never saw him. He's too old to have gone to school with Christopher. My God, Paula—did you *look* at him? I'm scared. I'm so scared. He's not gone. He didn't leave. He's out there waiting."

Paula looked for the flashlight. For batteries, a lantern, more candles, anything. Dora stood watching her. "Go on upstairs," Paula said, "if you're not going to help."

"You don't believe me."

"I don't know what I believe. I want this night to be over and I want more light. And an end to this fucking blizzard. And right now there isn't anything else that I want."

"A person couldn't just hide out there in that cold and wind, right? A person would freeze to death."

"Yes, Dora. A person would freeze to death. Go upstairs."

The other woman made her way up out of the meager glow of the candle flame. And Paula was alone. She had been thinking of taking her two boys and leaving. She had been thinking about the end of her marriage, the troubles, the discontent of the long nights, sleepless and worried, wanting not to hurt anyone. She stood for a moment in the chilly gloom of the basement and had the thought that this day's badness was the beginning of something more, an unfolding. She didn't even know what it would be about; she wasn't even sure it was coming. But her blood told her it was, and she had to be ready for it, whatever it might be. She moved to the workbench at the far

end of the basement and, still holding the flickering candle—
which seemed about to go out—she opened the heavy wooden
drawer there, and held the candle over it. Here was Kent's tar-
get revolver. She brought it out, opened it, and saw that it was
loaded. She closed it, checked the safety, then moved to the
other end of the bench, where she found a terry cloth rag. She
wrapped the gun in it, and then looked for something with
which to conceal it on her person. There was an old Baltimore
Orioles jacket hanging on a hook at the other end of the room.
She moved there, placed the revolver in its rag on the little
lamp table against the wall, lifted the jacket down, and put it
on. It was way too big for her. The ends of it drooped to her
thighs. She rolled the too-long sleeves up. It would do. The
storm outside made a terrible thudding, cracking roar that
made her jump, and she crouched down for a second. She
waited. There wasn't any other sound now but the storm.
Finally she picked up the revolver in its wrap and placed it in
the deep left pocket.

She was a woman in a little rural house in Virginia, in the
middle of a big snowstorm, wearing a baseball jacket, armed,
expecting grave business. There could never be anything so
strange, so brutally exact, as experience, and she knew it. She
had only wanted to go. She had only entertained the idea of
leaving this house.

She made her way up into the dark cave of the stairwell,
lighting it as she went. Dora and the boys were back at the windows in the living room, hunched there in the uncertain light
of more candles, staring out at the unabated agitation of the
storm. It wasn't even midnight. She went past them, upstairs,
to the master bedroom, where she could have a good view of
the road, if anything that had headlamps came down it. She
watched the white expanse, through the fantastic churning, the

eddies of wind made visible by the solidness of the swarming flakes. Nothing moved out there. But it was coming; she sensed it. Whatever it was. It was near.

She took the revolver out of the jacket and set it on the windowsill, where she could reach it if and when she had to. She didn't know, now. And there was so much time to go through until sunrise. Her sons were downstairs with their great-aunt, barricading the doors.

She had begun this day, this very day, wholeheartedly believing in goodwill, work, contracts, commitments, friendship, helpfulness. She had believed that she might say to Kent, "I want to go. I want to move out for a while, and see what happens." And he might be upset, but would accept it, too, because people did so in the circumstances; people came to these changes and suffered them quietly, or at least civilly. And nobody came looking for you with the intent to hurt you.

She leaned into the icy glass, put her fingers on the cold handle of the revolver, and watched the distant commotion of the storm for any sign of light, hoping for it even as she understood that when she saw it, if she saw it, she would have to try to determine what it meant—safe arrival, help, someone seeking shelter, or intending harm.

BLOOD

Walker Clayfield's older brother, Max, started the subcontracting business—house painting, carpentry, and wiring—upon his return from a hitch in the army in 1998. Back then, he and Walker and Sean, the youngest, all lived with their mother, Minnie, in the old place on Highpoint Terrace. The house had been added onto decades ago, when Minnie was a newly married lady, and happy. It had a narrow backyard, at one end of which was the partial spine of an unfinished boat under a cracked plastic tarp—the failed project of Theodore Clayfield, the boys' sad excuse for a father. The old man had begun to build it out of wood from scratch before his madness and his drinking and other forms of excess got him—a fatal heart attack at fifty-one. Growing up, the old man had apprenticed to his own father as a boatwright.

That man, too, had mental troubles—and bottle troubles.

Walker, after he entered high school, began helping Max during summers. By then, Max was chasing after Jenny Glass, whose family didn't like him. Once, when Jenny was having dinner at Paulette's Restaurant with Bill Jonas, whom she had started seeing, Max stormed in and overturned the table where they sat, and then went after Jonas. The two of them fell over another table, breaking several plates and glasses. Max ended up in the hospital. Jenny forgave him for it because he was bruised and beaten and because he was so contrite. But when, with her mother's encouragement, she went out with Jonas again, there Max was, wet-eyed and penitent and hurt—still wanting to fight.

Max is like that. Like his father at least that much, Minnie will say. Whatever he sets his mind to can wither from the force of his attention. And of course Jenny Glass possesses her own kind of stubbornness. Even after Max finally won her, she wouldn't live in the old place with the family. So Max bought a small house in a little neighborhood of World War II housing over by the river, and fixed it up for his mother and younger brothers to live in. The house is the last one on Darwood Avenue, a blind street beyond which is a field of wildflowers and, in the middle distance, an abandoned railroad trestle and the stone columns of what was one of the first bridges to Arkansas from this part of Memphis. Minnie made a garden out back and put white curtains in the windows and flower boxes on the windowsills across the front. Jenny helped her.

Jenny and Max were married within a month of the completion of the little house. Jenny has always liked the Highpoint house, and the neighborhood, with its little corner grocery store only a block away. She and Max have had some very happy times there.

Last year, Max got it into his head that he wanted to finish the old man's boat and start a charter fishing business in the gulf, which is more than two hundred miles away on the interstate. People often pay up to fifteen hundred dollars a head to be able to say they fished the Gulf Stream. It's big business down there. This can be freedom. Free at last. That's what he'll name the boat. When he talks about it, you can see that the whole thing has already been accomplished in his head.

Free at last.

But shortly after Christmas, Minnie suffered a mild stroke, and she requires some care. Also the real estate market has hit a bad slump, putting a big hole in the contracting. Max and Jenny have had to take jobs, Jenny tending the counter at an antiques store in the Cooper-Young district, Max working in the service bay at the local Chevrolet dealership, performing oil changes and lube jobs. Now every single minute of his free time on weekends goes into work on the boat. He's given up softball league and sold all his hunting and camping gear. He no longer goes to ball games with his brothers or to movies with his wife or to restaurants with the family—or even to the occasional contract job either, though he does include himself in the process of preparing the estimates. He has left most of the actual work to Walker. He's also become tightfisted, and he doesn't want to talk about anything but this pet project of his. He goes on about rot-resistant oak and cedar planks and carvel construction of the hull and spar, though he hasn't even finished the frame.

The catafalque, as Jenny calls it, sits there in the backyard, an enormous rib cage of wood amid scattered scraps and piles of packed-down sawdust. Max tells anyone who will listen that when it's finished it will be a cabin cruiser, eighteen feet long, with an inboard motor and all the modern equipment. Of course finishing is years away.

Walker keeps up with what business there is. He puts in an occasional ceiling fan or paints the inside of a house or builds bookshelves—but mostly he helps keep his mother's little place, and he has more free time than is healthy. He lifts weights, plays basketball with Sean, goes more often than he should over to the Highpoint house, and then tries to keep to himself, a young man with too much room for thinking, as his mother would put it. Casting about, she would say. And he rides off in the truck to Mud Island, alone, and walks the long concrete model of the Mississippi, and stands on what he knows to be the Highpoint area of the black bronze-crossed representation of Memphis. He goes on down the fake river to the little park at the end and eats an ice cream and looks at the fountain. People walk by him; children play in the water. He sits there. Idleness and worry all the time, fidgeting, nervous, unable to think about anything but the one thing that has come to occupy him above all else, with a constant pressure under the breastbone. He's continually brooding about it and turning on it in his thoughts, even in sleep, this affliction that came out of nowhere, this terrible surprise and misery, this secret hunger and aching.

He has fallen desperately in love with Jenny Glass Clayfield.

When he and his mother and Sean visit the old Highpoint house, they all end up sitting near the big wooden frame, try°ing to talk over the noise of Max's labor. Walker watches his sister-in-law move back and forth from the house to the end of the yard, and the rib cage of blond wood there, and then he tries hard not to watch her. She's a shape in his peripheral vision, and he hears her voice, that softness coming from her throat; he could pick it out of a crowd of people all talking at once. When he glances at her he sees the soft curve of her breasts in the little area of the open collar of her blouse. He hates his own mind, his own senses, because they are so attuned to every nuance of her being—sound, breath, touch, the fragrance of her, the physical power of her proximity, bones and flesh and the dark shine of the eyes and the hair with its perfect straight shimmer in sunlight.

Work on the boat takes up the hour before dinner. The family moves through the shade of the lawn in the sound of it. Finally their mother shakes her head and makes her slow way into the house, to sit with Jenny and play gin rummy. Walker tolerates Sean's teasing and banters with him, not really attending to what is said, feeling only annoyance with the other's constant chatter. Sometimes they toss a baseball back and forth. Walker wonders if Jenny can see him from the window. Now and then Max joins in the talk—that is, when he's not rattled and aggravated, trying, he says, to focus on the work. He allows Walker only a boy's tasks, really: holding tools and fetching things.

Jenny serves the evening meal out in the yard, and they all sit in the striped shade of the unfinished boat, and Walker attempts to see past her, around her, away from her. He knows that this thing he's struggling with is not a crush. This is a passion so deep it has taken everything else out of him; it feels like a form of starvation—or, no, a form of drowning. Something wells up in his spirit, and leaves him inwardly gasping. She talks about trying to sleep in the ruckus at night, Max with his boat, his manic dream of maritime riches, the floodlights pouring in the window, her weekends and evenings sacrificed to this set of ribs on scaffolding. Her husband treats the talk as a form of mockery. Nothing gets through to him. It occurs to Walker that Max has one obsession and he, Walker, has his. Walker desires to set the older man straight, and then, like part of the same thought, hopes that Max will never get it and that Jenny's discontent will grow. This thought makes him sorry and sick inside.

Most days now, after Sean gets home from school, Walker will play a little distracted basketball with him, and then leave him with their mother and, when there's no job site to go to, will drive over to the park or into the city center to walk around, and finally he ends up at Max's. He tells his mother and his younger brother that it's to help with the boat. Sometimes he can find a way to believe it himself: a brother is supposed to be there for a brother.

"They're gonna get tired of seeing you," his mother says. "They *are* a married c-couple you know."

"I'm helping out. You want me to stay here?"

"They both work all day. They n-need time alone."

"I'll stay here if you want me to. I won't go anywhere at all."

"I'm t-talking about what *they* might want. Stop it."

"They're fine with me coming over. Max says he wants my help."

"Let's hope—so." She manages well enough on the cane, and her speech, which was slightly damaged by the stroke, is getting better fast. She's a lady who has little tolerance for weakness, even in herself. Having lived through a bad marriage to a mentally unstable, increasingly alcoholic, and sporadically violent husband, and having raised the boys mostly alone, she's got a streak of iron in her. Max, who is fourteen years older than Walker, remembers a lot of what went on before the old man died. More than he likes. He understands Minnie, and admires her, and he calls her by her first name, as if they are old friends rather than mother and son.

Minnie would side with Max.

Walker keeps having this thought, while trying not to think at all.

Max and Jenny have been married nine years. Sean, who just turned fifteen, doesn't really remember them any other way. Walker can recall the years of their going back and forth, the two early miscarriages, several of the bad fights, and a trial separation, when Jenny took a bus to Florida to be with her parents for part of a winter, trying to deal with the fact that she was still childless and that her husband wasn't the romantic she'd thought he was. This is how she has recently described it to Minnie and Walker, casually, standing in the kitchen with a glass of orange juice in her hand and gazing out the window at Max working on the boat.

One afternoon Walker goes over to help Max with some hand-sanding, and Jenny comes home early from her job at the antiques shop. Walker hears the car, and keeps his eyes fixed on the sandpaper under the heel of his hand. She stays in the house for a time, and then comes to the door and calls out: "I need something, Max."

"Put me down for tonight," Max says.

"Funny. And you wish."

"Go see what she wants," he says to Walker.

She watches Walker approach, and holds the door open for him. "I wouldn't want to get in the way of the effing boat," she says.

He goes into the house, turns, and waits. She leans out the door and says, "Hey Max, did I tell you I'm running away with Walker?"

"Good," he calls. "Tell him to leave the truck."

She slams the door and comes by Walker, who follows her through the kitchen. He sees her supple, curved, solid shape under the lime-green skirt and white blouse. They cross through the small parlor, with its pictures of Jenny's family on the walls and its magazine baskets, three of them ranked next to one another in a row under the one window, stuffed with issues of *O* and *Redbook*. She stops at the entrance to the living room and puts her forehead softly against the door frame, holding on there. "Oh, hell," she murmurs, and then straightens and gives him a weak little sad-eyed smile. He imagines putting his arms around her. Then he hears Max drop something outside, wood clattering against wood, and everything seems to collapse inside him. He's stripped clean under the skin, raw and stinging.

"Jenny?" he says. "Oh, God."

She says, in almost the exact same instant: "Boy, I'm tired."

He waits.

She says. "Did you say, *Oh, God*? What's going on, Walker?"

"Can I do something, Jenny?"

"Something wrong?" she says.

"Can I do anything *for* you," he gets out.

"Tell me I'll get through this boat business. It's killing me."

He takes her gingerly by the elbow, feeling despondent and false. "You okay?"

"I'm not great," she says, then lightly, unmindfully, casually pats his shoulder. "I'm very, very *tired*." She leads him to the dining room, the hutch, and indicates a Crock-Pot on the top shelf.

He carries it back into the kitchen for her.

"Coming back for dinner?" she says.

"Mom said she wants to cook tonight. Wants me to be there."

"Oh." Jenny bows her head slightly, disappointed or simply, as she says, tired. Her eyelashes are so long and dark. "Well, I guess I'll go to bed and read, then." She moves one strand of hair away from her forehead, and smiles, as if it costs her. "See you tomorrow?"

"I think Max is out of his mind," he tells her, just able to breathe the words out. "Staying out there with you in here."

Now it will happen, he thinks.

But she steps offhandedly, face turned to one side, into his arms; the embrace is sisterly, like all the others. Still, he holds her for a second longer, saying nothing, feeling her pull back. He breathes in the scent of her hair, the sunscreen on her neck and shoulders, his hand wide on the small of her back. Finally he lets go and she dismisses him, almost brushing him away with her hands, busying herself with the dinner. "Tomorrow, then. There'll be barbecue left over."

"Good," he starts to say. But his voice catches, and he makes his way out of there.

Night, and sleeplessness. Ablaze inside. Fever. Fright. He drowses, and comes out of it with a start, wide-eyed, breath-caught, sick. The ordinary objects in the room seem to expand, and his mind presents them to him as grotesque twisted shapes, though they are perversely only themselves, giving forth nothing but their plainness: dresser, lamp, lamp shade, alarm clock, books, the half-open door, the sliver of light leading into the hall. He hears Sean, one room away, shifting and turning in his bed, and he hears his mother's late-night television.

He closes his eyes and sees Jenny standing with him in the kitchen of his brother's house.

He tries to make his mind go elsewhere, but it keeps showing him her face, with those eyes—that look, the something confiding in it, yearning. *I'm his brother*, he says to himself. *I'm his goddamned brother. But she's closer to my age than his. She's only four years older. Stop this. Stop it.*

The slow hours of the night pass this way, and if he sleeps at all he is aware of it only as a kind of stupor, waiting for the real thing or some semblance of it, something like rest—a lull that will make him sink past the constant play of her image across his mind, and stop the sudden waking, those repeated stirrings, looking at the strangeness of what he knows, to his horror, is nothing more than a plain, quiet bedroom at night.

. . .

His own brief romantic history is complicated. He's had several girlfriends, none of whom stayed long, and he was engaged to one, Milly Sparks, a couple of years ago. Milly Sparks had been a friend of the family, the youngest daughter of Minnie's best school chum, and she changed her mind the day before the planned wedding, with several members of her far-flung family having spent considerable sums of money gathering from distances.

She was institutionalized later in the summer—disambiguation, psychosis, schizophrenia of the delusional variety. Walker visited her in the hospital, and her ravings seemed so classically nutty that he found himself wondering if she was staging them for his benefit. But no, she was gone, believing her visions utterly and simply, stridently, with the confidence of a child. Minnie said it wasn't much different from her own history with his father, though, she said with some relish, having survived it all, he was never diagnosed as anything but a drunk.

They do not, any of them, speak of Milly Sparks anymore. And Walker sometimes senses the others being careful not to mention her in their talk when he's present.

He never thinks of Milly Sparks. Not ever.

Saturday morning he rises from the badness of the night, puts on the clothes he wore the day before, steps out in the hall, and looks at Sean in his cluttered little room. Sean's still asleep, blankets tangled around him like something tying him down, sun pouring on him through his window. Walker gazes at the boy, envying his ability to sleep through anything. Then he walks into the living room, to the screen door that looks out onto the little front porch. His mother's sitting on the top step there, sipping coffee and watching the trucks crossing the bridge to Arkansas. There's clean, clear light up high over that way, where the sun is just hitting the spars of the bridge. Arkansas is a strip of bare trees and dirt yonder, across the far, gray running of the Mississippi in the early morning mist. He opens the door, and it protests slightly.

"You want b-breakfast?" she says without looking back.

He lets the door slap to. "Not hungry," he says.

"You got a—l-lot on your mind."

He steps below her and sits on the bottom step, reaches and pulls a stalk of knife grass from the lawn. He plays with the whitening green blade, stretching it and looking at the color of it in the light.

"Talk to me, son."

"Pretty morning."

"I'm not t-talking about the-thc gu-goddamn weather."

"Okay, then what are you talking about, Ma?"

"You been going around here like a—z-zombie. What's got h-hold of you?"

"Well, damn. You tell me. Because I don't have a clue."

She sighs and leans back. "Ok-kay. You'll tell me when you're ready."

"There's nothing to tell. I'm fine. I feel fine."

"Half the time y-you don't know what day it is."

"That's not a sign of anything, is it?" He has the upsetting thought that Jenny has gleaned something, too, from watching him. "Have you been talking to somebody?"

"Who?"

He shrugs exaggeratedly, meaning it to be sardonic. "I wouldn't know that."

"N-nobody."

"Well, you're imagining things, I guess."

"Don't insult me, boy." Her gaze is direct and cold. "You got something on your mind y-you don't want to t-talk about. That's fine. But don't—lie to me about it. I ain't s-stupid."

He gets up and walks past her to the door. The telephone is ringing in the house. "It's personal," he says. "So can we please drop it?"

"Like it's r-radioactive," his mother says.

It's Max on the phone. "Can you pick Jenny up at the dealership? She took the car in there to get it inspected and they found a problem with the water pump. Says it'll take at least two hours and that she'll wait for it, because she knows I don't want to stop work on the boat. I hung up before I realized I could call you. You don't mind, do you, man? I mean, I can't do anything anyway unless you drive the truck over here. And she's sitting there with two hours' dead time. You're not doing anything right this minute, are you?"

"Sean and I were going to go play ball in a while. And I got a call about a carpentry job. Supposed to go over there and talk about it."

"Big job?"

"Apartment complex. Twenty stories high. Swimming pool on the roof. Helicopter pad for emergencies. Twelve billion dollars for the oak floors and framing alone and more than that for all the roofing and wiring and painting. You working on the boat today or coming with me?"

"We're millionaires."

"Just about. You coming?"

"How 'bout you tell me what it really is."

"Kitchen cabinets. And maybe knocking a wall out. If we get the bid."

"I'm coming with you—so please pick Jenny up. I don't

want to interrupt things now. She'll be waiting for the car in the maintenance and repair shop."

"I told Sean I'd take him to play ball."

"You'll have time for that," Max says. "Come on—it's for a good cause." This has been his phrase over the past year, to excuse himself. "I can't keep track of the time here, anyway," he adds.

"I'll be there. But I've got to shower and dress." He hangs up. It's fifteen minutes to nine. His mother has gone out into the little garden in back. He sees her there from his bedroom window. She's put on a big floppy cloth hat. She bends, with the help of her cane, and pulls a weed out, then straightens and gazes toward the pond on the other side of the road. Lately, all her movements have this faintly pensive feature, as though she's trying distrustfully to commit everything to memory. Often, in midmotion, she pauses, as if listening for a sound she can't be certain she heard. Walker watches her awhile, and then he hears his little brother moving around in the other room. He gets out of his clothes, showers, dresses, makes his bed, puts his dirty clothes in the hamper in the hall. In the kitchen, he makes coffee, and takes it out on the front porch, where he finds Sean sitting on the top step, tying his tennis shoes.

"Don't tell me," Sean says. "You have to go over there."

"I have to pick Jenny up in town." Walker rejects the enticement of this chance to be alone with Jenny. "You want to ride along?"

"Whatever."

Their mother comes around the house from the garden, and as she nears them, Walker tells her where he and the boy are going.

"Well, tell them—I said 'H-hey.'"

He finishes the coffee, and she walks over and takes the empty cup from him. Habit. Living at home is hard sometimes.

He taps the horn as they make the turn out of the drive, and Sean waves to her from the back window. The morning has remained cool and bright, with little breezes and the scent of new grass and flowers in the air. Walker leaves the windows open. His younger brother climbs into the well behind the front seat, lying back on his neck, wrapping weighted leather bands around his wrists: he's readying himself for shooting baskets. The bands will improve his strength; he wears the same sort of thing around both ankles. He's exactly five feet tall, and hopes to grow much taller, though Walker and Max have both told him he probably won't, that he'll have to learn to take advantage of being small. It's Max who got all the size and strength in the family—the only son to inherit those genes of their father.

"I've got an idea," the boy says, concentrating on getting his wrist wrapped tight. "Let's go over to Max's tonight and burn the thing to the ground."

"You're just mad because we're picking Jenny up instead of playing ball."

"You'd tell Max to pick her up himself if it wasn't for Jenny. You like being around Jenny."

"Okay, maybe. Yeah. I like her. But if I didn't like her I'd still do it for a brother. *You're* a brother, and as a brother I'm suggesting that you shut your stupid mouth."

Sean concentrates on the wrist bands.

"Okay, little bro?"

"*Okay*," he says. "Take it easy. I think she's hot, too. God."

In Midtown, there's a flea market going on, and traffic is slow. They wait behind a line of cars going up past the court-house. The traffic moves, and they travel forward a few feet. The air smells of exhaust. Everything is stopped again. Sean gets to his knees, folds his arms on the seat back, and rests his chin on his forearms. "We're gonna be late."

"Well, then we'll be late," Walker says.

"You don't have to be mad at me anymore."

"Quit breathing down my neck," Walker says.

A little later, Sean says, "You do think Jenny's hot, though."

"Yeah," Walker tells him. "And? You? What're you telling me?"

"You know."

"Hey," Walker turns to glare at him. "If you think you've got a handle on something why don't you shake it and see what happens?"

Two blocks before they reach the dealership, they see her.

She's talking to a man in jeans and a cowboy hat and boots. They're standing by a small red car. "Get a load of Disco Bill," Sean says, as Walker slows the truck.

Jenny is clearly very surprised, even upset, to see them. She moves quickly away from the man, who stands there motionless, watching them pull up in the truck.

Walker reaches over and opens the passenger side door. She glances back at the cowboy and then gets in.

"What're you doing here?" she says.

"Who's the cowboy?" Sean wants to know. "He looks like Disco Bill."

The cowboy has gotten into the red car and is already backing out of his space. Jenny glances back at him and then rights herself, smoothing her denim skirt in her lap. "Try not to be such a teenager, Sean."

"Where were you going?" Walker asks her.

"Nowhere. God. I walked Bill to his car."

"Oh, God," Sean says, laughing. "That's *freakish*. His name *is* Bill. It's Bill. Oh, God. I totally got it right on the nose."

"Who's Disco Bill?" she says, trying to look over the seat at him. There's a shine across her forehead. "Some cartoon character you watch on TV all day?"

"I called it," Sean laughs. "Disco Bill. *That* guy's Disco Bill. It's perfect. Oh, ha—perfect."

She turns back around, folding her arms and staring out the windshield. Walker has come to the corner, and is waiting to turn. He looks over at her, at the side of her face. "So who *is* Bill," he says.

"A friend I met working in the antiques store, okay?" There's a brittleness in her voice. "Is that okay with you? I mean, do I have your permission to make a friend?"

Sean is still congratulating himself behind them. "I so totally called it. I got it. I freakin' called it. Disco freakin' Bill."

"Who the hell is Disco Bill?" Jenny says. "And shut up."

"I made it up. That's what I'm telling you. Disco Bill. I made it up and the guy's name is Bill. It's too good."

"Shut up, Sean," Walker says. "Christ."

Jenny pushes the hair back from her flawless face. "I swear, it's exhausting. Everything's a joke with him."

Walker makes the turn, and drives for a time without looking at her and without speaking. The image of her reaction at the sight of the truck plays across the surface of his mind, and then sinks into him.

"Those were actual cowboy boots," Sean says. "Right?"

She gazes out the passenger window and doesn't answer.

"Who is he, really?" Walker says, watching the road.

"He's just a guy," Jenny says. "He works across the street. In the computer store."

"Well, and he's so dressed for *that*," Sean says.

"Sean, please. Really. I'm not in the mood."

The traffic is heavy going out of town, too. They sit behind a smoking charter bus. The truck's engine begins to shake, idling roughly, as though it might stall.

"Hey, but you do need cowboy boots in a computer store, right? I mean you gotta look the part," says Sean.

They are all silent for a moment.

"Does he have a medallion on his chest? I didn't look—"

"Sean—if you—"

"It really needs a medallion."

"Why're you—" She turns and glares at him, then shakes her head and faces front, apparently having decided that whatever she was going to say is pointless.

"Really," Sean says. "I know what the fashion-conscious geek is wearing these days in the computer stores."

The traffic moves a little, and as Walker edges the truck forward, it stalls. He restarts it, gives it gas, and a cloud of exhaust billows out behind them.

"You're welcome," Sean says as someone behind them honks a horn. "We aim to please."

"Is this one going to break down, too, now?" Jenny says.

"It needs a tune-up," says Walker, grinding the gears. "Everything falls apart at once."

They're moving again. And now some cool air comes in the window.

"Let's get a movie," Sean says, lying back in the well behind them.

Walker looks over his shoulder at the boy, then glances at Jenny. Her hair is blowing across her face, but he can see that she's crying. *What the hell?* She looks out the window. The traffic is thinning out a little now, and he picks up speed. They're quiet again. Walker takes the back road toward the Highpoint house, and as he approaches a country store, pulls into the lot and stops.

"What," Sean says.

"Anybody want something cold to drink?"

"I'm dying," Sean says.

Walker opens his door and steps from the truck, holding the seat up for Sean to climb out. "Here." He gives Sean a ten-dollar bill. "I want a mineral water." He looks in at Jenny. "You want anything?"

She shakes her head.

Sean is staring at her now, though she's looking down, and her dark hair hides her face.

"Go on," Walker says to him.

"I'm going to get a couple hot dogs, too. It's my God-given right."

"Help yourself, Sean." Walker says. "Jesus, you can be annoying."

The boy starts across the lot, jumping and fake-shooting an imaginary basketball, watching his own shadow on the asphalt. Walker gets back into the truck. Next to him in the seat, his sister-in-law wipes the tears from her eyes and sniffles. "I'm sorry," she says.

He's quiet, expecting her to go on. He wants to reach over and put his hand on her face.

She dips into her purse and brings out a handkerchief. The makeup around her eyes has run down her cheeks. She sniffles again. "I bet I look like a raccoon."

"You're fine. What's going on, Jenny?" The moment feels dreamlike, fantastic. He feels rage climbing his spine about the computer store cowboy, and understands that the rage is for himself, and not his brother. All this surges in him, and stops his speech.

She turns the rearview mirror and tries to get the mascara off.

"Were you getting into his *car*?"

She frowns at herself, wiping the dark makeup from her eyes. "God," Walker begins. He might start crying himself.

And now she turns to him. "I wasn't getting into his car." And the crying starts again. "God—I've got to quit this before Sean—" She stops, sniffles, wipes at her eyes again.

He watches her. There's more, but she's clearly holding back whatever it is. "Jesus Christ," he says.

"What?" she says. "It's been a bad day. Leave me alone."

He draws in air and hears himself ask, "Is that guy somebody important to you?" His own voice sounds terribly thin to him, someone else's voice.

She sits back, clutching the handkerchief; her eyes are wild. She's looking out at the lot, where three men are crossing. One of them is talking and the other two are laughing. It's a joke. Walker has a moment of seeing this as separated out from everything else he has ever seen or observed in his life. He knows that he'll never forget it as long as he lives: three men laughing at a joke walking across a parking lot and it was when Jenny sat next to him, crying because he caught her with the computer salesman. He can't breathe, thinking this, watching the men move on by. His sister-in-law says, "You mean *Disco Bill?* He's a *friend*. Okay? It's just that Sean—everything's a comedy act to Sean, that's all. I just get tired of it."

They're quiet a moment.

"You don't have to run to Max with it, you know? The guy's just a friend."

"You acted so weird seeing us."

"Don't be ridiculous."

"You were upset. I saw it, Jenny."

"What do you want me to tell you? You want me to say something that isn't true? I'm not having a good day. God! Sean gets on my nerves, okay?"

"Me, too." Walker says. And when she doesn't respond he says, "I think you're the most beautiful woman I ever saw in my life. Movies, magazines, dreams, just watching people in the street."

She says, "Oh, Walker."

He's astonished at the soft worry in her voice, the obvious wish to believe him. "Really," he says.

"You're sweet." She wipes her eyes with the backs of her hands.

"I mean it," he says. "I'm not being sweet."

She glances at him, then leans over and peers at herself in the rearview mirror again, wiping the makeup from her cheeks. "I'll be all right."

"You can tell me," he hears himself say. He gazes at the smoothness of the backs of her hands. Something is about to change forever. He wants to kiss her.

"Walker—really."

"Tell me," he says. "Come on." It's as though there's no one else in the world, as though they have no history, no established pattern of speech and gestures between them. He puts his arms around her and hears himself say her name. "Jenny."

She pulls away. "Don't."

"I'm sorry."

She lets her head rest on the seat back and regards him. Then she touches his chest. "I'm such an idiot," she says.

"Don't apologize."

He can't speak.

"It'll be all right. I'm tired of the work on the boat. I never see him."

"But you love him." The words sound ridiculous. He feels like a kid. He wants her to say she doesn't love him anymore;

he wants her to say it's not Max now, but Walker. He listens to her voice in his imagination say *You. You.*

But she sighs and seems to laugh a little. "I don't know anything anymore," she says. "Can we just not talk about it now? Trust me, everything's the same."

He looks out at the facade of the store, and sees Sean coming back with his hot dogs and the drinks.

"I think I'd like something to drink," Jenny says.

"You can have my water," says Walker. He feels the words as meaning that she can have anything she wants that he can humanly give her, no matter what anyone—brothers, mothers, family, friends, and strangers—has to say about it.

"I wasn't talking about water," she says, and gives forth a little laugh.

"Will you take my water?" He feels the oddness of wanting the situation to go on, her tears, her trouble, this instance. He doesn't want to let go of it.

"Water's all we can get for now, right?"

"I could go in and get some beer," he says.

"You're sweet. There's plenty at the house if I want it."

"You can have my water." He gets out of the truck and heads across the lot to meet Sean, who is about to drop the bottle of mineral water. Walker takes it, and then stands blocking the boy's way to the truck. "Cut the smart remarks, okay?" He can't keep the shaking out of his voice.

"I'm just kidding her."

"Well, it's not funny—so quit it."

The ride to the house is quiet. Sean sulks in the back. Jenny looks out the passenger window, and then tries the radio for a while. Nothing of interest is on. She turns it off. Walker grips the wheel. When they pull up in front of the house, he gets out and moves to help her down from the truck, but she has already made the step down and is holding the seat back for Sean, who gets into the front. She closes the door on him.

"See you both later."

"We'll be through in an hour," Walker tells her. She has already started for the house, and she simply moves one hand away from her side, waving slightly without looking back.

He and Sean go to Pumphries, a recreation center near St. Catherine's Catholic Church. The court is in the shade of tall oaks and sycamores, and the baskets have chain nets that clang when the ball hits the rim. Walker can't concentrate. Few of his shots go in, and the shooting around becomes a series of misses and chasing the ball. Sean is irritable and sullen, and they do not speak much. Walker loses two games of Horse and another of 21 to the boy. There's a puddle of stagnant water at one end of the court and with one of his misses the ball rolls there and splashes in. The stink of it is on his hands when he drops Sean at the river house and heads to Highpoint Terrace to pick up Jenny and take her back to the car dealership. She's been waiting for him. She walks out to the truck as he pulls up. "Go ahead and get in," he tells her. "I've gotta wash my hands." In the kitchen, alone, he looks through the window over the sink, hearing the power saw: Max cutting another rib for the hull. Max is out there in the noise with the shade and the sunlight falling through the leaves. The wood chips fly, white in the brightness. Walker discovers himself feeling sorry for him, as if he has betrayed him.

In the truck, Jenny sits with her hands folded in her lap. Walker gets in and looks over at her. "Why don't you tell him how you feel?"

She seems annoyed at the question. "I don't want to talk about it. Please?"

He backs out, one arm on the back of the seat, near her shoulder. When he shifts gears and heads out of the neighborhood, she sniffles.

"You okay?" he says.

"Fine."

She says nothing else. Just sits looking out at the passing houses and streets. It's as if, with time to plan her response, she has gained a kind of cold equilibrium. When they get to the dealership, she thanks him, opening the door.

"He and I have to see some people about a bid," he says. "Kitchen cabinets."

She looks back at him. "Great."

"If you want to talk," he manages to say.

She reaches over and touches his arm. "Thank you."

He nods, and watches her go into the dealership. She doesn't look back.

At the Highpoint house, Max is still working. Walker honks the horn and waits. There's the sound of the power sander. He leans on the horn, holds it down. Then listens. The power sander is off. But then the saw starts up. He gets out of the truck, fuming, and stands half into it, still leaning on the horn. When he stops now, there's silence, and he leans on it again. Max comes from the house, putting on a clean shirt, his body gleaming with sweat. Walker lets the horn go and climbs in again. "You stink. Great. We'll get this bid all right."

Max gets in on the passenger side, buttoning the shirt. "Just drive. Christ. You couldn't come around back and get me? What is it—forty feet?"

"You should've been waiting for me. Showered and ready, goddamn it."

"What the hell's the matter with you?" Max says. "Jesus."

The house they are going to is in Harbor Town, past the turnoff to their mother's river house, and on, to Mud Island. They cross the bridge with the enormous, silver-looking pyramid on the left, reflecting the sun and too bright to look at directly. The road winds to the right and along the river. They turn into Harbor Town, and go over the first little bridge there. The buildings here are very close together, with very little lawn space, and shade trees line the road. The house they are going to is a tall, narrow place with two verandas, one above the other, and a lot of windows. Walker parks the truck and gets out, and Max reaches into the glove box to get the clipboard and pencil. His blue shirt hangs on him, with dark splotches.

"You look like you just got out of a pond," Walker tells him.

"It's a hot day. Shut up."

"You ought to pay more attention to things."

"What?" Max stops and looks at him.

"You heard me."

"Hey, just keep your end up, you know?"

Walker starts to move off. "I'm not just talking about the goddamn business."

"Okay." His brother takes his arm at the elbow. "Then what? Tell me what's on your mind."

Walker pulls his arm away and goes on.

"What the hell're you talking about? What's got into you? You've been moping around for weeks. Everybody's noticed it."

"Jenny," Walker says. "Has Jenny noticed it?"

"What *about* Jenny, cowboy?"

"Why 'cowboy'?"

"Do you want to tell me what the fuck you're talking about?"

He doesn't answer. They go along the walk, which leads

Blood

through a row of forsythia bushes to an atriumlike structure, at one end of which, perhaps twenty yards away, is a wrought-iron door. A tall skinny man with big round green eyes stands there waiting, holding the door open. There's something about his face. "Hot enough for you?" he says. Walker realizes that he's wearing makeup; it's adhering to his hairline, a bad job of it, as if it were slapped on by somebody not interested in getting it right.

"Plenty hot," says Max, who, if he has noticed, is keeping it to himself.

"Name's Ron Podrup," the man says.

Max and Walker introduce themselves. They step past him, into the cool shade of the front room, which is refrigerator cold. A woman sits there, at the edge of the couch, hands folded over her knees. Walker bows slightly, seeing her, and then he sees that she's been crying. She stands, and looks him up and down. She has a thin, lined face with deep-socketed eyes, and a down-turning mouth. Her hair is parted in the middle of the top of her head and combed straight down either side, and her ears stick out of it—they give her whole countenance a vaguely goofy look. "You're the workmen?" she says.

"Yes, ma'am," Max says, coming up beside Walker.

"May Podrup." She offers her hand, and they shake, and then her tall husband leads them to the kitchen. "We're actors," he says. "Community theater. Dress rehearsal."

"Excuse me?" Max says.

"The makeup." The man indicates his long face. "She wasn't really crying."

"I'm sorry?" Max says.

"They're actors," Walker tells him, with barely suppressed anger. It seems to him that building the boat has robbed his brother of the ability to see anything else at all.

159

Podrup straightens, clears his throat. "Well, anyway. Here's what we'd like done."

"Should I go get the calculator, dearest?" she says.

He turns to look at her. "Why, no."

"Do you need me here, then, dearest?"

There's an edge to her voice. It's as if she's having fun with it, standing there with a faint smile playing at the corners of the bitter-looking mouth. It's a smile. Her very white teeth show. It changes her entire appearance; she's actually quite pretty. Walker has a moment of wishing he could feel anything for anyone other than what he does feel, and for whom. It slices through him like a blade. She goes on: "Or will you go it alone on this one?"

"I'll brave it," he says. "Why don't you wait in the living room and we can finish for today in a minute."

She says, "All right, dearest." Then she nods at the brothers and leaves the room. He gives them a look, as if seeking some sort of lighthearted commiseration from them. Walker has the sensation of not knowing what to do with his face. He tries a little smile and a nod, but then Mr. Podrup's made-up face returns to its blank seriousness. He begins describing the remodeling he's planned—one side of the kitchen to be expanded by knocking down a dividing wall, cabinets to be put all along that side, an opening in the far wall, looking out to the den.

Mrs. Podrup is moving around in the other room. Walker glances back at the entrance there, and sees her cross the frame. She's carrying a small table. Beyond her is a shelf full of books.

"Can I take some measurements?" Max says. "Walker?"

They work together determining the length and height of the wall. They have always worked together well. The man goes back into the other room with the woman and they're talking low. They're practicing, rehearsing. The woman clearly wants not to do this now, but the man insists. She calls him David, but that's the name of the character he plays. It's a drama about a man and a woman on a bus, lovers on a journey somewhere. They are both married to other people. The word *trap* keeps getting repeated. Max scratches a little schematic drawing onto the pad, to show it to them. And he winks at Walker, who thinks about these people pretending so badly for the benefit of the visiting contractors.

Then he thinks of Jenny, and her friend from the computer store.

As they walk back out to the truck, Max says, "Was that weird or was that *weird?*"

"It was weird."

"I don't think I want to do the work for them."

"You wouldn't be the one doing it."

They get in, and Walker turns the ignition. His brother sits staring at him. "You've got something on your chest, and I sure wish you'd let me in on it."

"I don't know what you're talking about. I wish everybody'd let me alone a little, Jesus."

A little later, Max says, "You really want to be there doing work with those two in the house?"

"They were rehearsing. What's so weird about that?"

"With us *there?* I think they just wanted an audience. I bet we never hear from them again."

"Let's just make the bid and see what happens."

"A couple of screwballs."

"Really?" Walker says. "No kidding. How screwball is it to be building a fucking cabin cruiser in your backyard?"

"Hey, is *that* what's the matter with you?"

"Nothing's the matter with me. Just forget it."

"No come on—let me have it. Everybody else seems to want to take a turn. Here's your chance."

"You're talking about Jenny."

Max says nothing, and they ride on for a few moments in silence.

"Are you talking about Jenny?"

"Just drive, okay? I don't feel like fighting with you, too."

"You're gonna lose her, Max."

"Really. Who to—you?"

Walker doesn't respond to this. They arrive back at the Highpoint house. Walker pulls into the shade of the big willow in front. He leaves the motor running. He feels his own heart stamping in his chest. Max gets out and slams the door. Their car with its new fuel pump is in the driveway, so Jenny's home.

"I'll call you with the amount when I've figured it, and you can call them," he says, without looking back.

Walker drives away, fast.

That night, he has a dream: he's in the truck and she and the cowboy are in the back, doing it. The cowboy is ranged behind her and her belly is big, and she looks at Walker and smirks and says his name. He wakes with a start, breathless and for a moment unable to shake the sense of it, the ill-seeming air of it, turning in the bed, the image still too clear, shortening his breath. He rises and walks into the kitchen to pour himself some milk, and there he finds Sean, sitting at the table with a glass of orange juice and the last piece of the cake Minnie baked yesterday afternoon.

"You were moaning in your sleep," Sean says.

"Let me have some of that."

"What's the deal with everybody lately?"

"Nothing."

"Something's screwy."

"Nothing's going on that I know of."

"You're so not a good liar."

"Hey, why don't you just mind your own business."

"That thing with Disco Bill this morning. That was funny."

"You don't know shit about anything, so shut up."

"It *was* funny."

"Not everything's part of your own little jokey world, Sean, okay?"

The boy drinks his juice and then sighs and stands. "You don't need to go ballistic on me about it."

"Well, grow up a little."

"Yeah. Me grow up. I'm out of here when I turn eighteen. And look at you, you're twenty-seven and still living at home."

Walker ignores this, cutting a small piece of the cake and lifting it to his mouth.

"I'm sorry," Sean says. "That was shitty."

"Apology accepted."

"But you know what? I'm sick of that stupid boat. If there's anything going on with her, *he'll* be the last to know." There are tiny flecks of white in his eyes—one's blue and the other's brown. An anomaly, of which he's proud. His eyesight is also extraordinarily good, has been measured at 20/10. The joke between the brothers is that for someone with such nearly supernatural sight he's pretty thick. But in fact the boy never misses a thing, and about this that is now going on he has come very close to the truth. Walker slaps his shoulder and then boxes the side of his head lightly, and tussles with him a little, trying to get him off the scent. "Go to bed," he says. "And stop imagining things."

"I can't help the way you look at her, dude. But it's, um, *evident*. And she was crying today. That was hard to miss."

"I don't look at her any way—and what the hell."

"Maybe she needs something you can give her."

"What'd you say?" Walker takes him by the front of his shirt. "You got a smart mouth, you know it? And you don't know what you're talking about."

"Let go of me. Christ! I just meant somebody to talk to."

Walker loosens his grip, but keeps his hands on the boy's arms. "You shouldn't stick your nose in where it doesn't belong."

Their mother's voice comes from the other room. "What's g-going on in there? I'm t-trying to sleep."

"We're going to bed, Ma," Walker says. He lets the boy go.

Sean moves away from him, making a show of adjusting his shirt front and rolling his shoulders.

"Remember what I said," Walker tells him.

"Fuck you," says the boy.

"She's my sister-in-law. And yours. She's family. Just because I'm not torturing her every minute like you are."

"Whatever," says the boy. "Just fuck off."

"And watch your language."

"Fuck off."

"I—can hear you," says their mother. "Sean, I'm going to come in there and wash your mouth out with soap." The fact that she now has nothing like the physical strength to accomplish such a thing shuts them both up. They look at each other, hearing their mother's voice. "Go to bed," Minnie calls, "b-both of you."

"Good night, Ma," Sean says.

"Just let me sleep, dear," says Minnie.

A little later, lying down again in the quiet of his room, Walker's afraid to go back to sleep, afraid the dream will come back out of the dark of himself. But it's still there, anyway, the image of Jenny on all fours in the bed of the truck, the body that in the dream is nothing like hers—hanging breasts and great rounded belly, the fleshy shaking of her. He puts the light on and tries to read. Useless. The image keeps swimming at him through the drowsiness that never quite closes him down.

The actor couple, the Podrups, accept Max's estimate of two thousand dollars, with a deposit. And it becomes Walker's job to spend the next two days buying materials, taking delivery, and going to Harbor Town to tear down the wall. It rains on and off both days, and in the late afternoon of the second day, the alarm siren sounds across the city—a tornado warning. The Podrups are out, because of the noise and the dust. He breaks through the drywall and pulls out the studs, sweating even in the air-conditioning and resisting the temptation to go spy on Jenny. Max is at the dealership. Walker talks to him on the phone, but the talk is confined to the project. Max's voice is full of the frustration he feels not being able to work on the boat. The rain has stopped him. But he says nothing about it, nor anything about his wife. The conversation is clipped, direct, cold, and without the slightest hint of the kind of blood-simple chatter that has always existed between them.

The third day at the Podrups', Walker uses his lunch break to drive into Midtown, to the Café Olé which is half a block from the antiques shop and the computer store. There's a window looking out on the street, and he sits at a table there, watching the entrance to both buildings. Jenny's car is in the side lot next to the shop. The Miata convertible is on the street. He watches for an hour, but doesn't see Jenny, or Disco Bill. He waits past the hour, thinking one or the other or both of them might come out and cross the street. People walk by both places and some of them go in. There's a lot of traffic. But no sign of the two people he has come to look for. He pays for his lunch and sneaks back to the truck, feeling small and dirty. He knows quite well that it's not for Max's honor and pride that he watches, but for his own; he doesn't question it now. He tells himself Max doesn't care anymore. But a suffocating sense of his own failure and shame follows him back to work. In Harbor Town again, breaking up the last of the wall, he sees himself there in the shards of plaster, imagines that this is his body, made of his weakness and cowardice, beneath the blows. He hammers away at the pieces.

The sun is out again. The storms have left a cool, sunny late afternoon, with breezes that carry the fragrances of magnolia and crape myrtle and dogwood. It's a rare, mild spring in Memphis. The family gathers for dinner near the shadow of the unfinished boat under the new tarp that Max bought using the advance money from the Podrups. Minnie wears her floppy straw hat, and a new, bright blue flower-print dress that Max bought, also with the Podrups' money. Jenny does most of the preparations, and Max cooks the hamburgers and hot dogs. They sit at the long picnic table and drink cold beer from the cooler, while the meat broils on the flames. Walker stands there with Max, sipping a beer, surreptitiously watching Jenny, who wears a light green sleeveless tank top and denim shorts that are tight across her middle. She goes back and forth from the house, carrying plates. Sean helps her.

Walker and Max say little to each other. Max will have to help with some of the work in Harbor Town this weekend, and he complains about that. Walker ignores this. There isn't any way around it. It will take the two of them to put together the frames for what will be required. Minnie presides over a quiet dinner. There's obvious tension between Jenny and Max, as well. Sean chatters about the *Simpsons* reruns he's been watching— Minnie bought him DVD sets of the first two seasons.

"I watched a c-couple of them," Minnie says. "They're funny. You know your f-father was funny. It's why I m-married him."

"That show never even amused me," says Jenny. "Or diverted me, either."

"I never liked it much," Walker says.

"For someone who didn't like it, you watched it enough."

He feels the rush of blood to his cheeks, and so he hauls himself out of his seat and walks over to the grill to get another hamburger. He glances back at her, and sees that she's oblivious to what she has just done to him. He finds himself imagining that she falters in some way, and needs him for something he can refuse. It's stupid, he tells himself, even as he entertains the thought. He returns to the table and endures their talk, wolfing down the hamburger. The talk has been about the boat, but now it's about the old man again, and the days he spent on it, and the way he was.

"W-when I first knew him he was—well, beautiful. Like I said h-he m-made me laugh. He was always—thinking of something fun to—do. And then one y-year it just t-turned."

"Was it after he started this?" Jenny indicates the boat frame under the new tarp.

"B-before that," Minnie says, thinking. "That was—late."

"Sometimes I think it's cursed," Jenny says. "Like it's got hold of us."

"It's got hold of me, all right," says Max. "That's what you mean anyway, isn't it?"

"If you say so."

To the table, Max says, "I guess it's no secret that Jenny wants me to quit on this thing."

"Not just Jenny," says Sean, with a thin smile.

"Right," Walker hears himself say.

"Your father couldn't figure how to get r-rid—of it," Minnie puts in. "Wished he'd never s-started it. That's true."

"Free at last," Max says. "I'm the one who's going to finish it."

"Nothing's gonna stop *you*," Jenny says, and throws her napkin down.

"You've hit the nail on the head," he tells her.

Minnie says, "It's n-not good to spend—so much time on one thing."

"What is this," Max says, "some kind of intervention?"

They all trade looks with one another, and there's a pause, during which they hear the distant blast of a train.

"I'm working toward something," Max says. "I've got a goal." He's looking right at Jenny. "What've you got if you don't share this goal?"

She's staring down, completely beautiful, the long soft strands of her hair shining in the sun, being stirred by the little breeze that comes. Her smooth hand holds her fork, with which she moves some of the green beans on her plate.

"I'm your goddamn husband."

"That's all," Walker says.

"What?"

"Everybody sh-shut up," says Minnie. "I h-have a headache."

They all turn to her.

"Not l-like that. Christ. Every—every h-headache isn't a—stroke. You—you all just—make me t-tired lately with th-this squabbling."

"We're not squabbling," Max says. "We're just having a little debate."

Jenny gets up from the table and quietly strides into the house, carrying her empty plate with her.

"You wanted to say something to me?" Max says to Walker.
"Yeah," says Walker. "I wanted to say I love you, bro."
"That's more l-like it," Minnie says, smiling.
"Peace, brother," Sean says. "Dig."

Max lightly cuffs the side of his head, ruffling his hair. "Get me another burger off the grill, squirt," he says.

Walker waits a few seconds and then goes into the house, too, carrying his plate. Jenny's not in the kitchen. Her plate is in the sink. He sets his own on top of it, and moves to the entrance of the living room. She has gone into the back part of the house. The bedrooms. He says, "Jenny?"

Nothing.

He steps to the middle of the living room, and pauses. Her voice comes faintly from the master bedroom. She's talking, low, on the telephone. He wants to sneak closer, to listen, but the others are coming in, too, now. He goes to help his mother into the house. Outside, it's threatening to storm. Lightning flickers in the sky beyond the trees that line the opposite side of the street.

Saturday, he and Max work efficiently and without much tension on the project at the Podrups' house. Jenny calls Max on his cell to say she's gone in to work at the antiques store, and has decided to stay there all day. Max's voice is cold as he talks to her, and when Walker reacts to it, he goes into the next room. He's gone for a good twenty minutes. Walker can hear his voice, but no words. Finally he comes back in, folding the cell with a snap, with temper. "Women," he says.

Walker says, "If I had a wife—" He stops himself. He was going to say that if he had Jenny he would not treat her that way; he would do everything he could, all the time, to please her.

"Yeah?" Max says.

"Nothing."

"I get that boat finished everybody's gonna wanna take a turn at the wheel. You'll all thank me."

"Free at last," Walker says.

"Watch it happen," says his brother.

They work on in silence. It has threatened rain all morning, but now the sun comes out, the sky widens, no clouds.

Just after noon, Max decides to go work on the boat. Walker drives him to the Highpoint house without speaking, and when they arrive Max simply opens the door, gets out, and slams it. He doesn't look back, walking toward the rear of the house. Walker taps the horn, so that he turns, and then Walker waves at him. He shakes his head, smiles, lifts one hand, and then heads on. Walker drives back to Harbor Town by way of Central Avenue. He takes a left on Cooper, and goes the mile out of his way to the Café Olé. But then, driving past the antiques shop, he turns around and heads back to the worksite. He continues what he and Max started in the morning, building the framework of the cabinets, and doing some of the wiring. The Podrups arrive and say they'll stay out of his way. But Mr. Podrup keeps coming into the room to watch the work. He wants to talk, is curious about Walker's situation. Has he always lived in Memphis? Yes, sir. Does he like it? Yes, sir, always did. He doesn't mind the heat in the summer? Sometimes, but it's like that most everywhere else.

"Well," says Mr. Podrup. "That river makes it worse."

"But the river runs all the way down the continent," Walker says. "Right?"

"I guess you've got a point there."

"Ron," Mrs. Podrup says, from the other room, "let the boy work."

"It's all right, ma'am," Walker tells her. "I was about to take my lunch break anyway."

She comes to the entrance and stands with her hands on her hips. "He called me ma'am."

"Yes, he did," says Mr. Podrup. "I heard it."

"Just being polite," Walker says. He wants to hit something; the feeling rises in him like heat, a column of fire where his spine is. *I'm no goddamn boy.*

"Well, lunch breaks are necessary," Mr. Podrup says automatically, not even attending to his own words. Walker moves away from him, surprised at the strength of the urge to strike him.

"Can't work on an empty stomach," she says.

Apparently they both think the fact of the lunch break means they'll all sit and talk. The disappointment shows in their faces as Walker heads for the door. He can't get away from them fast enough. It's as if he is the harm that might come to them if they keep talking and keep getting on his nerves as they are.

He goes out and gets into the truck in the bright sun. They're the ones with the money, doing the remodeling; they're the ones settled into their lives, certain of things and full of smug assumptions about people like him. Driving too fast to Midtown, he thinks of Jenny and the computer store geek. She couldn't see anything in him. How could she see anything in him?

At the corner of Cooper and Young, he parks the truck. Children are playing some game in the soft dust of the churchyard up the way, making a racket, and a woman stands watching them, arms folded. He walks up to the Beauty Shop Restaurant, goes in, and sits at the bar. There isn't anyone else in the place, yet, and for a moment he wonders if they're open.

But then a woman, square and bulky-looking, with long black hair and a brown, round-cheeked face, comes from the back and walks behind the bar, with some wineglasses to put up. "Be right with you," she says, in a voice that's surprisingly soft.

He looks out the window at the other side of the street, the Café Olé, and the gas station, and then the computer store, a few doors down from that. When the waitress comes to him, he orders a hamburger and a beer. There doesn't seem to be any business at the computer store. He watches the entrance. The street itself looks abandoned just now, the leaf shade moving on it in the breezes. He can still hear the voices of the children in the churchyard. The waitress brings him an iced glass of beer, and he drinks most of it in one long gulp, then finishes it, and asks for another. She brings it to him in another iced glass, and he drinks that, too. It's so cold and crisp, and it goes down smoothly.

"Thirsty," she says.

"Bring me another one."

"Really thirsty."

He slides the empty glass down the bar toward her. "You can just fill that if you want."

She takes the glass and puts it under the spigot.

A woman with a little boy comes down the sidewalk and crosses to the other side of the street, through the shade and sun. They go by the open door of the computer place. The waitress brings his beer, and he cradles it with his hands, watching the progress of the woman and boy down the way. He drinks the beer without tasting it now. His hamburger comes and he orders still another beer. The waitress smiles at him, but seems a little doubtful, holding the glass under the spigot and not looking directly at him. He bites into the hamburger, and eats a french fry. He sees Disco Bill arrive at the store, in his red Miata. Bill skips around the car and into the store, looking happy. The sun blazes on the little silver buttons of his shirtsleeves. Walker takes another bite of the hamburger, but finds that his hunger is gone. He keeps watching the entrance to the computer store. Some women come into the restaurant, four of them, all dressed as if for something important—suits, needle-point high-heeled shoes, bright-colored scarves, lots of makeup. They're talking about another woman, someone they all know, and by whom they are all evidently appalled. They go on in excited whispers, following the waitress into the restaurant to a booth.

He finishes his beer and heads to the men's room, past them. They're rattling at the waitress now, and it's clear they are visiting the city for the first time. They ask about Priscilla Presley—is this really the beauty shop where she had her hair done? Walker goes into the restroom, which smells too sweet. He only glances at himself in the mirror. When he's finished, he returns to his place at the bar, and he sees Bill sitting near the door, talking low into a cell phone. Walker orders another beer and sits half-turned on the stool, hands clasping one knee, looking out at the street but seeing the other man out of the corner of his eye. Watching him, trying to hear. The voice is murmurous and conspiratorial, secretive, and the laugh is low and, Walker thinks, lewd-sounding; there's something obscene about it. He leans a little in the man's direction, then stands, moves to the window, and he can hear the words now. "I'm glad for it," he hears. "Bless the world for it all." He puts his hands in his pockets and waits, rocking slightly on the balls of his feet. "When can I see you? Can you get off early? We could have a couple of hours this afternoon."

The waitress brings the beer—another iced glass—and sets it down. "Last one, pardner," she calls to Walker.

"One more after this," he tells her, and smiles.

"Okay, one more."

He moves to the bar, takes the beer, and drinks half of it, then goes back to the doorway.

The computer store man laughs softly, looking out at the street. He says, "You wouldn't." Then, "You would not."

"I know who you're talking to," Walker says to him.

He doesn't know he's being spoken to. He's listening to whatever she's telling him. "Describe it," he says. "I bet you can't." He laughs again. "Well come on over. The whole rest of the afternoon."

Walker finishes the beer, and puts the glass back on the bar. The waitress picks it up, takes it to the end, and puts it under the spigot. She brings it back and sets it down. "Last one."

"Keep it," Walker says, and turns, takes three unsteady paces to where Bill sits talking that way into his cell phone, and with a sweeping roundhouse motion of his right arm, punches him on the forehead. The impact sends a shock of nerve-pain all the way to his shoulder, and Bill falls from the chair with a tremendous crash, the cell phone flying from his hand, bouncing from the glass of the window and falling, where it slides the few feet to the side wall. Walker stands there holding his hand, which has already sprouted a big welt. Bill is trying to get up, turning to all fours, groaning and beginning to splutter words. "The fuck—what the—"

Walker puts the heel of his foot at the base of his spine and pushes, so that he lies on his stomach. He hears the waitress yelling behind him, the other women making a commotion of alarm. "Don't get up," he says to Bill. "Really. Don't do it. Don't even try to. I'll kill you if you do."

He steps to the cell phone and brings it to his ear. It's silent. No one on the other end. He tries to push the button that will show, in the little window, the last number dialed, or the last call received. He can't find it, and now Bill is getting to his feet. Walker picks up a chair with his good hand and brings it down, hard, on his head.

At the Podrups' house, he finds that he can't work very well with the injured hand. It's very swollen and red, probably broken. Driving with one hand through traffic, coming here, he felt almost happy, elated, utterly without an idea as to what might be next. He's in the Podrups' opened dining area, where the cabinets will go, and he can't do the work, can't cut away the last of the wall that was there. He's surprised by how completely the expectation of going on with the day has taken hold. Bill lay very still after the chair. Walker stepped over him and looked at his face, and his eyes were half open; he looked dead. But he was breathing. His lips were moving.

The work is impossible to accomplish with one hand. Podrup has come to the entrance of the room and is watching. "Something wrong?"

"I'll have to come back," Walker tells him.

"Are you all right? What'd you do to your hand?"

"Nothing, man. Never felt better."

"Apparently," says Mrs. Podrup, coming into the space next to her husband. "And you've had some help with how you feel, haven't you? A little something to numb the pain." They've been talking about him in the other room; it's clear from the looks they exchange now, mutually acknowledging that their suspicions have proven to be true.

"Had a beer," Walker mumbles.

She speaks to her husband. "He can barely stand."

"Look," says Mr. Podrup. "We need this done in a timely fashion."

Walker feels everything falling to pieces. He wants to strike at them, at everyone and everything. "I'll come back," he says. "Or my brother will."

"We'd like to talk to your brother," says Podrup.

"Yeah," Walker says. "You do that." And he stands very close to the other man, so that he can smell the sourness of his breath—onions mixed with coffee.

Podrup does not give way. The flesh around the thin line of his mouth is white.

"Go right ahead," Walker says, then turns unsteadily and moves toward the door. Mrs. Podrup gives him a wide berth, and he finds that he can't quite stay straight down the hallway, has to put the good hand out against the wall to support himself. He makes it to the door, and stands there, vaguely realizing that this is all wrong, all far from him and the kind of person he has always been—a good boy, a hardworking young man. He wants to say something to put things right, but there isn't anything to say. "Sorry," he mutters, but the uselessness of the word makes him sputter and laugh. "Shit," he says. Then he's outside in the blinding windless sun, cutting through the atriumlike space to the lawn, staggering across dry grass to the truck. They're standing in the doorway, watching him. He sees them as he gets behind the wheel, and he has the impulse to wave before he starts it up. But they turn and close their door and he is now alone on the street, the rows of houses that look abandoned in the bright light, nothing stirring, all the windows closed and the curtains still as stone. He turns the ignition with his good hand, reaching around to do it. He can't use the other at all, and the pain is growing worse by the minute. Keeping it sideways on the top of his right thigh, as he would if he were going to do a karate chop with it, he drives through the ponds of shade and sun to the Highpoint house, parks in front, and then sits for a while, his damaged hand held up to his face, where he can examine the swollen redness of the knuckles. Something's broken, that's clear. He can't even bend the fingers.

Carefully he gets out of the truck, and walks around the house, holding the pulsing hand with its prodigious welt. Max is where Max always is at this time of a Saturday, sanding a plank, sitting near the rib cage of wood, his back to the house. He hears Walker and turns, and stares.

Walker comes toward him out of the sunlight. The shade moves over him, no cooler than the sun, and he's getting the headache he knew would come from drinking that much beer midday.

"What're you doing here?" Max says.

Walker stops and waits for him to say whatever he will say. But Max just stares.

"Why don't you quit this?" Walker says to him.

"What the hell are you talking about?"

"This," Walker says, indicating the structure. He bends to pick up a piece of cut plank, and tosses it at the boat. "Christ. Do you know what's going on?"

"What's wrong with you?" Max says. He gets to his feet, and now he sees the injured hand. "What in the world?"

"She's fucking somebody else, Max."

"You're not making sense."

"Jenny, goddamn it."

For a long time neither of them moves, or speaks, and a summer-soft breeze blows over the tops of the trees, raising a little swirl of dust and stirring the shade on them. Walker begins to cry, and he wipes his good forearm across his own face, standing there.

"You better go on home," Max says. "Sober up. Maybe have a doctor look at that."

"Didn't you hear me?"

"Go home," Max says. "Before something happens."

"It already has, Max. Didn't you hear what I said? Your wife's screwing somebody else."

Max picks up a piece of wood and steps toward him. He comes close, and Walker backs up. Max holds up the wood like a club. "Get out of here, now. Before you really get hurt. Go home."

"You don't get it, do you."

"I'm telling you," Max says, pushing him.

Walker stumbles back a few paces, then turns and tries to make his way back around the house, but an unevenness in the ground betrays him, and he falls. His older brother stands over him. It comes to him that he is only trying to hurt *her*, now, by telling Max; it has nothing to do with Max.

"Get up," Max says.

"You don't even care what she does," Walker says, trying to rise.

Max strikes him on the back of the head with the flat of his hand, and Walker, rising, begins flailing at him, even with the broken hand. Max has to fend him off with the piece of wood. They grapple and fall, and roll, and Max hits him, and hits him again with the wood, the size of a policeman's nightstick. Walker feels the blows, and keeps on, swinging both arms, tasting blood, feeling it run down the side of his head, kicking at the other and trying to hit at him, and being hit, with fists and the club, and then, without any kind of sense of time passing, he finds that he's sitting against the wall of the house, hands in his lap, feet straight out, looking through a lot of shadow-figures at the skeleton of the boat, and still tasting blood. The shadow-figures are people, standing or moving around him, getting in the light, and the light is blinding when they step out of it. He shades his eyes with the good hand and tries to see who everyone is, all the shapes moving across the light.

"What time is it?" he says to them. "Is everyone all right?"

It's his mother who tells him, as he lies on the gurney in the emergency room, that the computer salesman may not live. She cries, telling him, in that slight stutter, that the poor man, Bill, has a wife and two children, that his heart stopped at the scene and was restarted; that his skull is fractured. The police are outside, everything's gone all to pieces and what were you thinking, what were you thinking, oh, what got into you? She cries, her fists down on the blanket over his legs, How could this be? How could this have happened and why, why didn't you talk to me? Why? He's all blankness, lying there, looking at her from a far place, a depth of solitude and numbness.

"W-Why, son?"

Faces move around him. He requires stitches in two places, twelve above one eyebrow and seven behind the left ear. He wakes and sleeps while all this is done, and in his sleep he sees himself standing over himself, a tableau from across a room, and the room is white, empty, nothing on the walls, no doors or windows, everything white, the floor and the ceiling, too— white. And he's outside himself, free, and none of the last few weeks has taken place. It's as if he's a little boy again, until he wakes, and sees, through an opening in the curtain that's been drawn around his bed, two men watching him, and waiting. Police. Walker sees his mother speak to them, and the pleading look on her face as she moves by them and goes on. And then Max is there, talking to them, with Jenny on his arm. Jenny's crying, looking at the men and not bothering to wipe the tears from her eyes. But then this is all gone, too, and he's in the dream room again, standing over himself, except that it's no longer himself, but his mother, and Sean, too, all of them, one body containing everyone, and he wakes to a voice, no voice he knows, a man standing close, with white hairs coming from his nostrils.

"Can you understand me, Mr. Clayfield?"

"No," Walker says, low. He can't tell whether he has actually spoken. "Have they given me something for the pain?" he asks. "I hurt my hand." He holds it up. It's in a temporary cast.

"We'll have to do this later," the man says, across him. Walker turns his head to see that it's his mother and brother.

"I hurt my hand," he says to them.

"Oh, W-Walker," says his mother, crying. "That poor man didn't do anything."

"I'm okay," he tells her. "My hand." He holds it up again. He sees Max move away, putting his own hands to the sides of his head. But then Max is there again, frowning at him, mouth slightly open, a dumbfounded man. "I love her, Max," Walker says, or thinks he says. "I couldn't stand him talking to her that way. She can't love him, Max." His older brother doesn't move or change expression, and Walker comes to know that no sound at all has issued from him, no words. He looks back at his mother, crying there, faltering, being helped to a chair. And now everything dissolves, crumples, and he can't open his eyes, can't see. "Where is she, Max?" No answer. Max is gone, everyone is gone but the man with the silver hairs in his nose, who sits in a chair at the foot of the bed, looking through a magazine.

"Sir?" Walker says. But he still can't utter a sound. He closes his eyes and feels everything falling from him, as though he has begun rising on a cloud, but then very quickly the sensation changes, and it is he who is falling, drifting away, sailing down. He sees Jenny standing near the frame of the unfinished boat, arms folded, hair pulled back, eyes half closed, unseeing, as the half-closed eyes of Bill the computer salesman were, and Walker turns in the cavernous darkness of himself, searching for that other time, far away, when he was himself, not a man who would fall in love with his brother's wife; not a man who would cheat or steal or lie; not a man—not that man—who would ever think of causing the slightest harm to another human being.

OVERCAST

Here is how Elaine Woodson attempted to describe things to herself one predawn:

It's like those times when the whole sky is one smooth whitish dome and you're not aware of it as cloud cover until the thing glides off in the wind and gives you blue sky. It's like that. A form of walking pneumonia of the spirit. I'm not even quite aware of the thing until it has lifted.

She did not speak of it. Not to her mother, or her father—who lived alone in Santa Monica now—or her two married sisters, or her younger brother; not to friends. It was bad manners to make yourself and your troubles the subject of conversation, even with family. More than fifty percent of all marriages end in divorce.

She had never wanted to be defined by marriage anyhow.

Since the divorce—from Sean, who was pretty but unfaithful and lazy, had a drug habit, and doubtless everyone wondered what she must have seen in him to begin with—she had been working behind the counter in the Memphis Belle diner, which was close enough to Beale Street and the Peabody Hotel to remain fairly busy most of the time. She would say that her life was too hectic for her to feel sorry for herself, though this wasn't really the case. Life was in fact not all that crowded with events. And, as everyone knows, when there is brooding to do, people who are so inclined will make the time. She simply wasn't the type to agonize about her own situation. She was what a friend in school once described as fortunately curious; her focus was always on the world outside herself.

The divorce was final almost a year ago, and aside from a dinner here and there, or a movie, she hadn't been seeing anybody. She had been surprised to learn that Sean was getting married again, but that was something she thought was rather entertaining. She joked about it with her sisters, her mother. The poor sad girl, whoever she was.

Elaine remarked with a kind of serious mirth that for herself, she wanted some time to rest up. And that was true.

She did miss sex sometimes. Well, she missed closeness. She had never been able to be casual about intimacy, even as everyone else she knew tended to that, or seemed to. You couldn't tell really what people were like alone. But for her, she had to feel that her heart was involved, that it all came from there.

These days, when she left work in the evenings, she went straight back to the little house on Cleveland Street, with its flourishing indoor plants and its book-lined walls, its neatly stacked collection of popular and classical music, and its little flower garden in back.

Home.

Where, she would say, she could breathe easily. Her life was simple. She had been telling people that she rather liked living alone. She cooked for herself, and enjoyed a good crisp glass of Sancerre or a little Bordeaux in the late evenings. Her sisters, like her father, lived far away—Belinda in Maine and Chloe in Vancouver, and they had families that kept them busy. Belinda had three children, and Chloe had two; Belinda, a dental hygienist, was married to a dentist; Chloe used the term

homemaker to describe herself and had married a tax account-
ant who bought and sold antiques. Both men were handsome,
blond, steady, and usually warmhearted, though they had never
thought much of Sean, and had been fairly vocal about that at
times. And withal, Elaine never once implied to her sisters that
in her own estimation their husbands were chokingly smug
and finally rather humdrum. Everybody was good friends from
a distance, as their younger brother once put it. He was in college, now, at Vanderbilt, three hours away. The whole family
was scattered in distance for Elaine, except her mother, who
lived just across the river, in Arkansas. Now and then her
mother drove over to Memphis to visit, but she seldom stayed
long, since Elaine had no television. Elaine's entertainment
was reading, listening to music—particularly opera—doing
some gardening, and occasionally writing little notes and snip-
pets she was too modest to call poetry, or prose either.

Sometimes what she wrote really did take the form of a kind
of playful verse:

Call that song all morning from the trees
A word that's far from song. Say antifreeze
Croons to the dawn, then winterize your car
With music from the puffed throat of a bird.
A word's a sound, too—thought, quick-fetched from far,
In use before we counted Time. Absurd.

But mostly they were more in the nature of notes to herself.
For instance, this evening, she wrote:

Said I felt fine automatically politely to the man in the straw hat
today, and was surprised that in fact did feel fine, after a
morning full of bright sun in which I hadn't quite noticed the

inner clouds. Such a strange sense seeing him coming. But we spoke and my little private cloud cover sailed off in the wind. Bright sun inside all afternoon. Pack for Mother's. Water.

That last word was a command, stemming from long-standing trouble remembering to do daily tasks like watering. She had always been objective about her own nature. She was thirty-three, and single again, and Sean was out in Las Vegas, working as a blackjack dealer. Always good with his hands, he'd done a little of that down in Tunica, Mississippi, before the divorce. He loved the game. But he was never very happy being married. She always had the feeling that he was only partly there. And then she had thought fondly she would have a child someday. For a while it was an area of serious tension. She hoped for it, longed for it. He dreaded even the slightest trace of the idea, said it gave him the willies. "You have a child and in a week you're old and getting ready to die. It just makes it all go so much faster. Bang. Like that, you're a grandfather and it's all basically over."

"No," she told him. "It goes exactly as fast as it goes. And you look up and it's gone bang all right, and you're alone in a room with a urine smell coming from you because you haven't had a shower for a week and there's nothing but the TV. And you still die."

Then he would resort to the old ersatz morality: "I don't want to bring an innocent child into such a terrible world."

"Don't lie about it, Sean. You're afraid. Admit that you're afraid."

"All right. I'm afraid," he said. "You bet I'm afraid. I'm so scared I can't take in a full breath, you know? I can't sigh. It's all stuck right here in the middle of my chest, the place they usually point out as the seat of emotion. And my number one emotion just now is fear."

The truth was that she had been afraid, too.

Eight years of that, and she was ready to call it quits. They were both ready, the two of them. Childless, and aimless, too. They had met in college. He dropped out soon after. She finished, but didn't want to teach or do any of the other tasks for which her education had prepared her. She took the classes because she wanted to read the books. She had a hunger for good books. Even so, she and Sean spent a lot of time smoking dope and watching television over the years, while he worked for the county keeping order among case records, and she went from job to job, mostly editing the dreadful failures of expression rife in the work of people who wrote for trade publications, in-house newsletters, and the occasional greeting card summary of a family's year. *And this past December, when Tammy's daddy chided her ever so sweetly for eating like a horse, Tammy looked up at him and said "neighhh." So cute. And, we all agreed, advanced for a four-year-old.*

Mind-numbing.

They had been together almost five years before they married. And the day they went through with it, she had to resist inwardly the sense of it as a probable mistake; things were already going south. She had come to think of these eight years as the time it took to admit the truth. They were both happier separate from each other. He called now and then to tell her how he was and to ask how she was. Everything was still friendly. And of course he would never change. He was scarily like her father, both of them locked in a kind of perpetual adolescence, except that her father seemed proudly aware of the fact, and poor Sean didn't have the slightest intimation of it. Occasionally, through the past few months, speaking from the noise and clamor of a Vegas hall, he would say he missed her, and he wanted to know, with that nearly childlike straightforwardness, if she missed him.

She would tell him, quite honestly, no. "You be happy," she'd say. "I'm happy."

And he was happy; that was true now. He was about to be remarried, and was moving on, and she was glad of that, truly. And yet there had been these passages lately, under the cloud. They had nothing to do with him; she was certain of that. All this started well before he announced his new situation. But something was changing in her heart.

Today, at the diner, she watched the man in the straw hat come walking from far up the street, beyond the trolley stop, out of the shadow of the big YMCA building, his white shirt showing bright in the sun, and the straw hat looking new, a perfect yellow color with a black band. She saw him, and abruptly had an unbidden strong sense that this morning would be important, that something momentous would take place. It stopped her. She stood holding the coffeepot, paused, examining the thought. What was it about the image of a man in a straw hat, walking in sunlight, that should cause her to have such a premonitory jolt? She sought to dismiss it, but she watched him come on, anyway. He carried something under one arm and as he neared, coming up the hill, she saw that it was books. She assumed he would turn down Third Street, or walk by when he got to the block where the diner was, but his gait increased slightly, and he strode up to the door and looked in, looked right at her as if he were looking specifically *for* her, one hand held up to hold the hat on his head in the breeze. Then he pulled the door open and entered. The motion of him, stepping to the window and looking in, startled her. It was ridiculous.

He nodded at her, took a seat at the counter, and picked up one of the menus from the little rack of them there. He asked for black coffee, and when she brought it, he ordered eggs over, with no bacon and no toast, and a small bowl of grits with cheese. They chatted pleasantly about the weather, the hot day. Nothing out of the ordinary about it. There was gray in his beard. He was fifty-something. A soft-spoken gentleman from the city, no one she knew. Her heart was beating in her cheeks.

She left him alone, and went to the register, where a very old woman was waiting to pay. She did not look at Elaine, but just handed her the check, with the money for it in exact change. "Was everything all right?" Elaine said.

The old woman nodded and shuffled out the door. The sun beat down on her head with its loose strands of white hair, and it shone on her scalp. Elaine looked away.

The man in the straw hat was reading one of his books. She worked around him, cleaning the counter, and tried to imagine how people got through. She and Sean had spent so much time stoned, out of it, sitting in front of the television. She got him to take the TV with him when he left. She did not miss it, even a little. The dramas they had watched before he took it away went on, and the depicted lives changed as they would, and it meant nothing to her and she would never be able to explain to herself how it could've got hold of her the way it had. She would spend a week worrying how something was going to unfold in a fictional life, and it was all soap operas, except the operas had come to prime time and the dialogue was better. She decided that what she felt about the approach of the man in the straw hat was a holdover from those hours of watching the television dramas, where everything had a meaning and the camera eye, so much like a human eye, never looked at anything that didn't mean something was about to happen. She was tired; she hadn't been sleeping well.

The man was gazing at her. "You all right today?" he asked. It was customary in Memphis to put it like this—it was a rough equivalent to "how are you?" except that it was also infused with a friendly concern quite absent from the other expression. She had always loved it. You didn't encounter it anywhere else, as far as she could tell, except Memphis. "You all right today?" As though the questioner and the person being asked were in an ongoing conversation about something through which both were struggling. It was part of the charm of where she lived.

"I feel fine," she told him. And she did. She noticed it; the cloud had lifted again, was gone again. She wiped the counter and gazed at him. "Everything all right?" she asked him. "The food, I mean."

"Just right," he said. "The food, I mean." He smiled.

"Wonderful. How's everything else?"

"I've just moved house. Everything's in boxes. Just went back to the old place to make sure everything was out of it."

"No fun," she said. "But the coffee's good, right?"

"Perfect."

A moment later, she asked if he would like a refill.

"Thank you," he said. "It's good coffee."

"I make it myself," she told him. "Because I drink it, too."

He held the cup to his lips and blew across the lip of it. "Very rich."

"Yes. Some people think it's too strong."

"They pour a lot of cream into it?"

"And sugar."

"Never liked it any other way but black."

"I used to put a lot of sugar and cream in it when I was young," she said.

"You're still young."

"Well."

He turned the pages of the book and sipped the coffee. When she asked him if he'd like still more, he nodded, and held out his cup. She poured it full again.

"Thanks," he said. "I've had some good news this morning."

"Really."

He nodded, still smiling, though she thought she saw a kind of sad light in his eyes.

"Is it something you can share?" she asked.

The smile stayed. "I'm not gonna die just yet."

"Oh," she got out. "That *is* good news." She believed he might say more, but he went on eating, reading one of the books. She watched him. He did not look ill. Probably some routine medical exam had showed him to be healthy. Or maybe he *was* ill, and in some kind of remission. She caught herself trying again to imagine how people got through. There was work, and she went about it with a kind of heavy concentration, glad of him there, but not wanting to bother him, either.

Presently, when he got up to pay she went to the register and he handed her a twenty. "That was very good," he said while she made change. "You made me feel like I was in your kitchen."

"You're very kind." She handed him his change, and he was already on his way out the door. He stopped where he had been sitting and put ten dollars down. "Thank you," she called after him. He waved. She watched him walk on up the sidewalk, toward Main Street and the trolley stop there. He trotted the last few steps because the trolley was arriving. He got on, and rode away toward the loop leading around to Mud Island

and the river, and for some reason this gave her a sudden strange sense of abandonment, as though she were watching the departure of a precious part of life. She went to the big sink and washed her small hands and wondered.

Perhaps a minute later, she found a playbill on the floor by the stool where he had been sitting. It was for something that was showing that week at the Orpheum. Inside was a ticket stub, and a little piece of notepaper with writing on it, not quite readable, and what appeared to be a phone number smeared to illegibility by moisture; it looked like running mascara. She put the playbill and its note in the little box her boss, Mr. Green, kept for lost and found. To her knowledge, nothing had ever been put there before.

Pack some books. Set alarm for seven. Pack to go straight from work. Curious that he would say that about dying.

Men think about it more?

That's the orthodox way of seeing it, I believe. Read that somewhere.

That evening, she had an extra glass of Sancerre, and went to bed a little groggy. She tried to read, but kept nodding off. Yet as soon as she shut the light, she was wide awake, lying there open-eyed in the perfect dark—her bedroom windows were covered by heavy curtains; no light from the street and no bright moon could get through. She kept thinking of the man in the straw hat. It was such a funny, wide-brimmed hat, and he'd worn it at an angle. It shaded his face, the little beard and mustache, the green eyes, friendly eyes that were also somehow rather gloomily piercing. The irises didn't quite reach the lower edges, where the little pouches drooped, the color of old bruises. It was a strange face; it was very interesting, even unforgettable. But no one would have thought it was good to look at. Indeed, at first glance, one might have said it was ugly.

She kept seeing it, trying to go to sleep. And sleep wouldn't come. It had felt so strange, standing there watching him come, as though he were her future itself. She couldn't shake the idea. Nothing important had taken place. She had served breakfast to him and he had left a large tip and gone on his way. And the little playbill and note had dropped from his pocket.

> *Those faces that we see once and think we'll*
> *Forget, come back sometimes at night to keep*
> *Us company. Night's stare, bereft of sleep,*
> *The black pause that never quite takes you deep*
> *—because a human face stays and is real.*

> *What is it in my mood that turns on clay?*
> *What hooks me, wriggling—*
> *I'm not unhappy, we say, she says, they say*
> *Night comes on, jiggling*
> *While this wide sky forms more clouds day by day*

> *You'll probably never see the man again and you know it and it*
> *doesn't make any difference if you do see him again. Why did*
> *seeing him and talking to him do that to you? And why, why*
> *can't you go to sleep?*

At dawn, tired and bleary-eyed, she finished packing for the visit to the house in Arkansas, drank a big cup of coffee for what she knew would be a long day, and drove her little car to the diner. Yesterday, last night, she decided, was an anomaly, weariness, and then too much wine, and perhaps the start of a fever. Insomnia sometimes did give her a feverish feeling; and songs—passes in her day, voices, things people said or did, images, instances—replayed themselves with the persistence of delirium. She recalled the way it felt, pausing to watch him walking along, from nowhere, it seemed. That sense of life shifting in the very moment. She thought about him all the way to the diner. After she parked in the lot, she stepped to the side of the road and looked toward where she had first seen him. Preposterous. The sun was brightening there, rising to the level of the far trees yonder. At the top of the farthest hill up that way there was the YMCA building, and she decided that he had probably spent time there, and walked out looking for something to eat.

She said aloud, "What the hell is the matter with you, girl?"

Her shift mate, Colleen, had warned her that she would be alone in the first part of the morning. She opened the diner, went inside, and looked in the little lost and found box. The playbill with its scribbled note and name and number inside was still there. She got things ready for breakfast, and drank more coffee as she brewed it. Colleen called just after seven to say she would be later than planned. Her boys were in trouble at school, again. She had conferences with teachers this morning, and one of the teachers would be delayed. She couldn't possibly be in until after ten o'clock. "Are you so busy?" she said.

"Not a soul yet."

"Oh, I hope it's a light morning."

"Mr. Green won't like that."

"Is he there?"

"You know he never comes in before noon."

But Mr. Green came in scarcely five minutes after the conversation with Colleen. There were only two customers in the place. A boy from the high school on his way to early swim practice, and an Episcopal priest, a regular, who had spent the night in the emergency room with one of his parishioners.

"Slow?" Mr. Green said to her, coming in.

"You're early."

"I thought you'd need help. Doesn't look like you do." He took an apron from the hook on the wall, tied it around himself, then went to the grill and turned the bacon that she had put on. She made an English muffin for herself. The place was always a little slow on Friday mornings. The tourist crowds would start wandering in toward noon. But when the priest paid to the penny and left, they were alone for a time. They talked about the skinflint priest, with his dour morning moods.

"He has an excuse this morning," Elaine said.

"It's your tip," said Mr. Green.

She leaned against the counter and gazed out at the street, the prospect of antiques shops, boutiques, restaurants, the line of stores, the public parking lot up that way, and the trolley stop. She expected to see the man come walking along. But there was only the ebb and flow of traffic gliding past Third Street, the shine of the cars out there. People began to trickle in: several men apparently on their way to some kind of landscaping job; a woman with two preschool children; a couple who had clearly come from the superhighway, their car full of boxes and clothes, with a portable carrier on the roof, and two bicycles on a rack behind.

Through the rest of the morning and into the afternoon, she was too busy to think. At her lunch break she walked up to the sushi place, Bluefin. This part of Main Street was closed to automobile traffic, and she sat out on the patio in the warm breezes and watched the trolleys and the horse-drawn tourist carriages go by. She was aware of herself purposely not looking into the trolley cars that passed. The waiter was a tall willowy girl with a stud in her nose and an enormous pair of rings expanding the lobe of each ear. Looking at the stretched-thin flesh of her ears undermined Elaine's appetite. She kept her attention on the street, with its stores and attractions, and the girl bustled around her, bringing edamame and water and chattering about the weather, which was in fact seasonably unremarkable: Memphis was always this hot in late July.

> *Where we go, leaving the rooms*
> *of others, is "away."*
> *Arriving here, bearing the glooms*
> *Of worry, why, we say*
> *"Here I am, glad of this dome*
> *Of instances & fright,*
> *This dim place I now call home.*
> *The insects screech all night."*

When she was with Sean, the two of them used to come to this part of town and walk down past Beale Street and the Orpheum Theatre to the galleries along South Main. A man who worked in a boutique near the train station was a source for Sean. They'd buy a nickel bag from him. Sean would make four joints out of it, and Elaine would put it in her purse. They'd go into some of the galleries, walking back toward Union Avenue. And sometimes they would take a table on the outdoor patio of Bluefin. Sean would light a joint. They would pass it back and forth under the table, while they waited for the food to come. She would watch the young families walking by—couples with babies in strollers or toddlers tagging along. Sean called them "citizens" in a dismissive tone and with a little tilting back of his head, as though the word itself contained some power to cause a recoiling, like the kick from a pistol shot, and his phrase to describe what they were doing, sitting there on the open patio, was "watching the citizens."

She ate her edamame and some soup. The sky above the city was gray, and that fit her mood. When she got back to the diner, she peeked into the lost and found box. The playbill with its unreadable note and number were still there. She took it out and tried to read the writing. She could make out one word: *can't*. She was pretty sure that was the word. The rest of it was smudged ink, draining down the little page. She put it back and turned to Colleen, who was carrying two plates on one arm and one on the other, crossing to a table by the window.

"Am I glad to see you," she said.

She was run ragged, and Mr. Green had stayed to help at the griddle. As the hours wore on Elaine lost herself in the bustle and stress of keeping up with it all.

Just before the end of her shift, the man in the straw hat entered.

She looked up from taking the order of two women from the university, and saw him. Something turned over in her blood. He went up to Mr. Green and said something, and Mr. Green reached for the lost and found box.

"Excuse me," Elaine said to the women. "Be right back."

She moved down the crowded counter to where the man stood. He had retrieved the contents of the box and set them down. He was nearsightedly holding the note up to his eyes, very close.

"Hello," she said to him.

He only glanced her way. "Hi."

"You were gone by the time I found it."

Now he stared. "Do you expect a reward or something?"

"Oh, no." Her heart sank. And then she seemed to pause in herself and observe that fact. It made her repeat the phrase, with exactly the same emphasis. "Oh, no."

He looked back at the note. "Can't read it anyway." He folded it into quarters, and put it in his pocket, then rolled the playbill. "Well, thanks."

"Don't mention it," Elaine said. "I think I'd call the number. You can read the number."

His eyes narrowed, and he took her in. "Pardon me?"

"Just a suggestion." She thought how foolish to suppose that yesterday had made any kind of impression on him, or that it meant anything. "Never mind," she said.

He took the note out again. "The number's mine. My new one. I wrote it down so I wouldn't forget it."

She said nothing.

"The note, well, that's something else. Something my daughter wrote. She came through town and left it on the door of the house I just left. I was out getting tested for a tumor that wasn't there. She comes through town. She hasn't spoken to me in three years."

"I'm so sorry."

"Yeah," he said. "Well."

"Order up," Mr. Green said behind her.

"I'm sorry," Elaine said again to the man, because it was all she could think of to say.

"What do you reckon her note says? Did you try to read it?"

"I only looked at the number. I thought if you didn't collect it in a couple of days, I'd call it."

"Maybe you'll call it anyway."

"Well, I didn't memorize it."

He handed her the note. "Here. You can have it. You've got it now."

She held it up to the light. She read again the word *can't*. She thought to say that to him, but he had turned and was moving to the door and out. He walked on down toward Third Street.

She put the piece of paper in the pocket of her apron, and then brought it out and looked at it again.

"Well?" Mr. Green said. "You work here or not?"

She put it in her jeans pocket, and went on with her day, avoiding eye contact with Mr. Green.

By the time she left for her mother's, she had tried to put the whole thing from her mind. It was perfectly silly, and she was more interested in her reaction to it all than to the thing itself. She drove across the bridge into Arkansas, thinking about the strangeness of stumbling into someone's private life. Then she was thinking about the secrets of a lived life: the chain of events that made up the desperate seriousness of the private self, all that worry—everyone had some version of it. How did Keats put it? "The weariness, the fever, and the fret." Something about the temper of her own last few days must have produced it—that bizarre sense that things were about to change because a stranger walked up from three blocks away and looked at her through a window, a man peering into an establishment, looking to see if it was open. This little moment, mingled with the genial exchange that followed and the fact of the twice-abandoned and unreadable note, with its one clear word, had brought her to her present state of odd disturbance and speculation.

By the time she reached her mother's house, the sun was

going down among flaming red and orange and burned-looking clouds, and she was sleepy, tired, and putting the whole stupid business behind her. She got out of the car and started up the sidewalk, talking to herself.

"Ridiculous. Stop it. It means nothing."

Her mother stood in the entrance, holding the screen door open.

"I hope you didn't eat," she said. "Who the hell are you talking to?"

"Myself."

"Well, don't do it so publicly. People will think you're crazy."

"Maybe I am." Elaine stepped up on the little porch.

"Hungry?" Mother asked.

"Not really, yet." Elaine kissed her cheek.

"Have I got a shock for you, kiddo. Guess who's here?"

She looked into the dim space of the living room, with its clutter of antiques and its heavy-curtained windows looking out on the back patio, where her mother spent most of her time.

"Come on," Mother said, leading her inside. "You won't believe it."

They walked through the living room and the little kitchen to the patio doorway, and there, seated on the lounge chair next to the TV tray full of bottles and glasses, was her father.

"Hello, kid," he said, without rising. It was as if this were a normal visit, and he was sitting in his normal place. It had been more than three months since she'd heard from him, and that was a bought birthday card, merely signed with his full name under the word *love*. Long ago, she'd stopped wondering about him. He sent cards on birthdays, at Christmas; she flew out there one Thanksgiving, and he introduced her to his new wife, whose kindness made Elaine hope for her, knowing her father. Within the year that woman, too, was gone. He had been married twice since then. The old man went about life cheerfully, without the slightest concern for anything but his own requirements. There was no malice nor any conscious greediness in anything he did. That was just how he was: a happy, funny, appealing man congenitally unable to sense in the slightest way the reality of other people. What she had from him was what all others ever had from him. A kind of customary attention, something that he knew intellectually was the expected norm by the society in which he lived, but which he did not truly feel. In all this, he could have been the standard Sean aspired to, if Sean had it in him to aspire to anything. But thinking this made her feel petty, and mean, and she put it away from herself. People were what they were.

"Good to see you," he said, smiling. He had gleaming white, straight teeth. This was part of his charm, of course.

She stepped out onto the patio, but did not cross to where he was. Suddenly, her breath had seized up. She drew in air and held it. "You're a ways from home," she managed to say.

"Long time," he said. "Why're you hanging back on me? What's going on?"

"Nothing," she told him.

"Don't I get a hug?"

She walked over and embraced him, bending down into his reaching arms. He still did not get up, and she had the thought that maybe he couldn't. She smelled the coffee he had drunk, and the bay rum he always wore. Mother looked at her with something like expectation. "Aren't you the slightest bit hungry?" she said. "You didn't eat already." But her eyes said *Please don't say anything mean.*

"I'm fine," Elaine told her.

"I'm on my way east," the old man said. "Driving. Been on the road for four days, taking it slow. Going back to visit my uncle Freddy. You remember Freddy?"

"No."

"Well, you were young."

She nodded, then watched Mother pour him a glass of water on ice. The ice bucket was full and a lot of melting had taken place; apparently, the old man had been sitting here for some time. Elaine's mother sat next to him, in her own lounge chair. The TV was on without sound.

"Uncle Freddy's having his seventy-fifth birthday party."

"Actually, to be honest, I don't think I've ever even heard of him," Elaine said.

"Sure you have," said Mother, rising. "I've got to tend to dinner. We're having pork chops."

"My favorite," said the old man. He leaned slightly toward Elaine. "I know we've talked about this, but I think Sean's out of his mind."

They had never talked about it. Elaine said, "Well, you know, Dad—it was mutual."

"I know, but he should've fought for you."

"He might've done that but I didn't want it."

"Well, I always said you're a match for anything."

A pet phrase of his. She reached over and touched his wrist. "Excuse me," she murmured, and followed her mother into the kitchen. There, she picked up the spatula and opened the oven to turn the chops. Her mother sliced a carrot, and two stalks of celery. They worked side by side for a minute, without saying anything.

"I think he wants to stay a few days," Mother said.

"And you're gonna let him."

She shrugged. "Kind of nice having him around."

"You're really thinking of it."

"Hey—he's your father."

"A biological accident."

"Oh, stop it, Elaine. For God's sake."

"You aren't thinking what I think you're thinking," Elaine said.

"It's a visit," Mother said. "Leave me alone."

They worked quietly for another few minutes. Elaine began cutting up the potatoes her mother had set out, and placing the pieces on a baking sheet. The old man liked to pour the juice of the chops over potatoes broiled in garlic and butter.

Her father walked in, looked at them both, smiled, opened the refrigerator, and stood there staring into it. He was already making himself at home. He reached in and got a beer, glanced at them again, and then went on outside.

"I don't like being alone," Mother said. "Okay? I've decided that I *hate* being alone. For you, now, it might be just the thing. I'm sure it is. I'm proud of you for it. And I was all right with it myself for a good while after we—after he was gone and you all were out in the world. I really was. But I'm tired of it now, Elaine. I am. I'm sick and tired of it all the way into my bones. And I like the sound of him in the rooms. He's a mess. He'll never be anything but what he is. And I don't care anymore. I've tried with others and you know I have. And it was always so dull. Always so tense all the time and having to learn the new habits and running around pretending all the time, and I missed him and you can look down on me if you want to. But if he wants to stay, I'm going to let him stay. And you all will just have to live with that."

"God, Mom. Okay."

"Well, don't look at me like that."

"I'm sorry."

Mother opened the refrigerator and brought out a bottle of salad dressing.

"How long's he been here?" Elaine asked her.

"He got in yesterday morning."

From the patio, he called to them. "You guys gonna stay in there all evening?"

"Do you want me to ask him how long he's staying?" Elaine asked.

"No! Have you been listening to me?"

"I'm sorry."

"I've already told him he can stay as long as he likes."

"Have you talked to the others? Chloe?"

"Why would I want to do that? Look, this is my house."

"I'm sorry," Elaine said, and leaned over and kissed her cheek. "You're absolutely right. I really am sorry. And good for you. Good for both of you."

"Don't patronize me either. I don't need that from you or the others. This isn't cute or sweet. It is what it is. It's my life and my well-being, and I won't have you all talking about me behind my back. I have a history with this man that none of you can know. I have a life with him. A whole life you all never saw. And whatever his faults have been, we got along pretty well, usually."

"I know," Elaine said. "I *am* sorry. I know. I know."

Mother looked like she might cry, but she sniffled into a crushed paper towel and waved Elaine away, moved to the sink and washed her hands, then went back to working on the salad. Elaine finished cutting the potatoes, then walked over and hugged her.

"Sweetie," Mother said to her.

"Actually, it makes me happy," said Elaine, forcing a smile.

A little later, she excused herself, claiming a headache, and went up to her old room. It always surprised her, coming back, how small it was; her memory kept adding length and breadth to it. The closed feel of it now made her a little breathless, so she stood out in the hall for a spell, breathing slowly. Her mother and father began laughing at something out on the patio. Back in the room, she sat at her old night table.

> *The pictures on the walls*
> *Are as they have been since*
> *I lived here: dusty halls—*
> *Museumlike with prints*
>
> *I hung at seventeen.*
> *The lady's quite archival,*
> *Oh, she wants the scene*
> *Outside of time, Time's rival*
>
> *Pinned & held, the curved*
> *Edge of the moth's bright wing*
> *Itself quite still, preserved,*
> *The thing in everything.*

On the night table was her old telephone, with the clear plastic dial. She stood and took the little piece of paper out of her jeans pocket, sat on the bed, and gazed at it. She murmured the word: *can't.* She tried to parse the others. It was all just too blurred. What was it that the woman scribbling tightly on the little piece of paper said that she could not do, or see, or feel, or understand? The daughter who hadn't spoken to her father in all that time. *Can't. Can't. Can't.* How deeply Elaine wanted to know the answer. And the very depth of her desire to know it appalled her. She looked at the phone number.

Her mother came to the foot of the stairs, asking if she wanted something brought up there to eat or drink.

"No, thanks."

"You coming back down?"

"In a while," Elaine said. "I have to make a call."

"Are you all right?"

"I know it's hard to imagine I'd have anyone to call."

"I can't hear you, honey."

"It's fine," Elaine said, loud enough to be heard. "I'm fine."

"We'll be out on the patio."

"Okay."

She sat on the edge of the bed and reflected that she was not fine, after all. Her hands were shaking. She looked at them. She would never have believed she could be so frail inside, sitting here shivering, the inner cloud settling over her.

She picked up the phone and dialed the number, and waited through five rings. No answer. No machine. She put the receiver back in its cradle, then stood and moved to the window. The street was melting into darkness, and the reflection of her face. She called the number again, and again there was no answer. Finally she turned the light off and lay down with her hands folded across her chest, as she used to do when she was a devout teenager, and wanted to pray herself to sleep. She thought of those nights she lay wide awake in the dark trying to dream up her life out in the world, wondering and worrying about where she might go, who she might come to be with, what she might find to do or be, and whether or not she would be happy there, so far away, in the magical distance, the future that was taking so long to arrive.

ONE HOUR IN THE HISTORY OF LOVE

Here are some people sitting in partial sunlight at one end of the Fresh Café patio, on Queen Street in the beautiful city of Toronto. Early fall, shades of burnt orange and red and bright yellow in the trees lining the street. The café is not crowded. The lunch hour hasn't quite come into full swing. It's not quite noon.

At one table two young couples sit facing each other: Dale and Tracy, Gabe and Martha. The two couples are having a reunion. Dale and Tracy are newlyweds, and Martha introduced them. They have come north from Niagara, where they now live. The girls have gifts for each other in little designer bags, and are exchanging them—soaps, scented candles, scarves. They've been friends since grade school. The men, who haven't known each other that long, have ordered a bottle of Viognier, and while they wait for it they sip water from tall glasses, and talk about flying in the post-9/11 world. When Dale rests his elbow on the table, it wobbles toward him. He sits back and folds his ruddy arms. A moment later, Gabe leans on it, and it wobbles back. So Dale tears off the end of a book of matches, folds it tight, and reaches down to wedge it under the bottom of one leg. But the table's still wobbly.

His new wife, Tracy, says, "We could move to another table."

"It's better now, isn't it?" says Martha. "I don't want to move. I'm tired."

Tracy and Dale were married this past April, only one month after they met. It has been six months and four days since the wedding, and Martha's the one who's counting. She and Dale worked together for a time at the Canadian Broadcasting Corporation; she introduced Tracy to him on the three-year anniversary of her first date with Gabe. Gabe has yet to commit.

"Martha's tired," he says. "Call the media."

There's a beautiful windless warm cloudless sky above the patio, sun blazing on the shiny cars, reflecting in the sunglasses of passersby and in the windows of the stores across the way. It makes the shadows sharp under the angles of brick and steel and stone in the facade of the bank at the corner, where some men are lined up to use the automatic teller. A perfect day, and Martha's all darkness inside.

"It's supposed to be a mild winter," Dale, the happy new husband, says, looking at the men stepping up one by one to get their money. He thinks of a place where you just say how much money you want and they give it to you. It looks that way. His present joy is such that thoughts like this enter his mind as possibilities. Why not?

The waiter brings the wine and presents it with the demeanor of someone who believes that it's hardly worth the show. The wine is thin and watery and without character, and he knows it. He's a middle-aged, divorced father of two grown children who seldom visit him anymore because of his failures when they were young, but his expertise with wine is impressive to everyone he knows. He pours a little in the bottom of Gabe's glass, and Gabe, glancing at the others, tastes it, then nods. "Very good." The waiter is certain that Gabe wouldn't know if it was bad. He pours the two others' glasses full, then comes back to Gabe's. There are only three glasses, because Tracy has said she's not having any wine. The waiter sets the bottle in its metal bucket of ice, arranges the white towel around it, and walks off, glad to be done with them. This isn't his table.

Gabe offers a toast. "To the new married couple. Let's hope they never become an old married couple."

"Oh, that's awful," Martha tells him. "Listen to what you just hoped for them: divorce or—God—worse."

"Okay," Gabe says. "Happiness for the married folks." He smiles out of one side of his mouth. "I think I hoped for them always to be as fresh and in love as they are today."

"To us," says Dale.

They drink, Tracy sipping her water.

When Gabe leans on the table, it tips again. "Hell," he says, folding another matchbook and reaching down.

Tracy says, "I think we should get another table." Her silky blond hair is tied in a bun at the base of her neck. The sun catches it, little filaments of fire. At the open collar of her blouse a small diamond ring hangs like a pendant on a little silver chain: her wedding ring, too big to wear on her finger. She hasn't had time to get it sized. Dale put it on her finger at the ceremony, and then they took it off for the honeymoon. This is how she explains it proudly to friends.

"This wobble is fixable," Martha says. "We're all situated. Let's ignore it. God." She's not told anyone, not even Tracy— especially not Tracy—about this, but she's begun thinking she might break things off with Gabe. She slouches down in her seat, feeling the sun on her shoulders, and watches him try to improve on Dale's effort with the table. She's wearing sunglasses with wide mirror lenses. When she turns to Tracy, Tracy sees herself in the lenses, and drops her gaze.

She and Dale are expecting, and they haven't told the other two about it yet. "I wish you wouldn't wear those things, Martha," she says about the sunglasses.

Martha grins. "I'm like one of those rappers with car windows you can't see into."

"Rappers," Gabe says. "Where'd you get that?"

"There's always rap music coming from those cars, right? Tracy, why aren't you having some of this wine?"

"I listen to Andrea Bocelli," Gabe says. "That doesn't make me an opera singer."

"You know what? Shut up," Martha says in a honeyed voice, smiling sweetly at his back as he continues working the matchbook, folding it even tighter.

Gabe came east from Vancouver four years ago to work public relations at the art museum. He's not an opera singer but has worked as a musician, a guitar player—rock and roll—and he once wanted to make a career out of it. But he hasn't played anywhere or even practiced in more than a year. Too busy with work. And Martha doesn't really like the late nights. They've found other things to do in the city.

Tracy says, "I thought they passed a law against that kind of window on cars."

"I think that was only in the States," says her husband.

"Maybe they ought to make them illegal for sunglasses, too," Gabe says, sitting up at last.

"Not two days ago you told me you thought they were sexy," says Martha.

"I never liked them. I think of them as a sign of the times. You know, like those cars only one person can fit into. Selfishness personified."

"Oh, boy, a theory from Gabe," says Martha with a smirk.

"All those little gadgets and games and iPods," Gabe continues, "that people use to shut themselves away, even on a city street."

"Well, I like being inscrutable," says Martha. "And pardon me all to hell. But the sun hurts my eyes." She feels like crying. She can barely hold it back, a form of courage that is seldom appreciated. She wishes for love, craves light and laughter, and the sounds of the street seem oppressive and discouraging. She feels too small and dark, with her tight black curls and her chewed, unpainted fingernails. She looks at the red polish on Tracy's and recalls that Tracy makes regular visits to a manicurist, even on her tight budget. She rejects the thought that there's something shallow in that.

Tracy pats her arm. Martha smiles at her.

Tracy, smiling back, feels inexplicably sorry— sorry past the awkwardness of this little moment. Something is afoot. She turns and gazes at the shining street. She grew up here but spent several years in New York, and another in England, doing what the advertising executives call focus groups, a form of conferencing to sell products or services. She and Dale moved to Niagara only last month—he's working for the Ripley's Believe It or Not! Museum as a ticket taker, and she's still doing focus groups, only now it's called group marketing. It's true that she and Dale are a little worried about money, but they've made it a romantic thing, the charming poverty of young marrieds starting out. This visit is something they arranged, spending money they don't have, to tell their friends the news. Dale keeps looking across the table at Tracy, wondering with his eyes when she'll say it. She will when it seems right. But there's something indefinable stopping her, having to do with the air between Martha and Gabe. Just now, oddly, it seems too big to say.

Martha says to Tracy, "Why aren't you having any wine?" She feels, with her sinking heart and her dejection, that she knows.

Dale thinks that now Tracy will tell them. But his wife only shakes her head slightly and says, "Just didn't feel like it. I'll have some." She pours an ounce or two into her empty water glass, and sips it. Dale stares at her.

A tall, big-boned waitress wearing a white bandanna over bright red hair approaches with her pad and pencil. She's in late pregnancy, and she explains that the waiter was spelling for her while she took care of a small emergency involving her condition. She is having some contractions, she tells them. Braxton Hicks. She wears a black vest over a white T-shirt, and black jeans with an elastic front to allow room for the bulge of her belly. Tracy sees Dale, the expectant father, looking at her, and gives him a little wink.

To the waitress, she says, "When's your baby due?"

The waitress, who lives alone in a flat above Bloor Street, smiles and runs one hand lightly over the tight cloth at the level of her navel. "Not for another month." In the late nights she hears the Turks and the Armenians arguing below, smoking and drinking in the light of the all-night grocery, and she dreams of having her child somewhere far away. The father of this baby is a married man, an Episcopal priest; they've broken it off. He doesn't know about the baby, and she wants to keep it that way. She's through with him. She has what she wanted when she started with him—this child, from a healthy strong man. She's determined that she'll find some way to get to Tuscany, and she'll be happy no matter what life presents her with. The baby keeps her focused on the future. She runs her hand under the bulge, and then back up, sighing softly, contentedly, and then asks, all business, what they wish to eat.

They order.

. . .

Three other people, two men and a woman, are seated across the opening to the sidewalk, near a large potted plant. The plant provides spiny shade, brittle-seeming, not enough to be true shade in the brightness.

These three actually got here first, and were seated first. On one side of the table are Jesse, a sharp-featured, slightly graying American in his middle forties, and Benjamin, a British-born Canadian in his late fifties. Across from Benjamin the woman, Laura, sits with her elbows resting on the table. She is thirty, very slight, with pretty dark almond eyes. Benjamin has a photography studio here in Toronto, and Laura was once his assistant. He has ambitions, but in fact he supports himself—has supported himself all along—working as a wedding photographer. He's having a show now at a small gallery just down College Street. The American is a writer who hasn't finished anything in several years and has managed his anxiety about this fact in the usual ways—drink, self-pity, aimless reading, idleness. Laura and he have been together for almost a year now. They're going to be married, though they haven't decided on the date. The plan is that they will move to the States and get married there. Recently, she helped him start something new, and she herself is also writing something. They are at that pitch of loving where the world seems to have been made only for them. They're often filled with a kind of sympathy for everybody they see. They came down to College Street to make the gallery walk and to celebrate the new work they're doing, and to shine the light of their happiness upon the world. They ran into Benjamin, who invited them to the café for a coffee. Jesse has never met Benjamin, and until a short while ago didn't know he existed, had no idea of this aspect of his future wife's past work life.

When they sat down, Laura put her bag in the chair next to her and placed herself across from Benjamin. Jesse noted this—it knifed through him—but said nothing.

"Jesse's from America," Laura says now, leaning a little toward Benjamin, because Benjamin has held out a print of one of the photographs he's chosen not to exhibit at the gallery, but which he wants her to see. Jesse can't see it clearly from this angle, so he looks at the street. An elderly couple make their way past, headed down toward the intersection, the woman walking slowly to compensate for the man's unsteady shuffle.

"You're from America," says Benjamin. "Really." He turns the print toward Jesse, so he can admire it if he wishes to.

Jesse looks at it as if at a passing car. "Yeah," he says. It's like the first one in the show, the one you see entering the gallery: all lurid colors, so bright as to seem almost out of focus: a very heavy dark woman in dominatrix getup—black stockings, black panties, black conical spike-studded bra that barely contains all her flesh—brandishing a whip and wearing a bridal train, standing in front of a wall poster of Niagara Falls.

"Jesse's published three novels," Laura says.

"Would I have read them?"

Oh, boy, Jesse thinks.

"Well, they're published here, too," says Laura.

"Titles?" Benjamin only reads whatever is on the best-seller list and is therefore quite certain that he's never heard of Jesse, but he wants to try being polite.

"I don't think you'd have seen them," says Jesse. "They're very specific. For a specific kind of reader." This is what he says to people who ask him that question. If the other person persists, he'll say, *You know, somewhere past the fourth grade.* He wishes Laura hadn't brought up the books. He looks at the chair across from him, with her bag on it, and adds, "Actually, I haven't seen them here. Not a single title, as a matter of cold fact."

"Well," says Benjamin, "the booksellers are so timid these days. They want only tried and true stuff—major writers."

"Danielle Steele," says Jesse. "Right? Robert Ludlum. Masters of the form?"

"Jesse's very well known in America," Laura says quickly.

"Really. Do you mean, like, famous?"

"Famous among friends," Jesse says.

"I'm writing now, too," says Laura, a little shyly. She glances across the space of sunlight at the man trying to steady a table by stuffing something under one of the legs. The woman there who's wearing mirror sunglasses looks this way and the reflection of sunlight is blinding. Laura turns her attention back to the next print Benjamin's holding out for her to see. It must be from the same shoot: the same model. He shows it to Jesse. The backdrop in this one is a motel room in pink light, a heart-shaped bed, photos of brides and grooms on a low-slung dresser that looks like the slim-lined, self-consciously space-aged furniture of the fifties. It's so pretentious, so studiedly ironic, that it's funny. Jesse laughs. It comes from him involuntarily, and he covers his mouth. He sees from the expression on the other man's face that this is a mistake.

"It's so startling as an image," says Laura, because nothing else comes of her search for words to describe it. And because this is supposed to be a friendly visit, she convinces herself that it *is* a startling image, or that its ugliness startles, and so must be a good thing. The artist's intention.

"I'm trying to get an effect," Benjamin tells her, believing that at least he has impressed *her*. He remembers having the feeling that she could be his if he wished. It seems to him that she admired what she called his work. The long hours he spent this summer photographing the endless sameness of weddings seem far away just now. "I want to take the forms of expecta- tion and turn them upside down," he tells her, speaking only to her.

In truth, the gallery show is something he's paying the gallery owner for, renting the space for an appalling amount of money. He doesn't know where the next dollar is or will come from, and he has already paid for the coffee—funds he intended to put toward cigarettes. All of this because he felt the desire to impress Laura. He knows she thinks he's having this success and she's beautiful and he wants to show off, especially with the American sitting here. The American is looking at him. So he presses on with his explanation. "I want to do wed- dings with a twist, you know—show the couple stark naked, say, in front of a picture of the Falls. Like that first print."

"Naked wedding photos," Jesse says flatly, staring.

Benjamin concentrates on Laura. "I think it might get to be a fashion, you know, taking these darkly candid pictures of bride and groom—and doing angles, too. I have one in mind where the camera angle is down low and you see deep shad- ows, all darkness and flesh, and it takes a moment to realize you're looking at the genitals of the bride and groom. Unaroused, of course, but, you know, together." He looks at Jesse, who simply continues to stare. "It's going to be my next show, I think."

"Well, I love your work," says Laura, a little automatically. She has noticed that Jesse's becoming agitated, biting the cuti- cle of his thumbnail and glaring out at the street. She doesn't want anything to ruin the sweetness of this day. She had felt caught, running into Benjamin that way, had walked into the gallery because she was so surprised to find his name on the card in the window. "I know this photographer," she said to

Jesse. And Jesse followed. She hadn't thought Benjamin would be there, in late morning.

Now Benjamin feels his cell phone vibrate in his pocket. "Excuse me," he says, and moves off to take the call.

The other two watch him go.

"Jesus Christ," Jesse says.

"Well, that's Benjamin." Laura remembers Benjamin's neediness, and his tears, his troubles with his then wife, whose name Laura can't recall. Benjamin had put his head on Laura's shoulder and wept, looking at her all moony-eyed, and wanting love. She nearly gave it to him.

"And you *love* his work," Jesse says. "Jesus goddamn."

"I was being kind."

"You *volunteered* that you love his work, Laura. That picture. That bullshit idiotic piece of naked pompous asinine pretension."

She says nothing. She feels caught out, even a little ashamed. And she doesn't deserve these feelings at all. It brings her close to anger, except that the morning has been so beautiful. She will let nothing ruin it; they're going to America to live, and she used to think all sorts of ill about America and Americans.

Jesse says, "You want to tell me why you put your bag in the seat next to you and then sat across from *him*?"

This stuns her. "I—I thought you'd sit next to me."

"You thought I'd sit on your bag."

She glances at the bag, lying there like an allegation. "It doesn't mean anything, Jesse. I didn't know I did it. I'm sorry. I used to think he was a big deal. I was his assistant."

"You mean you were *with* him?"

"No—I worked for him. That's all. He used to confide in me a little."

"What's that mean? He'd cry on your shoulder?"

This shakes her, too, a little. She blinks, looks down. "I used to think of him as an artist. Okay? I was young."

"You can't tell me you like those pictures in the gallery."

"Some of them, yes." It's true, she tells herself. It's as if he's attacking her taste, now, and by a strange implication her past, that she could ever have thought of Benjamin in that light, someone she might love.

"You're kidding," Jesse says. "Right?"

"Some of them *are* interesting, Jesse. Yes."

"Jesus Christ."

She stands and puts the bag in the chair she was sitting in, then sits across from him and takes his hands into her own. "I'm sorry. Okay?"

"What're you sorry for? It's your past. And your past adds up to you." Jesse wishes he could feel the words as he speaks them, wanting all others, anyone else she has ever thought of as a lover to be obliterated, to have never happened. He understands the irrationality of the feeling—the huge selfish loutishness of it—and he gives her hands a little squeeze, forces a smile.

"There is no past with Benjamin, Jesse. I worked for him. That's all. I thought he had talent."

"There's more talent in your little fingernail than in his whole fucking family tree."

Benjamin, standing a few feet away on the sidewalk, sees them lean across the table for a kiss and decides that he has wasted the money for the coffee. He's talking to Sheila, who's on the other side of the city, lying in bed, not alone, though she hasn't told Benjamin this. What she does tell him is that there isn't any sense talking it out or trying anymore; she feels claustrophobic all the time around him. She wants out. The words feel automatic. She's said it all before and he hasn't believed her.

He says, "I'm so elsewhere right now, Sheila." And she breaks the connection. He folds the phone up and puts it in his pocket, watching the slow progress of an old couple toward the end of the block. He watches them for a moment, until they get to the crossing. They go on out against the light, and across the street, and into the coffee shop there. The sight of them depresses him, and it's something deeper than simply that they are old and slow-moving.

At the other table, Martha has consumed her sandwich and lighted a cigarette. She watches Tracy pick at her salad—it came with a lot of peppers, which she doesn't really like. She's putting the peppers on the edge of the salad plate. Both men also watch this, quietly.

Gabe says, "Every time I see someone light a cigarette I want one."

"And a lot of the time you have one," Martha says.

"I'd say two out of eight."

"Is this one of those times?" Dale asks. He still smokes, and has pulled the pack out of his shirt pocket. He extends it to Gabe, who holds his hand up, and then takes one from Martha's pack, and lights it, smiling across the table at her. There's something mildly defiant in it.

"That's rich," Martha says.

They have been talking about the corruption that is apparently inherent in all forms of conservative government. To Dale, it seems that they are carefully avoiding the subject of their own future. He smokes his cigarette and looks at Tracy, one eyebrow up, waiting for her to see the question in it. *Why haven't we told them?* It seems odd now, this delay in telling the news. He wishes he could contrive a way to get her alone, just for the few seconds it would take to ask her about it. He thinks there must be something she has perceived about Martha and Gabe, something that has made her hesitate.

Martha, having hardly eaten, fusses with the scarf that Tracy gave her, running it through her fingers. Then she puts it over her head, clasping the ends of it tightly around her neck, the cigarette dangling from her lips. "Look," she says. "I'm the madonna from hell."

"You look like a peasant," Gabe says, blowing smoke. He wishes she could find a way to be less shrill. What frightens him is that, when they were first together, he liked this about her, liked the quick movements and the high pitch of her emotions, her high-strung reactions. All morning, he's been thinking of asking her to marry him, and little incremental changes in how he sees her keep stopping him. Just now, while she holds the scarf over her head and smirks at his remark, he believes he sees how she'll look in fifteen years.

"Should we order another bottle of wine?" Dale asks.

"Let's," says Martha, pulling the scarf off, crushing her cigarette out.

Tracy excuses herself and leaves them there, crosses to the entrance of the place, and asks the pregnant waitress where the restroom is. The waitress indicates an opening in the near wall, but then gives her a confiding little nod, a direct gaze. The refusal of the wine has not gone unnoticed by the waitress either. Within the space of a few seconds, Tracy feels as if she has made a new friend. She says, "Yes."

"How far along?" the waitress asks. "Isn't it the most marvelous thing? Have you been ill? I haven't been—not once."

Tracy says, "What's your name again?"

"Stephanie."

"We're two and a half months, Stephanie. And I've felt a little nausea."

"That goes away. Really."

"I can't wait for that."

"Anyway, congratulations."

Tracy accepts her little embrace—one arm coming across the bridge of her shoulders—then heads into the narrow hallway to the restrooms. The lady's room is small, closetlike, smelly, and fairly dirty. There are iron-colored stains on the sink. She sees herself as if by accident in the smudged mirror there. She steps close to look into her eyes, and with the little finger of her left hand, removes a tiny kernel of sleep debris. It's probably been there all morning. She shakes her head, steps back, and regards herself again. A mother-to-be. It's time to tell Martha and Gabe.

Returning to the table, she finds them all engaged in a passionate discussion of the war in Iraq. Gabe believes that it is the right thing to do and that the Americans will eventually be vindicated by history. The militant Muslims are still in the eleventh century, held there by cultural mores that deny the new and the modern. "Imagine," he says, "putting *Hamlet* on in Kabul. It's like thinking of eating steak and drinking wine on the moon." Dale agrees with this but sees the war as another Vietnam, America as the dinosaur being slowly sucked down by the quagmire. Martha has lighted another cigarette, and she disagrees with both men: the war is just the human appetite for some excuse to kill. She says this, then simply stares at the street, blowing smoke.

Tracy wants to tell them. She understands the necessity and the celebration, the fact that the longer she keeps it back, the more awkward it might seem. But the talk has turned to such dark matters, and in fact her nights are filled with trembling at the thought of bringing a child into this terrible world, with its mushrooming catastrophes, expanding horrors. She takes her seat, and watches the pregnant waitress pour more water for everyone.

Down the street a little, in the small coffee shop on the corner of Queen Street and Dovercourt Road, the two old people sit. His name is Patrick Glenville, almost eighty, still with all his hair, dyed brown and cut in a flattop, and all his teeth, too. At this moment he's pretending to listen to his wife, Helene, who is two years older than he and wears a black wig. She's complaining about their grown sons, three of them, all living far away—Dickie in Alberta; Roger in Calgary; William, the youngest, in Vancouver. None of them have called or written in weeks. He's unhappy about it, too, but doesn't want to let it become a thing, won't complain when they *do* call. They have their own families, and nobody has a lot of money. For the first time in their lives, none of the boys have plans to come home at Christmas. Helene smokes a cigarette and talks about neglect; her voice has gotten so thick. They've been married fifty-three years. She's hurting. He doesn't want to think about it all now. It's a pretty fall day; they are healthy and together. That's true. He wishes to ease things for her and has tried to remark on the fine clear weather, the pretty turning leaves on the maples in the park, but he's also growing weary of how she keeps tormenting herself. And the cigarettes, all these years, have given his darling the voice of a very gruff old man—a change so incremental that it seems, only this morning, to have caught him. This, too, grates on his nerves.

"You give them everything," she says. "And what do you end up with?"

"Let it alone," he says. "Please, dear. You're not doing yourself any good."

She blows smoke, and looks at her own hand holding the cigarette. It seems to her that he's the reason the boys don't want to come home anymore; he's the one who grows contentious over drinks and the talk of sports, the very mention of politics. She says, "If you showed even a little more enthusiasm, they might change their minds."

"Me?" he says. It's all he can manage. But then the question occurs to him: "Have they said something to you?"

She returns his stern look with a passive fixed gaze.

"Tell me what was said."

"All you do is criticize them," she says. "They talk about that. William and Roger both spoke of it when they were here last Canada Day. And Dickie agreed with me over the phone when I asked him how *he* felt."

Patrick waits as the waiter brings his sandwich and Helene's soup.

"You know you squabbled the whole time."

"You're all talking behind my back?" he says.

She spoons some of the soup into her mouth, still holding the lighted cigarette. The soup tastes like the cigarette, so she puts the cigarette out. As long as she has known him, his worst temper has been roused by such little surprises as this. She wishes she hadn't said anything. They eat quietly for a few minutes. He takes the tomato slices from his sandwich, and the lettuce, which looks wilted. Olive oil trails down the side of his palm. He's staring out at the street, chewing.

"It wasn't behind your back," she says. "I'm telling you about it."

"How's your soup?" he asks.

"Now you're going to pout."

He puts the sandwich down, reaches into his pocket, brings out a twenty-dollar bill, and puts it on the table. Their whole

SOMETHING IS OUT THERE

lives together, the mornings and afternoons and nights, and the troubles with the children, and he has loved her through it all, been faithful and loyal to her even in conflicts with the boys, and they are all talking about him like a third party, someone to whom they barely owe the respect of direct speech. "Well," he says. "You can go see them. One by one. Spend as long as you want with them."

"Patrick," she says as he rises and heads for the door. The anger has actually put a spring in his step; he's moving faster than he has in days, head tilted forward, hands shoved down into his pockets, face grim with angry determination.

"I'm going to finish my lunch," she says. "Just so you know."

He pushes out into the street. Helene lights another cigarette, almost in retaliation. He moves to the corner, a big baby, she thinks. And she knows exactly how it will go. It's the only time he moves with any alacrity or energy, now: when he's angry. He's on such a short fuse these days, this man whose patience was a quality she always admired and depended on; he'll walk home alone, go in, and pour a drink. Maybe he'll have several, and he'll be waiting for her on the steps when she arrives, sloppy and sorry and wanting her to put her arms around him and saying he didn't mean it, he doesn't know what gets into him.

Back at the Fresh Café, Tracy says it out, in the middle of their talk of war: "We're going to have a baby."

Martha turns to her, and her whole face seems to open, mouth wide, dark eyebrows showing above the mirror frames, which she now takes off. She makes a sound, a yell, and throws her arms around her friend.

"I knew it!" she shouts. She looks across the table at Gabe, and in the sudden brightness of not having her sunglasses on, her eyes play a trick on her: his face has taken on an aspect of sharp-jawed leering, the cigarette smoke escaping from the corners of his crookedly grinning mouth. He looks cruel, and full of eerie joy, or a kind of evil satiation—someone happily contemplating terrible events, glad of suffering, and a proximate cause of it. She has a flash of thinking about depictions of the devil; but then his face rearranges itself. It is Gabe, putting out his cigarette and reaching across the table to shake hands with Dale.

"I'm so happy for you," she says to Tracy, and begins to cry. She's indeed happy for her friend, and this news has given her some resolve. She'll go looking soon, and her mind constricts on the image of Gabe with the smoke curling from his teeth. She puts the sunglasses back on, offers her nearly empty wineglass for a toast.

At the other table, Benjamin shows another print to Laura. The breasts of his dominatrix model, Sheila, so close up and lighted in such a way as to appear to be landscape. But this is only a routine gesture now—how he is with everyone or anyone who will look at his photographs. He's irritable, thinking about Sheila hanging up on him, the spent cigarette money, the hopeless hours taking photographs of people he thinks of as happier than they will ever be again, and now Laura says something else about Jesse, and America—how she would love to see his next show, the wild wedding photography, but that she and Jesse are moving to Montana. He can't help himself. "You're going to live there? America? Everybody carries a gun there. Especially in Montana. You won't be going out much, will you? I'd be afraid of getting shot, or worse. The Americans are so violent. They're like children. They're a holocaust waiting to happen, aren't they."

Jesse studies the side of the other man's face during this little speech, and is at first rather surprised at the vehemence of it. Also, he's faintly puzzled at the apparent deficiency of tact, until he realizes that, consciously or not, this tirade is aimed at him.

"They're all so naïve about the world," Benjamin goes on, as if Jesse isn't there. "With their idiotic president, and their war. A holocaust in the making."

"You're from England," Jesse says. "Right? Didn't you say England?" he asks Laura, who nods, looking at him with a blankness. But she thinks she knows what will happen now.

"Yes," Benjamin says. "England, yes."

"*Great* little country," Jesse says. "Really. *Terrific* little country."

Benjamin looks at him, sees the brightness of his eyes, the intent there.

"I mean it. Marvelous little place," Jesse says. "You can't beat those plucky little Brits for fuck all. Believe me, and I've known a fuckload of them."

"Well, I don't—I didn't mean any offense."

"Oh, hey—no, really. I always said I thought England was a cool little fun place. With lots of interesting little things about it. Really."

"Well, I should get back to the gallery."

"Thanks for the coffee," Jesse says. "Seriously. Great little fucking cup of coffee."

Trying to recover something in the moment, Benjamin says, "I say outrageous things to people now and then, when I meet them. Just to gauge their character."

"'S that so," Jesse says, without the slightest expression in his features, the lidded eyes giving away nothing, yielding no doubt, no second thoughts. "Of course you realize, being an *artist*, that it's exactly your kind of generalized, shitty, abstract thinking about a whole nation of three hundred twenty million human souls that makes holocausts possible. That that's *just* where all the holocausts happen to come from. Speaking, you know, generally, about fucking holocausts waiting to happen."

"Well, I didn't mean all of them, of course."

"That's where they all come from, Jack. Those pesky little holocausts. They come from fucked-up weak-minded unoriginal people gathering to act on abstractions."

"Yes," Benjamin says, standing. "Well, as I said—I didn't mean it the way it sounded. And I really have to get back." He steps over and gives Laura a hug, then offers his hand to Jesse, who looks at it for a bad instant before taking it.

"Give me a call before you leave town," Benjamin says to them both. "We could sit out on my balcony and share a bottle of wine." He realizes, as he speaks, how lonely this makes him sound, and as he tries to find something else to say, some words indicating with the proper amount of casualness that *others* would also be there, Jesse cuts him off. "We'll do that, you bet," he says in the tone of someone already forgetting the invitation, and walking away with his lovely woman on his arm, and his obvious pride in being happy, in love. Benjamin walks down the sidewalk, past an old man—the same old man, he realizes, that he had seen earlier—who comes storming by him with that rickety walk, hands shoved down in his pockets. The whole world is bright sun, and the man's eyes are narrow, furious, the mouth deeply frowning. Benjamin finds that he can't go back to the gallery just yet. He watches the old man out of sight, and then lights a cigarette and smokes it. He stands across the street from the gallery, smoking and trying not to allow his mind to replay what has happened to him today. He sees three women enter the gallery, and watches them stroll from photograph to photograph. They seem to be talking about each one, pausing and remarking. He imagines, because he has to, that they are appreciating the brilliance of the conceptions, the colors, the angles.

Dale watches the progress of the old man as he comes by and goes on up the street. Martha and Gabe are leaving, hugging Tracy, who weeps a little. Her emotions have been so fluid these past few weeks, and of course every shade of her feeling charms him. She's his pregnant darling. When Martha and Gabe go off down toward the bank, arm in arm, Tracy sits sniffling, one arm on the still slightly wobbly table, one hand up to her eyes. Dale looks at her elbow, the bone there, solid, hers. Dimly it makes him feel the separateness of her—her body that is even now shaping another body, inside—and his own emotions have been unsteady enough, trembling sweetly on the brink of crying, or laughing. "I don't think they've got another month in them," he says about Gabe and Martha.

"Don't," Tracy says. "Please, Dale. You're always so negative."

"God," he says. "Do you really think that about me?" He's surprised at the force of his anger at her for the remark.

"You know what I mean," she says.

"I love you," he tells her, and strives to mean it as deeply as, in this instant—against the backdrop of his unlooked-for annoyance with her—he feels it. "Dearest," he says.

She sobs softly, then smiles at him. "Oh, baby. I wish they could be happy like us."

"I wish everybody could," he tells her. "That's not too negative, is it?"

"Stop it," she says, and reaches for him.

Across the city, miles away under the summery sunlight, the scattered tufts of cloud, the shifting forms of the moving sky,

Sheila lies in the lounge chair on her balcony, smoking and thinking of how Benjamin didn't call back—she feels both relief and regret about it. Well, something like regret—the old sense of something failing in the world, something obsessively, elementally wrong with the facts of existence. Her someone else sleeps heavily in the bed behind her, a nice man, good-looking, charming in a well-meaning kind of stumbling way, someone she met only last week and liked, and knew in the liking that it was going to be over with Benjamin, even as she also began almost immediately to know that this one too would not be the one—not, after all, oh, and again, the one. She knows so quickly by now, it seems. Last night, kissing the side of her neck, he said, "I love this about you, this downy little place." And she had a moment of feeling him to be so stupid that she almost laughed. She has almost ceased to believe it, that there is anything like love, real love, the kind she has hoped for since she first understood it in the movies and the songs and the talk and the stories people told each other when she was young, watching and listening so intently, a girl who couldn't wait to fall in love. Now she hears him stir, and there will be the work of having to get rid of him, unless of course he, too, is having the same thoughts and will want to get away as quickly as possible. Probably that will be so. It won't surprise her, though it will contribute to the morning's gloomy mood. But he wants to make love. He calls her into the room and she goes, lies down with him. He begins kissing her, and she kisses him back, trying to empty her mind. "I love this about you," he says, again. She can't quite believe it. She waits, and he keeps nuzzling and kissing.

"You love what about me?" she says.

IMMIGRATION

The middle of spring in Memphis and it felt like winter. Tonight, setting out the recycling, she got a chill and it took a good ten minutes to get rid of it. She had him hold her, and breathe warm at her neck. They lay in the bed under the ceiling light, because he said it would feel like warmth shining down on them. She thought of the waste of electricity. "Can you turn it off?" she said.

"I'm cold, too."

"Please?"

"You turn it off."

She was quiet. In a little while he got up and flicked the switch and then crawled in at her back, shivering. "I'd like to turn the heat on."

"Stay," she said.

"I'm dying."

"We'll be warm now."

"It's too bloody cold."

"Don't go, please."

He lay there shivering, and she reached back to pull him closer. The cold air of the room seemed to be flowing in at his neck, so he pulled the blanket higher, burrowing in, breathing his own exhalation for the warmth. It wasn't enough. He would never sleep like this, with the chill in his bones, and he wanted to be rested.

They had an appointment early the next day with the Immigration Office to prove that they were a real married couple. They had been married a year now, and his student visa was no longer valid; he would have to get a permanent residency card in order to work. He was from Ireland. Belfast. His parents still lived there. An elderly sullen couple whose exhaustive politeness to her, during her one visit to their house, seemed tinged with a kind of pity, as though they deplored her exposure to them; there was no other way to parse it. And the way they were together made it easy enough to believe. They barely spoke. Michael said they had been that way as long as he could remember, and not to worry about it. But she couldn't help feeling sorry for having disturbed their stolid existence in the green countryside.

While he finished his degree in history, she had supported him with her teaching job at the Memphis College of Art. She took the job at the end of their first year together, after a period that she considered spendthrift. They had spent a lot of money traveling around, and he was now past thirty, and things were tight. The economy was in the tank, and the administrators at the college were talking about furloughs—the delicate word in the academy for layoffs. He was going to have to find work.

He was ready. There was a need for history teachers at the high school. He had completed his degree, and written his thesis and defended it, and the book was in its tight green binding in the big long shelf of them in the university library. The thesis was about the Kennedy years, especially the problem of Berlin, and the Wall. He knew all about the cold war, and for many nights now in this winter and early spring he had been joking with her about *this* cold war, the trying to sleep while their teeth chattered and their muscles shook, and she claimed she liked a cold room and a warm bed, and of course it was nothing of the kind; it was her confounded fear of spending money. In the summer, she would insist that seventy degrees was too cold, and in blazing hot and thickly humid Memphis, she required that the thermostat be set at seventy-five degrees. They argued, back and forth. He made jokes about it in company. She swore that sixty-eight degrees in winter was different than sixty-eight degrees in summer.

He said, "Sure and you get the place down to thirty-two degrees Fahrenheit on any day of the year, summer fall winter spring, and the water'll freeze."

"It just *feels* different," she said.

"Either way, at thirty-two degrees, the water freezes and we die of exposure."

Now he waited for her to go to sleep, so he could get up and put the heat on. But she lay there shivering and murmuring about the things they would need in the morning for the meeting with the Immigration people.

He didn't want to talk about it. And even with the shaking he was beginning to be sleepy.

"The marriage license," she said. "Did we put that in?"

"Did you? Because I don't remember seeing it."

"The marriage license is the most important thing."

"I'll look in the morning."

"Can you check it now?"

"If you want to check it, love, you go right ahead."

She sighed again but did not move.

He sought to remember if he had seen the marriage license. There was too much to think about. He moved a little, and sighed, and shook.

She said, "Good night."

"I can't sleep. This is fucking daft. We might as well be in the Arctic."

She was silent. One of the things she found a bit taxing about him at times was his ability to concentrate on his own distress in any situation. He could be eloquent about it, spending energy delineating all the facets of whatever trouble had arisen, often enough trouble he had brought upon himself. She had never known a more disorganized man, and his lack of any kind of practical skill had worn her out during the process of gathering all that they would need for the morning's meeting: birth records and school transcripts, tax forms, proof of themselves as they were. The marriage license. She loved him, loved his humor and his voice and his soft brogue, but she was also exasperated by him.

"I'm worried about the pictures, too," she said to him now. "We don't have enough pictures, do we?"

"You want to get up and take a few more?"

"No. And stop it."

"I think we should bring stool samples," he said, sounding serious.

She didn't answer, but turned, facing him, and put her cupped hands to her mouth and breathed the warmth. "I won't be able to sleep if I don't know the marriage license is in there."

"Did you put it in there?" he said.

"I don't remember."

"Good night, Rita. We'll check it in the morning."

In the middle of the night, she awoke, sweating, and sat up, worried about the time. He was sprawled on his side, legs out of the blankets. She got up and went into the hall and flicked the light switch. He had turned the heat on in the night—probably while half-asleep. She turned it off and went into the kitchen. All the documents were arrayed on the table, with the two books of photographs: the many images of that busy first year. She looked through them again. Here were the two of them together and apart in many happy poses. The books were labeled WORLD TRAVELERS: him smiling clownishly on a sunny street near the Spanish Steps in Rome; the two of them embracing on the flat dirt lawn of a chateau in the Loire Valley; him seated at a café table outside a small village in Normandy, with bread and cheese and pretty shining bottles of red wine before him, and then her in the same pose, at the same table; both of them lounging and being silly in front of a *pension* in Paris, a gloomy-looking ivy wall and narrow windows behind them; and here were several from the rainy afternoon in Belfast at his parents' cottage with its heavy stone entrance and its low ceilings. And there were the ones from the year before, both of them by the fish market at San Francisco Bay, with Alcatraz brooding behind them in a cowl of drifting fog. And then there were several of them with her parents—who, last year, had divorced after thirty years—and her brothers and sisters in Virginia, everyone smiling into the camera, a sunny cool day in Fredericksburg, and he had said, when she showed it to him, "Ah, here we all are in happier times."

"What does *that* mean?" she said. "Are you talking about my mother and dad?"

"I have the thought any time I look at a picture like that, no matter who's in it."

"Well, everyone's here. Including you."

"Don't rile yourself, darlin'. It's a general thought I have every time I look at such a photograph, since I was a little tyke. 'Here we are in happier times.' And tell me straight from your heart, isn't that the truth of it?"

. . .

Now she closed the photo books and put them in the folder with the other papers. She supposed this would be enough. She worried about it all, nevertheless. The forms had been so daunting. And she remembered now that all the travel had been strenuous and had taken a toll on her nerves. In several of the pictures she looked carefree and glad, and she could recall the sense that it was something she put on, a ruse, to hide the stress of worrying about the money and the next flight.

Indeed, he would say that the strain she felt wasn't the travel but spending the money. And they had spent it, too, all of it— fifteen thousand dollars of an inheritance from his great uncle, who had made a fortune in the coal business and then lost most of it, and then made a lot back selling stocks. He left each of his surviving nephew's children a single flat payment calculated from an obscure formula he had devised that had to do with time spent in his company. Michael had lived in the old man's house one summer in Donegal before he started college. He often talked about him as a kind of natural force, a man who could be singularly unpleasant to be around, so strange and unpredictable, even volatile, but in the end hugely interesting: after you had been with him you realized that you hadn't been slightly bored. And he paid attention—the behest to Michael was accompanied by a note telling him that he should use it to study history. Michael was nearing completion of his degree at the time, and the advice seemed prescient.

Well, and a man who travels the world is in his way also studying the past.

He woke alone in the bed, turned, and looked at the faint outline of the door. He pulled the blanket up, knowing that she would've turned off the heat. Lying awake, he went over the arguments for sixty-eight degrees in the winter and seventy-five degrees in the summer. The whole thing was a perfect illustration of the economic anxiety of the lower middle classes. The phrase came to him like a quip he might use, but then he thought of her face, the sweet oval of it, and these little peccadilloes of hers were funny if you didn't let them annoy you.

He turned over again, wondering at the time and deciding that she must be seeking to reassure herself about all the materials they had gathered for tomorrow. Probably she had already located the marriage license, and probably it had been packed early, among the first things they thought about. How upsetting it was to think that you were going to be subject to the whims of the national government as manifested in the person of a single clerk—somebody working a job, with a desk and a computer and photographs of his family on the desk, and posters and paintings on his office wall. Michael pictured himself and Rita seated across a gray desk, with their lives before them in the envelopes and folders, while this little imagined balding gloomy man combed through everything, making little check marks on a legal pad as he went along. Perhaps he had lapsed into a dream, because her movement in the room startled him. She got into the bed very carefully, and lay with her back to him.

"Did we pack it?" he said.

"I'm sorry, I didn't mean to wake you."

"Did you find it?"

"It's there. You must've packed it."

"Well, if I did I don't remember it."

She closed her eyes and tried to drift off. He lay still, as if listening for her. She murmured, "Michael?"

Nothing.

. . .

It was a long night. She kept waking up, and she had a consecutive-feeling dream, a senseless narrative that kept unwinding. When light came to the window she gingerly removed herself from the bed, and put her robe on. In the hallway she checked the thermostat. Sixty-five degrees. She looked out the window at the street, with its shade trees and flowers. It was a bright morning, and dew was on the grass, sparkles everywhere, and the shade was dark blue. A beautiful day, cool and breezy, without a cloud in the sky. She put coffee on and sat by the front window taking it all in. She saw the neighbors come out and get in their van and drive away. Another neighbor, a woman she had only waved to now and then, came along the sidewalk with a big white dog on a leash, being pulled by him. She wore overalls over a white T-shirt and looked out of sorts. Rita laid her head on the back of the chair and closed her eyes.

And fell asleep.

He woke to the sound of her cell phone alarm, and said sleepily, "Turn it off, sweetie, please?"

When she gave no answer he said in a pleading and frustrated tone, nearly a whine: "Oh, come *onnnn*. I'm up. Turn it off." He opened his eyes, and saw that she wasn't there. So she was up and getting ready. "Good," he murmured aloud. And he turned the phone off and lay back down. He would wait until she came to wake him. He, too, fell asleep.

The INS office in Memphis is on Summer Avenue. Summer is a long street. It runs west all the way to Parkway North and the river, and to the east it goes all the way to Lakeland, and beyond. They both knew the street without being able to tell from the number exactly where the office might be. Their appointment was for eight-thirty a.m.

He woke just before eight o'clock. He got out of the bed and went into the bathroom and looked at himself in the mirror.

Then he looked at the clock on the wall to his left.

Rita woke to the sound of him moving through the house. They hurried into their clothes, barely speaking, and by eight-sixteen they were in the car, with him driving, speeding toward Highway 240, which was the shortest way to Summer. Neither of them spoke. They didn't know which way to turn on Summer. He thought *she* had looked it up, and she thought *he* had.

"It's your responsibility," she told him. "I thought you'd do it."

"Call them," he said. "Can you do that?"

"Why didn't you get up with the alarm?"

"I thought *you* were up. You *were* up."

"I had a bad night. I couldn't sleep. Christ. Sue me."

"Where were you?"

"I fell asleep in the chair."

"Call them. We're almost to the exit."

She keyed in the number, and got a recording, with choices. She had to scroll through them. He pulled over on the cloverleaf that would take them down to the light at Summer. Right would be west, left would be east.

She keyed angrily—sighing with exasperation and muttering under her breath—through the choices. And finally she was speaking to someone. He looked out at the highway and the parking lot of Garden Ridge Home Store, the drive-in theater screen beyond. The appointment form stated unequivocally that if a petitioner was late, the appointment would be canceled and all forms would become invalid. The entire process of seeking the card would have to be repeated. He tapped the wheel, listening to her.

She said, "We're at the 240 interchange. The light there."

"Take a left at the light," said the voice on the telephone, "and then take the first right and go to the end of the drive. We're right there."

"Thank you," Rita said. She snapped the phone shut. "We're in luck."

"I heard." He was already pulling the car out, but the blare of a truck horn stopped him. He slammed on the brake and she pitched forward. The folders on her lap fell to the floor at her feet.

He watched the truck, a big semi-trailer, go on past, down to the light. He looked back and carefully pulled out. He knew she was displeased with him. She hadn't reached to retrieve the folders.

"You're the one that fell asleep in the chair."

"It's your permanent residency. You'd think that would make you a little concerned for the details—like where the office is."

"We're in luck," he said. "Remember?"

The sound that came from her was not a word.

"Could you repeat that, please?"

"If you only had one—one—just *one* organizational gene."

"What would I do in that case? I would seek you out dead asleep in a chair in the living room when you're supposed to be getting ready for this appointment?"

"You just turned over and went back to sleep."

"I was depending on my lady," he said.

"Don't call me that. Your father calls your mother that."

"You thought it was charming when we were there."

"I thought it was sweet for *them*, since they're so unhappy and generally miserable with each other and in such obvious pain."

"Pain?" he said.

"Go," she told him.

The truck had pulled into the intersection and was also turning left. He idled forward, keeping a good distance behind it. "I don't know if I want a permanent residency here."

"Well, turn around then. Let's go home. You can go back to Ireland."

He pulled out around the truck and into the gas station there, and turned around, so that the car was facing Summer from the other side.

"What're you doing?" she said.

"You want to go home. Sure, and I can go home, too. I thought they were one and the same, but I see they're not."

"Just please stop this. I didn't mean it. We're going to be late."

"You said, Let's go home. And what's this about my mum and dad now?"

"We've got five minutes to get there, Michael. Do you want to go through the whole thing again?"

"Maybe I don't want to go through it now."

"*You* said they're miserable together."

"So they're to be pitied now, and you can't think of them except as something hostile to your well-being."

She looked out of the window and didn't answer. He made the right turn, and then the next right, and followed the drive to the building—a low gray institutional-looking place with aluminum-and-glass doors. She gathered what had fallen to the floor while he waited. Neither of them spoke. He watched her struggle with the papers. Finally she had it together, and they got out of the car. The heat of the morning had begun to bake the asphalt lot, and the air smelled heavily of creosote. She looked over the roof of the car at him, her face drawn and tired, already gleaming with sweat.

"Don't worry," he said to her. "We'll play the fuck'n love card."

"I didn't mean anything about your parents." Her expression was broken; he thought she might begin to cry, but then he reflected that she had brought it on herself with those cruel comments about two people who had taken her into their home and welcomed her to the family. He felt low and mean, but he was still angry, and he walked a couple of paces behind her, looking at the backs of her ankles against the cream white of her shoes and the blue cuffs of her slacks. His wife. He remembered being with her in a little tall-ceilinged room off the Piazza Navona, the two of them staring out at a rainy morning, the beginning of their life together, and she was talking with excitement about the Bernini in the center of the piazza, and he had turned to kiss her, a long sweet kiss, and when it was over she continued, without having lost the thought, a pretty girl still telling, still going on about her thrilling journey in the ancient town. It had charmed him so completely that he almost wept for the joy of it.

Now he opened the door of the ugly, single-floored building—it looked like a converted trailer—and held it, and walked in after her. This was a foyer leading to another glass-and-aluminum door. It had occurred to him that there was something unreasonable about his anger. He could feel himself holding on to it while opening that door for her. He dismissed the idea; he was certain that he was right about this morning. She was the one who had been unreasonable. He thought of his parents, saw his father sulking and seething over a plate of sausages, while the woman he had lived with all those years kept to her side of the table in silence.

There was a guard inside the inner door. They had to empty their pockets into a basket and step through a metal detector. The guard, a heavyset brown man with a permanent frown that showed even as he smiled, looked at their driver's licenses and then waved them into the room. Chairs were set in rows on one side. Five other people were there—a woman and two toddlers who looked to be twins, and a very young couple, teenagers. Everyone sat quietly, except the toddlers, who kept pulling against their mother, wanting out of her grasp. Another couple walked out of the central door, and the clerk there, a tall blond woman with very red lipstick, said "Mr. and Mrs. O'Keefe."

So they were on time, and if they had waited another minute, this woman would have called someone else. Rita thought of the tremendous overweening punctiliousness of this agency of the government—a reaction to 9/11, no doubt. The thought went through her as she followed the woman down a narrow hall and into a small office. On the desk was a computer, several pictures of the woman's children, and a tall stack of folders. Rita set her own folders on the desk.

The woman took their file from the stack and opened it. She used the eraser end of a pencil as friction to riffle through the pages. She asked for their passports and driver's licenses. Rita also had both birth certificates, and she handed them over.

"Do you have your marriage license?"

"Yes." She began looking through the folders on her side of the desk. "I'm sure I have it here somewhere."

The woman waited. Michael looked around the room, and his wife's little exasperated sigh told him that she wasn't finding the thing. "Maybe it's still in the car," he said.

"I packed it," said Rita. "I put it right in here."

"But the folders all fell on the floor when I had to slam on the brakes. Maybe you didn't get it when you picked it all up."

"Here," Rita said, pulling it out of the middle of the stack. "It got pushed in under some things. We almost had an accident coming here."

"Oh." The woman took the license and gazed at it. "You've been together . . . a year and two months."

"We've been together longer than that," Rita said. "We've been married a year and two months."

"You got married here in Tennessee."

"Yes."

"Do you have children yet?"

"No," said Rita. And suddenly a little sob rose up from the back of her throat. She was completely unready for it. She held the next breath back, feeling her throat close. Out of the corner of her eye she could see his face turned to her.

The woman had reached across to hand the license back, and she was frozen for a few awkward seconds, holding it out. Michael reached over and took it from her, and set it on the folder in front of Rita.

"Do you need some time?" the woman asked.

"Excuse me," Rita said, reaching into her purse and bringing out a handkerchief. She held it to her mouth. "I'm sorry." It wouldn't stop. She couldn't make it stop. She wiped her eyes, closed them tight, and sobbed.

The woman looked at Michael, who could only stare back. Perhaps he shrugged. And then he understood that she was expecting him to do something, to show some concern. He put his hand out and touched Rita's shaking shoulder. "There," he said.

"I don't know what's happened," Rita got out. But then it

came over her again in a wave, and she sat crying, now at least partly because of the fact itself—that she couldn't control it, make it stop.

Michael said, "We almost had an accident coming over here."

"I'll be back," the woman said. She rose, looking taller than he had remembered from first seeing her. She went out of the office and closed the door quietly.

He leaned over and said, "I'm sorry. Don't cry."

"I said that awful thing about your father and mother."

"I've said worse meself. Don't do this. Don't torture yourself." He was worried about the woman coming back. He searched his mind for something soothing to say, and his mind was blank. Again he saw her ankles, the white shoes, the pretty slacks. He felt a rush of affection for her and briefly it was as if he were looking at a child crying about some small thing.

"It's a wee thing," he said. "The lady'll understand. Don't worry."

"I'm fine," she said, resisting the thought that he really didn't know anything at all about her. "I love you." But she couldn't feel it just now, with him sitting there staring, his face white with embarrassment. Oh, how did people do it? How did they go from one place to another, and find some way to be happy? And she had been happy, so happy. And there would be children, that would come. They were together. A married couple in America. She thought of her mother and father, who had seemed so content all those years, and whose divorce had made her wish for something overwhelming to come, to make them see what they were to each other, to make them hold on to it better than they had. And she was not going to have a life like theirs, not going to lie about anything to anyone, not going to deceive herself. She took Michael's hand, reached for it, and looked into his green eyes, sniffling, gaining some control again. "I love you," she said, meaning it without quite feeling it.

"There," he repeated. "It's all right. It's going to be fine, you'll see. Nothing to worry about. I love you, too."

"I know," she told him. It was just that the truck had startled her so, and the morning itself had been upsetting. Things would be all right, would return to normal. She had packed the marriage license. All the other papers were in order. They were not terrorists, after all. He was going to get his permanent residency card. He would be able to stay as long as he wanted to.

SIXTY-FIVE MILLION YEARS

Because this was such a small parish, Father Hennessey knew many of the people who came to confess, and he was afraid that when he saw them on his daily rounds it might show in his face that their troubles and failures had lately, in spite of all his efforts to resist, been relegated to some zone of apathy in his heart. It was as if some part of him had come loose, and was in revolt.

His hours in the booth were an almost unbearable ordeal now.

The voices, one by one, murmured, droned, went on flatly in the confidence that what was being confessed was of interest—and through the long minutes he tried unsuccessfully to concentrate on the catalog of little cruelties, omissions, vanities, impure thoughts, petty indulgences, hatreds and angers, curses and unchecked passions of his completely ordinary parishioners.

He felt nothing. It was all the dread sameness of the self, all the old, recurring failures of control, the same rapacious desires, the same renegade appetites. Over and over and over.

But even beyond the worry about appearances, Father Hennessey was profoundly worried about the sensation itself. This spiritual lethargy, this torpor, this desolation—what other word could you use to describe it?—followed him into the restless nights. There were prayers and exercises to combat spiritual dryness, but nothing worked.

He spent the hours after confession on his knees, in his room, saying his office, and enduring the discomfort of the hard wooden floor. He took to denying himself his lunch, and often in the evenings he retired without drinking any water or juice, though the medicines he was taking for his arthritic hip gave him dry mouth. And he forfeited the little pleasurable habits that had formed over the years—the sip of cognac before bed; the occasional ice cream cone after dinner, Saturday- and Sunday-afternoon golf on television.

One evening, toward the end of his purgatory in the booth, after more than an hour of morbid anticipation that he might fall asleep, he closed one panel and opened the other to discover a young male voice that seemed already to have been talking: "Father, the dinosaurs lived here for millions of years. We've only been here for a little fraction of a second in terms of evolution. What was God thinking?"

Father Hennessey straightened and looked at the shape on the other side of the screen. "Yes?" he said. Then: "Begin again, please, son."

"Well, I don't get it."

"Tell me what you don't get."

"I don't get the millions of years. *Millions* of years, Father. What was he thinking?"

"How old are you?" Father Hennessey asked.

"Almost fifteen."

He began to talk about God's time being different from human time.

The boy interrupted him. "Yes, Father, but more than sixty

million years." There was an urgency in the voice; perhaps it was desperation.

"Son, remember the words of Saint Peter. 'Lord, I believe; help thou my unbelief.'"

"I know that one, Father. I know all that stuff. I spent a year in bed and there wasn't anything to do but read."

"I'm sorry," said the priest, because he could think of nothing else to say for the moment. But then he added, "If Saint Peter could doubt, think how much easier it is for us to fall into it."

"But he didn't know about the dinosaurs and the sixty million plus years."

"You don't know that—do you? You don't know that for sure."

"Saint Peter didn't know about the dinosaurs, Father."

The insistence in the voice annoyed him. He said, "We don't know that he didn't. We have no exact knowledge of that. There is no mention of it—although God himself mentions Leviathan in the Book of Job."

"I know that one, too," said the voice. "I read that one, too. He asks Job if he can draw the whale up out of the deep. He's bragging. It's a piece of petty belligerence."

"How old did you say you are?"

"I read a lot. I told you, I spent a year in bed. Juvenile RA. You know what that is?"

"Arthritis?"

"Rheumatoid. Yes. I got it two years ago. I missed a year of school. They thought I had leukemia."

"I'm so sorry."

"It's just my sister and me now."

Father Hennessey wanted to ask the name. He searched through the faces he could call up, the boys he knew. "Have you ever come to me before?" he said.

"I live with my sister. Our mother's in the hospital and she's the one who—well, no, I want to know. I want to know the answers to these questions."

"These are her questions, then."

"They're mine," the boy said. "I want to know."

"Are you from this parish?" He waited. But the shape was still; there was just the down-turning shadow of the profile. He saw a large, crooked nose, a round head—evidently the hair was cut very close to the scalp. "Well, are you?"

"Bless me, Father, for I have sinned."

Silence.

The priest murmured, "Yes?"

Nothing.

"Is there anything else you wish to confess?"

"Did he say, 'Let there be lizards?' Did he say, 'No voices, no music, no thoughts, no yearning for divine light. Just these big ugly scaly things roaring and grunting and eating each other or chewing up the vegetation?' What did he make them for? Could he have found them beautiful?"

"I've told you that we are not given that knowledge."

"You keep saying that, Father. But I want an answer. Job demanded an answer, and he got something, anyway. Don't you wonder about it?"

"No," Father Hennessey said, feeling as though the other might be less than sincere, and that this was all at his expense. "I don't wonder about it at all."

The boy sighed. Perhaps he was not almost fifteen years old, but thirty-five and mentally unstable.

"There is no perfect answer, son—except faith."

"That's what I keep say—" the boy began. But then he stopped.

"You keep—" the priest said. "Is this your mother again—"

There was a shuffling on the other side of the screen, and the shape was gone. Father Hennessey hesitated, and then got to his feet and opened the door to his booth, but there were only the three other people awaiting confession, standing in line under the Stations of the Cross. Two men and a woman he recognized, a member of the choir, who turned from him and seemed sheepish.

"Did you see that boy come out of here?" he said to her.

She stared, as if uncertain that he was speaking to her. "Excuse me?"

"The boy who just left here. Did you see him?"

"I wasn't paying any attention," the woman said, in a tone as if to say also that she had problems of her own.

The two men were shaking their heads.

With the second of these, who confessed to missing Mass for twenty years and committing all the mortal sins except murder, he gave a penance of Mass and Communion each morning for a month, and then couldn't remember the words of absolution—his mind, for that instant, was sheer blankness. The man either didn't notice or didn't care. He said his Act of Contrition, crossed himself, and left the booth.

Father Hennessey saw that the red light over the other screen was indicating a presence there, but hesitated a little before opening it. The prayer of absolution came back to him, and he repeated it, then reached to the sliding panel and pulled it back into its socket. The old woman, with petty concerns.

Later, he closed the church and went over to the rectory, where Mrs. Loring, his housekeeper, was holding dinner for him.

She was a big, graying, severe-looking woman who had raised a large family—seven boys and one girl, all of whom were now married, with children of their own. Her stern look was deceiving, for she was full of good humor, and she possessed the kind of practical piety that had always impressed him. He was even a trifle envious of it.

She said, "You look tired, Father."

"Yes," he said.

She reported to him about his phone calls and messages—several from parishioners helping with the week's events, and one from the hospital: a choir member had suffered an attack of appendicitis.

"Thank you," he told her.

It would be inaccurate to say that she mothered him. She would have been insulted by the suggestion. She had a life of her own, quite separate from the work she did here. Yet in his sleep he sometimes confused her with his mother, who had raised him alone, and lived now in a condominium in Orlando, Florida. Mrs. Loring answered the phone and kept the schedules and cooked the evening meal for him, and she protected his privacy when he needed it. Beyond that, she kept her own counsel. She went elsewhere for her confessions, too.

Upstairs, in his room, he took his coat off and got into a cardigan, then knelt by the bed to do his penance. The phone rang, but he let Mrs. Loring get it, and when she didn't call to him, assumed that it was something he could handle in the morning.

A little later, she let herself out. He watched from the window as her car pulled away into the dark, and he felt a surprisingly sharp pang of loneliness when the lights disappeared over the hill.

As had become the nightly pattern, he had trouble sleeping. He thought of the boy, imagined what the boy's night might be with such heavy doubt. And with arthritis. It disturbed him to find that his curiosity was merely intellectual; it was wholly without the grace of compassion: he couldn't make himself feel anything but the wish to know more. There had been an impatience, an earnestness, an edginess, in the boy's voice, and the priest had felt annoyed, even while being startled at the precociousness of the speech.

At the six a.m. Mass, he found himself unable to concentrate as he ought to. The whole ceremony was automatic. He felt as though he wasn't worthy of all those who had gotten up before light and made their way in the unseasonable cold to the church, expecting the consolations of the Mass. But then the sacrament itself was not harmed by the inadequacy of its priest, and everyone understood that.

He himself, of course, understood it perfectly, terribly.

He went back to the rectory and fixed himself a breakfast of cold cereal. On some mornings Mrs. Loring came to the six o'clock Mass. She had not come this morning. He sat at the kitchen table and drank a cup of coffee, listening to the radio, the weather forecast. Frost overnight. Mrs. Loring arrived, wearing a winter coat, which she took off and hung on the hook by the door. He offered her some coffee. She refused. She sat down and folded her hands on the table. "That phone call last evening after you went upstairs, a very strange call. A young man—just a boy, really. He said he wanted to speak not to you but to me."

"Did he give a name?"

She shook her head. "He wanted to know what my days were like here."

"What did you tell him?"

"I told him he was impertinent. And he hung up."

"Did he say anything about doubt?"

Mrs. Loring stared, and seemed to consider. But then she merely repeated the word: "Doubt?"

The cares of his week were not unusual, yet they drained him. He returned to the rectory and sank into his chair and wondered if he would be able to get up again. He took the medicine for his aching joints, and found that his appetite suffered. Mrs. Loring said nothing about any of this, but she waited longer before taking the plate away, and whenever he dozed off in the chair, she would unplug the phone. Several times he had seen her plug it back in.

Sometimes when she left in the evenings, he unplugged it himself. The answering machine could take the calls. There were usually quite a few, of course. More than any one person could handle on many nights. So much distress in the world. Everyone was so needy. He felt it, too.

That Saturday evening, after listening to four rather ordinary confessions, he heard the boy's voice again, and sat up straight. Somewhere in his mind was a sense of this being a chance to do better.

"Forgive me, Father. I have to confess the sin of doubt."

"Doubt is not in itself a sin," Father Hennessey told him. "Remember that, son."

"I keep thinking about the other planets, Father. Why put a planet way out in the middle of endless space and leave it with nothing on it forever. Did he know he was going to create us?"

Father Hennessey had a long history of answering exactly these kinds of questions, and he could not understand why they should cause him any unrest now, except that this child was so scarily precocious. And then, too, there was something in the voice, some element of sadness, and it had risen as it went on. Father Hennessey said, "This is a confessional." He took a breath. "It isn't sinful to question things."

"I know—right. I'm sorry. I'm afraid. I'm all hell inside."

"That's a feeling. It isn't the true situation. God is with you, son." The words felt empty.

"I don't believe it. And I can't fake it."

Had he heard a sob in the voice? Was the boy crying? This frighteningly intelligent presence? He leaned closer to the screen and said, "You must try to remember that you're in the hands of a merciful God."

Nothing.

"Pray with me."

He listened. Silence. "Perhaps you should come see me outside."

No sound.

"How—" the priest began. "How do you get here? Do you live near here?"

Again, nothing. The boy was out of the booth and gone. This time Father Hennessey walked out of the building, past the line of CCD students waiting for him, and on down the walk to the end of the block. But there was just the empty street. A chilly wind kicked up dust. Leaves flew from the maple tree on the corner.

The following Monday night, after religion class, he sat in the confessional and found once more that he couldn't pay attention. His mind failed him, tottered, lost its hold on every subject, over and over.

Outside, a steady drizzle fell out of a featureless black sky. People came into the booth in wet coats, smelling of the winter air and the rain. Most of them were teenagers from the CCD classes for public school children. Their sins were the same, the same, the same, and so it was a simple matter to hide his inattention through the usual portion of adolescent foment—all that forlorn and overwrought faltering with the unexpected and terrifying delights and demands of the body.

He kept thinking about the second failure with the boy.

And, well, this, too, was failure, this wandering away from the voices on the other side of the screen, and for a while, near the end of the time, he tried repeatedly—he did try, but without success—to haul himself back to them. Failure inside failure inside failure.

Another week went by. He tried—and did slightly better—concentrating on the confessions he heard Saturday, and again Monday. And he suffered the penance of sleeplessness in the nights. The first snow of the year hit in the middle of the following week, a dusting, not more than an inch, and when it cleared a bright moon shone. The world looked changed; there was a silvery softness to the light. He walked out in it, late, past midnight, unable to sleep. The church loomed over him, its shadow printed on the sifted dust of snow. He saw his own breath, and looked at the shadows of the houses beyond the trees.

That week, he read in the paper that a Mr. Alphonse Graham, a beloved high school teacher, had been caught engaging in a sexual act in the gymnasium equipment cabinet with one of his students, and was being charged for having contributed to the delinquency of a minor. The girl, not named, was only fifteen. The paper said that if she were a year younger, the charge would have been statutory rape. Her mother was a hospital patient, the article said, and the girl was living at home with her younger brother, who had juvenile rheumatoid arthritis. The two minors had lived alone in the house for several months, having been abandoned by their mother's live-in friend shortly after she entered the hospital. The article didn't say why she was in the hospital.

Father Hennessey knew instantly that this was the boy who had been coming to see him.

He asked Mrs. Loring to call the hospital and find out if this woman was allowed visitors. The hospital asked if Mrs. Loring was family, and when Mrs. Loring explained that she was calling for Father Hennessey, she was told that the woman was in the psychiatric ward and was presently in no condition to receive any visitors.

He went on with the increasing weight of what there was to do. He kept busy, and he prayed—or tried to pray.

Perhaps it was a mistake to deny himself so much—his own osteoarthritis was worse, and the sleeplessness was becoming a serious problem. He related this to his own confessor—Father Allenby, who talked of staleness and of ridding one's self of the earthly pull of ego. "It is always the ego that keeps us awake," he said. "Empty yourself of all that. Give yourself over to the spirit. We have to cross a desert, a spiritual wasteland, to reach him, remember that. Remember the forty years of wandering in the desert."

"Father, either it happened that way, or it didn't. I would like not to have to think of it as only a metaphor."

"You know quite well it is all a part of creation, and this spiritual journey," the gentle voice said.

"Forgive me," Father Hennessey murmured.

Concerning his problem with confessions, it was of course a very familiar thing. "Remember your training, Father." Still, it did not feel ordinary—it felt like a kind of secret quake, a collapsing, deep.

The following Friday evening, he poured himself a cognac, after turning it down during dinner with a parishioner, whose wife and two grown children were anxious to trade stories about the disgrace at the high school. They gossiped about it while Father Hennessey was sitting right there; and they kept on through his feeble and finally insincere attempts to change the subject. When he returned to the rectory, through a fine rain and a cold wind, he strode into the kitchen, poured the cognac and drank it down, and then poured another, which he later trickled back into the bottle, deciding not to allow even this small relinquishment of his hold on himself.

In the morning, he woke with a little headache, and took nothing for it. Penance. He said Mass as usual, at six o'clock, for the five people who came, and then he went back to the rectory and recited his office, kneeling on the hard wooden floor. He would construct something to articulate from the pulpit about gossip, one of the seven deadly sins. A sin nobody even thought about anymore, or paid the slightest bit of attention to, as if it had simply gone the way of weekly fasting before Communion.

He was fairly certain that he would never hear from the boy again.

But that evening in the confessional, the voice came, fraught with angry sorrow, going on again as if it had begun before he opened the panel. "I don't care why humans suffer or why the world is a place where living creatures have to kill and eat other living creatures in order to survive; that doesn't worry me. I'm worried about all the places in the universe where there's nothing going on, and nothing but silence. And stars that died out a billion years ago and you can't see the light of the explosion because it hasn't reached us yet or we can see the light and it's been dead for a million years."

The priest had begun to try to quiet him. "Shhhh, son. Shhhh. Shhhh."

". . . and the dinosaurs, the dinosaurs, Father. Sixty-five

million years of grunts and screeches and death, and these horrible things coming out of big eggs and laying big eggs. And then this meteor hits and the sun's blotted out and the vegetation dies and everything dies out starving for an eon. He must've caused it all to die out, so why did he do that? Did he make a mistake? He's faulty, isn't he, like all of us. He doesn't get it either. He's just blind power, like a force of nature. A person goes crazy and it's all just chemicals in the brain."

Father Hennessey said, "Listen. *Listen.*"

The boy stopped.

"How is your mother?"

"I don't want to talk about her now."

"Are your sister and you living with relatives now?"

"Forgive me, Father, for I have sinned."

"You can tell me, can't you, son?"

"We're in a foster home."

"I'd like to help."

"Bless me, Father, for I have sinned. It has been two weeks since my last confession. I have the sin of doubt. And it's the dinosaurs, the millions of years."

"The idea that a meteor caused the death of those creatures is something that has to be taken on faith as well, son. Don't you see? No one knows what happened. We have no way of knowing. But we do have the written records of Matthew, Mark, Luke, and John."

"Yes, Father—but you haven't really answered. John says in the beginning was the *word*, and that just isn't so. In the beginning was *millions* of years of meaningless grunting and screeching and roaring."

Father Hennessey murmured, "You were talking before about Job, right?"

"Yes."

"You're very advanced for your age. Do you know about the war in heaven?"

"Yes."

"What was the sin of the angel Lucifer?"

"Pride. Pride. *Pride.* I told you I already know all this stuff."

"Well, son, to question certain things too far is to commit the sin of pride, too, isn't it?"

The other was silent again.

"Isn't it."

Nothing.

"Do you see?"

"So doubt is a sin of pride."

"Yes," Father Hennessey told him, feeling a tightening in his chest. "If you *indulge* in it."

"I can't get out of it."

"You have to work at it. It's never easy. The path to holiness is arduous and full of traps. Remember there's an adversary, who would like very much for you to fail, and is working all the time to bring that about."

"She's not that."

"What did you say?"

Silence again.

"Please repeat that," said the priest.

"Never mind," the boy said.

"I was talking about the devil, son."

Another silence.

Father Hennessey endeavored to take a softer tone. "Son, you've brought this to confession, so you are acting on faith. Isn't that true? And isn't that a good thing?"

There was a long sigh. "I don't get anything out of it, though."

"All the more reason to pray for help."

❧ 260 ❧

"Nothing gets better."

"Pray with me," the priest said.

"It's all terrible empty space."

"Did you call my housekeeper?" Father Hennessey hadn't known that he would ask this, and now that he had, he felt weirdly as if he had entered some kind of unreality. He had crossed over a line, and would have to pursue it now. "Did you?" he said.

"I don't know."

"Who are you? Tell me that. You say you don't come from here."

The shadow moved on the other side of the screen, and the priest got up and opened his door, wanting to catch him, or catch sight of him. The others in line stood docilely staring. He saw the boy—close-cut blond hair, a ragged red flannel shirt—moving with a lurch along the aisle, on the far side, to the door there. "Wait," Father Hennessey said, trying to move quickly. But his arthritic hip caught him, and the boy was out. He limped to the door and looked at the empty alley with its puddles of rain. When he turned to go back into the church, he saw the others staring at him, and then trying not to stare.

"He called again," Mrs. Loring told him, and she gave him an oddly knowing look. "Last evening, while you were at novena. He asked what you were like. He said he was calling to find out what you were like. There was something very disturbed in the voice. It's a voice that's so grown-up, Father—I mean the talk is grown-up, and then it breaks on that little boy's falsetto. It's very upsetting. I told him to call you, and he said that he had."

"He hasn't called me," Father Hennessey said.

This was the following Saturday, after a week of exhausting tasks—the Knights of Columbus dance for the CCD classes, dinners with parishioners, several visits to the hospital and to homes of the sick, four baptisms, one extreme unction, and a wedding; he felt hollowed out from the inside. He was sitting at the table in the kitchen, in the hour before confessions were to begin. He dreaded it now for reasons that would have amazed him, even a month ago: quietly he hoped for boredom. Mrs. Loring had fixed him soup, and she had taken the seat opposite him, sipping coffee, and worrying, and looking at him. "I don't like it," she said.

"Did he say anything else to you?"

"He asked if I believe in hell."

"What did you tell him?"

"I didn't know what to tell him. I told him to talk to you. And that's when he said he'd called you."

"Did he put it that way? He'd *called* me?"

"He said he talked to you."

"If he calls you again, try to get his name for me, will you?"

"I did. I did that. He won't give his name, or where he's from. Just that he's not from here."

Father Hennessey stood. "I'll be in my room for a few minutes."

"If he does call you, Father, please tell him to stop calling me."

Abruptly, he had a reasonless suspicion that she knew the boy, and had put him up to everything. He couldn't help the thought—it was as if some part of him believed he might be able to trick the truth out of the very air. "Do you know the boy?" he asked.

Mrs. Loring stared—cold, dark eyes; a blank, concentrating face. "What?" she said.

"Nothing," said the priest. "I'm casting about like a man in a net."

Upstairs, alone, he said his office, but sitting on the bed this time. He heard Mrs. Loring leave. The kitchen was clean; the rooms of the house were in order. And still he felt as if something were intolerably wrong. The angles of wall and window and corner had kept their symmetry at the expense of some obscure, delicate aspect, whose absence made the whole house seem crooked. He knew this was pure imagining, and still he could not shake the feeling.

In the paper, there was the news that Alphonse Graham had pleaded guilty to contributing to the delinquency of a minor. There was no mention of the nameless juvenile, nor of any of the circumstances surrounding the admission of guilt—he had been let go at the high school; his wife had gone back east to stay with her aging mother. But Father Hennessey had heard the gossip. The poor man was finished. He would never teach again; essentially his life was over. The priest wished desperately, and with a kind of grieving appetite, to talk to him. He couldn't think it away, or pray it out of existence.

When he walked over to the church to hear confessions he resolved that if the boy came, he would stop being contentious. He would try to hear the anguish and respond to it.

But the boy didn't come. And he was not there the next week, or the week after that. Mrs. Loring hadn't heard from him either, and in her mind the episode, whatever it had been, was over. Father Hennessey feared that he had driven the boy away. And he had overwhelming curiosity as to his identity. In the slow passages between three o'clock in the morning and dawn, he lay awake and was partly convinced that there was some supernatural element to it all: the boy's appearance had been providential. Perhaps he hadn't been a real boy at all, but an angel or a demon. And why, the priest wondered, in his wakefulness and his confusion, should this seem so far-fetched, in a life built on faith? An angel had been sent to goad him out of his apathy.

Real winter weather arrived: a bad snowstorm that turned to freezing rain and ice. All the leaves were gone from the trees and he hadn't noticed. He spent Thanksgiving at a mission in the city, serving food to the homeless and hearing their confessions. He said a Mass at the center, and gave Communion. It was a struggle to feel it as the mystery he had always believed it to be. He was too weary, too tired of his own mind. When he heard confessions he kept listening for the boy's voice, that distressed, reedy, sorrowful, faintly angry voice mouthing startling phrases, and when it didn't come he felt low and depressed. He couldn't explain it, any of it—not even to himself.

He returned to spending an hour in excruciating pain each evening, kneeling on the hard floor to say his office. He recognized the essentially indulgent nature of the thing, yet felt compelled to do it anyway. The pain helped him concentrate; it felt, anyway, somewhat expiative.

The day before Christmas Eve, he had to pay a call on a parishioner, an elderly woman who had taken an overdose of aspirin. She was a patient in the psychological wing of the hospital. She had done well there, and was nearly restored enough to go back to her life. Father Hennessey's visit was one of the last things in her treatment, something her grown children wanted. She seemed unchanged from the gentle nodding presence she had been before the trouble: a little frenetic, but good-humored, even cheerful. It was impossible to believe that she could have tried to kill herself. He said a rosary with her, sitting at a window in the dayroom, overlooking the grounds. It was a bright cold day. He held her thin hand, gazing out the window, and he saw the boy approach the building from the far end of the parking lot, having come from the street over there; his coat was open, revealing a red sweatshirt. It was him, the one. Father Hennessey excused himself and hurried out and down to the front entrance. This was being given to him from on high. It was meant to be, and in this way, too—after weeks of worry. He was on the landing as the boy came up the stairs. The boy hadn't seen him, walking head down, muttering something to himself. When he looked up and saw the priest, he stopped.

"Hello," Father Hennessey said.

They stood there.

Finally the boy came up another step, hesitating, stopping again.

"It's me," the priest said. "Father Hennessey."

"What?"

"I believe providence put me here today, to see you. Why have you stopped coming?"

The boy shook his head. "I don't understand."

"I saw you," said Father Hennessey. "Remember?"

"No, I mean I don't understand about it. What good it's supposed to do. I'm not even Catholic. My mother is."

The priest took a stride toward him, and then sat down on the step, resting his elbows on his knees. He couldn't stand. The air stung his cheeks. He looked over at the boy and said, "Please, sit down."

The boy shook his head. "I can't. She's in there. My mother."

"Oh." Father Hennessey stood, with some effort. "Of course. I'm sorry."

"She's—not right in the head—"

"How long?"

"Since my father left. And now my sister's—well. She's gonna have a baby."

Father Hennessey said nothing. He felt something drop under his heart. He could not find the strength to draw in the next breath. He straightened and tried to collect himself.

"Yeah," the boy said, having seen the reaction.

"What's your name?" the priest managed to get out.

"I don't believe it, Father, any more than she does."

"Your mother?"

"No, that's not right; my mother *does* believe it. And it's put her in the bughouse."

"That isn't what's done it—" Father Hennessey said. And realized the note of pleading that had been in his voice. "Remember what we talked about, though—pride and des—" The priest stopped, having seen the impatience in the boy's countenance.

"Look, everything you said to me I said to her, okay? Jesus isn't around to chase the devils out of her."

Father Hennessey wondered at the force of his own feeling; he was close to tears. The boy seemed almost forbearing.

"Yeah," he said. "Well—I gotta go try again."

"I didn't help," Father Hennessey told him. "But—but faith—faith can help." He did not feel the words, and he saw the boy perceive this. He held his hands out slightly from the sides of his body, a gesture of helplessness.

"He made the angels, and they rebelled. Right?"

"Yes. That's right, son. And there's an adversary—"

"And then he made Adam and Eve and they were in the garden and the snake tempted Eve."

"Yes—the adversary—"

"How can he be perfect if he makes mistakes like those,

Father? Mistakes like me, and my mother?" There were tears in the voice. The priest was sure of it. He couldn't find his way to the words that would help.

"Faith," he got out. "We aren't given—"

"Stumbling along," the boy said simply, but without conviction, holding out his own hands. The priest saw that the fingers were knotted and curved slightly with the arthritis. There was something beautiful about them in their strange variance from the hands one expected a fourteen-year-old boy to have. Father Hennessey had a sense of having come face-to-face with a living sanctity. It stopped his breath again. He watched the boy go on up the stairs and into the building.

What disturbed him most that night, lying in bed thinking about it, was that he had gone through everything in these last few weeks only in terms of himself. That fact glared at him in his sleeplessness. He got up and paced the floor, and then knelt and tried to pray, and couldn't. His mind kept presenting him with a picture of the boy, walking up the steps of the hospital and in.

He began to wonder if he were not becoming unhinged.

In the morning Mrs. Loring arrived early, and went about her tasks with a certain briskness. Or had he imagined it? He said, "I met our friend."

"Who?" she said.

"The boy. The one who kept calling."

She said nothing.

"I'm sorry for what I said to you yesterday."

"I don't know what you're talking about, Father."

"Our caller—the one you talked to about me. He's going through a very bad time. He's a nice boy. A—a—well, a very special child."

"Everyone's special in their way," she said. "Usually." She smiled, and seemed to want him to take this as a joke.

"Is everything all right with you, this morning?" he asked her.

"Yes," she said, as if surprised that he would ask. "Everything's fine. Everything's just fine."

Throughout that day, he attended to his duties with her help, and when she left to go to her own house, her own life, he went for a long walk alone around the grounds of his church. The moon was out again, and it was clear and quite cold. The wintry chill went down through the cloth of his tunic and gripped him. He stood in the shadow of the church and looked up. He had a moment of being frightfully aware of it as mere stone; it was a building, the work of human hands, stone and brick and mortar and wood. The stars were ranged far and wide above it, sparkling.

This is Richard Bausch's eighth volume of short stories. He is also the author of a volume of poetry and eleven novels. In 2004 he won the PEN/Malamud Award for Short Fiction. He is a past Chancellor of the Fellowship of Southern Writers and lives in Tennessee, where he holds Moss Chair of Excellence in the Writer's Workshop of the University of Memphis.

A NOTE ON THE TYPE

This book was set in Janson, a typeface made by Nicholas Kis (1650–1702). The type is an excellent example of the influential and sturdy Dutch types that prevailed in England up to the time William Caslon (1692–1766) developed his own incomparable designs from them.

Composed by Textech, Brattleboro, Vermont
Printed and bound by R. R. Donnelley, Harrisonburg, Virginia
Book design by Robert C. Olsson